Suspects

International bestselling author Lesley Pearse has lived a life as rich with incidents, setbacks and joys as any found in her novels. After her mother died, Lesley spent three years in an orphanage before she was taken home when her father remarried. Resourceful, determined and willing to have a go at almost anything, Lesley left home at sixteen. By the mid sixties she was living in London, sharing flats, partying hard and married to a trumpet player in a jazz-rock band. She has also worked as a nanny and Playboy bunny, and designed and made clothes to sell to boutiques.

It was only after having three daughters that Lesley began to write. The hardships, traumas, close friends and lovers from those early years were inspiration for her beloved novels. She published her first book at forty-nine and has not looked back since.

Lesley is still a party girl.

Find out more about Lesley and
keep up to date with what she's been doing:

Follow her on Twitter:
@LesleyPearse

Sign up for her newsletter:
www.lesleypearse.com

D1262620

Suspects

LESLEY PEARSE

MICHAEL JOSEPH

MICHAEL JOSEPH

UK | USA | Canada | Ireland | Australia
India | New Zealand | South Africa

Michael Joseph is part of the Penguin Random House group of companies
whose addresses can be found at global.penguinrandomhouse.com

First published 2021
001

Copyright © Lesley Pearse, 2021

The moral right of the author has been asserted

Set in 15.5/18 pt Garamond MT Std
Typeset by Integra Software Services Pvt. Ltd, Pondicherry
Printed and bound in Great Britain by Clays Ltd, Elcograf S.p.A.

The authorized representative in the EEA is Penguin Random House Ireland,
Morrison Chambers, 32 Nassau Street, Dublin D02 YH68

A CIP catalogue record for this book is available from the British Library

HARDBACK ISBN: 978–0–241–42662–3
TRADE PAPERBACK ISBN: 978–0–241–42663–0

www.greenpenguin.co.uk

To my four gorgeous grandchildren,
Brandon, Harley, Sienna and Alicia.

I've missed you so much this year,
but we will make up for lost time soon.

Love you all xxxx

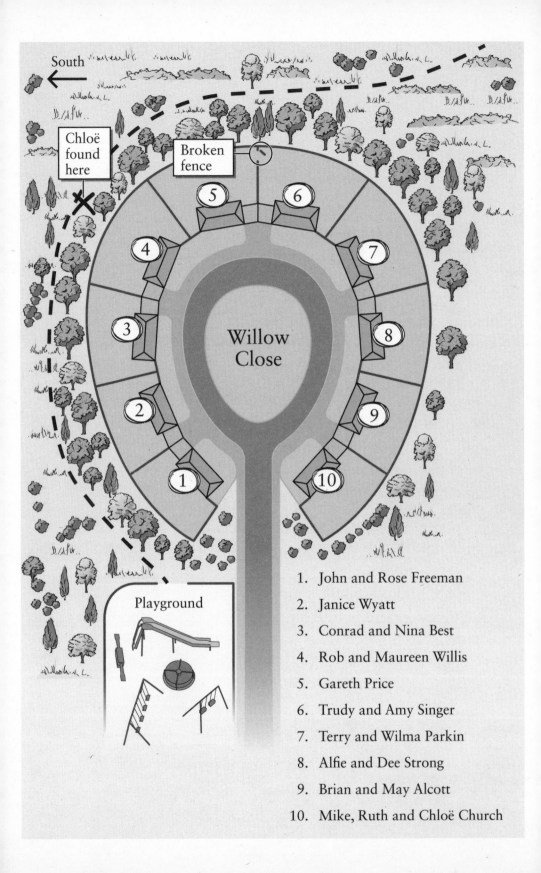

South

Chloë found here

Broken fence

5 6

4 7

3 Willow Close 8

2 9

1 10

Playground

1. John and Rose Freeman

2. Janice Wyatt

3. Conrad and Nina Best

4. Rob and Maureen Willis

5. Gareth Price

6. Trudy and Amy Singer

7. Terry and Wilma Parkin

8. Alfie and Dee Strong

9. Brian and May Alcott

10. Mike, Ruth and Chloë Church

I

18 July 2009, Cheltenham, Day One

'What on earth has Harry got now?' Maureen Willis asked her husband Rob, pointing to their Border Terrier, which appeared to have found something interesting a little way ahead of them under a bush.

'Harry. Leave it!' Rob yelled. He looked back to his wife, with a shrug of resignation. 'Please don't let it be fox poo. Seven on an already hot morning and we'll never get the stink off him.'

The couple speeded up to get their dog under control. Rob reached him first and Maureen heard him gasp in horror.

'What is it?' she called, panting a little with the exertion of getting her twelve-stone weight up the hill.

Rob had stopped short. Even from a distance Maureen could see, from the way he'd clapped his hand over his mouth, it was something gruesome.

'Don't come any closer,' Rob shouted, waving his arms as further warning, then he bent over to put the dog on his lead.

'What is it?' she called.

Rob looked down at the young girl sprawled on the ground, half under a bush. Her long blonde hair was matted with congealing blood, which also covered her bare arms and clothing. He could tell by her coltish limbs she was no more than twelve or thirteen. His stomach heaved at the savage attack.

Turning away, he said to Maureen, 'Call the police, love. It's a child who's been attacked. I'm pretty certain she's dead.'

2

At nine thirty the same morning, Conrad Best drove a hired van loaded with his and his wife Nina's belongings into Willow Close, and paused, taking in the carefully tended open-plan front gardens, and the serenity of the street. He turned to Nina in the passenger seat. 'Do you think we could be in swingers' territory?'

Nina laughed. She could always rely on Conrad to think of something smutty. But she could follow his thinking. In her opinion Willow Close in the bright sunshine was more *Stepford Wives* than swingers. Everything was perfect, from the neat borders of petunias and busy lizzies to the snowy white nets at sparkling windows, and gleaming, recently washed and waxed cars on drives.

But maybe Conrad had picked up on something else, a darker side to such perfection. Was it possible the residents threw parties where they swapped partners? If so, she hoped they weren't watching her and Conrad right now with a view to drawing them into it.

'Just keep that thought to yourself. I want to get on well with my new neighbours,' she said reprovingly.

Conrad had no filter: he was quite likely to come right out and ask someone which people were swingers.

'It's so good to finally get a house of our own. Even the sun's shining today.'

'And the police have come to welcome us.' Conrad pointed out a squad car parked just beyond their house. 'Unless, of course, a swingers party got out of hand?'

'You always think the worst.' Nina giggled. 'They might not be on criminal business. Maybe the policeman lives here and popped home for a coffee.'

Conrad parked the van outside the garage of number three, and looked thoughtfully across the road, where some neighbours had suddenly come out of their houses to get together. 'Look at that lot. They've come out for more than a lost dog or a broken window.'

Nina saw he was right. The body language and facial expressions of the people clustered together suggested they were discussing something distressing.

But the young couple had been dreaming of their own home for so long that their joy wiped out anything else that might be going on. They leapt out of the van gleefully.

They had first viewed the link-detached house back in January, and although they liked its space and the three good-sized bedrooms, they felt they were too young, in their mid-twenties, to settle for what they thought was a 'granny house'. They soon found, though, that all the houses they liked close to town were beyond their price range, and the cheaper ones needed far too much renovating, or had no off-street parking.

Then in the spring, when they heard the price of this one had been reduced for a quick sale, they viewed it again. Only then did they see that the south-facing garden was full of daffodils and blossom trees. They imagined having barbecues on the patio and, in time, a baby asleep in its pram on the lawn. They loved the way the whole house was full of sunshine. The trees beyond the garden fence had new leaves unfurling. It no longer seemed a 'granny house', but a for-ever home, with everything they needed.

Now they were moving in.

Conrad opened the front door and, regardless of people looking on, scooped Nina into his arms to carry her over the threshold. She giggled helplessly as he took her right to the French windows at the back of the house and dumped her rather unceremoniously on the floor.

'I didn't think they'd leave this carpet,' Nina said, stretching out on the floor, like a starfish. It was a light biscuit colour in exceptionally good condition. 'That'll save us some money, won't it?'

'They've left the stair carpet too,' Conrad said, as he ran up it. 'Wow, they've left all the carpets!' he shouted down to Nina. 'How great is that?'

Nina jumped up and went to join him. Sure enough the lovely neutral carpet was everywhere. They had very little money left after the solicitor's fees and they'd resigned themselves to living without carpets for months.

Conrad hugged Nina. 'I think I must be one of the luckiest men in the world,' he said. 'A beautiful wife, a job I love and now a house of our own.'

Nina thought she was the lucky one. Conrad was a care worker at what he liked to call 'a naughty boys' home'. Boys who had mostly been taken into care because they were running wild and getting into trouble. Conrad understood their underlying problems, which were not just poverty and neglect, but lack of self-worth caused by parental disinterest. He'd had a troubled childhood, though very different from the ones 'his' boys had, and kept his tough-guy image, muscles, tattoos and heavy-metal T-shirts because he knew it helped the boys feel he was on their side.

To Nina his true nature shone out of his kind grey eyes, his sense of fun in his wide smiling mouth. He was astoundingly sensitive too: he picked up on people's problems with barely a word from them. He kept in touch with many of his old boys, who had gone on to live in flats of their own. As he often said, that was the time when young lads could go off the rails. His mission was to make sure they didn't.

Nina had fancied Conrad, who looked at first sight

like a Gypsy, with his black curls and perma-tan, but when she found his soft centre, she fell in love with him. 'A bit of an exaggeration calling me beautiful.' She laughed. Nina had no illusions about herself: she was five foot five, slim, and had long mousy hair, which at present was dyed auburn. She saw nothing remarkable in her face – her eyes were brown, her complexion was clear and her nose small, but she wouldn't win any beauty contests.

But Conrad, her friends and family saw her differently. They said her enthusiasm for everything, the way she cared about people and her ability to make any occasion fun made her a human tonic.

Nina was a florist. She worked at Petals in the Montpelier area of Cheltenham. While kids who needed help were her husband's passion, she was passionate about flowers and hoped one day to own a floristry shop. She had already made quite a name for herself in wedding flowers, and she was lucky in that Babs, who owned Petals, loved her ideas and allowed her free rein with the designs.

A few minutes later the couple went outside again to get the first of the many boxes. In the last two years of living together their belongings seemed to have multiplied tenfold. As Conrad opened the van doors, a big, powerful-looking man in his late forties or early fifties, came across the road to greet them. 'Welcome to Willow Close. I'm Alfie, and I live at number eight. I popped over to warn you what's happened. It's about as nasty as anything could be when you're just moving into the street. A young girl was murdered this morning, right over there.' He pointed to the trees behind their house.

'No!' Conrad exclaimed in horror. 'Is that why the police car is here?'

'Yes. They're talking to Maureen and Rob Willis, your neighbours. They found the girl earlier when they were walking their dog. But we haven't heard yet who she is.'

'How awful for her parents.' Nina's voice shook with emotion. 'And a bad time for us to be moving in.'

'I'm sorry to spoil your day. Maybe I shouldn't have said anything.' He hung his head, looking contrite.

'There's never a right time to get news like that,' Conrad said, and touched the older man's forearm in understanding. 'Better to hear it straight away than to put your foot in it later. I'm Conrad Best, and my wife is Nina.'

Alfie had the look of a boxer, a nose that might have been punched flat, but still had thick brown hair with only a touch of grey at the temples. His voice was muted Cockney, as if he'd left London many years ago. Conrad felt he was going to like the man: the laughter lines around his eyes were a good omen, and his grey eyes suggested intelligence.

8

'Marge and Jack moved out of your house the day before yesterday, but they'll be so shocked when they hear what's happened, as we all are. But don't let me hold you up, and if you need anything, some milk, bread or an extra pair of hands, I'm just across the road.'

Conrad and Nina were unnaturally quiet as they unpacked the van, speeding up now, desperate to get all their goods inside and shut the front door. Nina looked out of the back window, and although the fence at the bottom of the garden was virtually hidden by bushes, the trees behind it were enough to remind her that a child had been killed there. She shuddered at the thought.

What if the murderer came over that way to kill her?

Later that day, Rob Willis glanced at Maureen, who was slumped in dejection on the sofa. He wished they'd done anything other than decide to walk Harry before setting off for their impromptu weekend in Lyme Regis. They were unaccustomed to making spur-of-the-moment decisions. Or, indeed, of changing their routine. Every Saturday morning they put the dog into the car at seven, drove to the park near Sainsbury's and exercised Harry before getting the week's shopping. They even bought the same grocery items each week, with only slight changes according to what fruit and vegetables were in season.

They had an annual two-week holiday each year in August, always the same cottage at Ilfracombe in north Devon. At Christmas they booked into a country-house hotel on Dartmoor.

It was the sweltering weather that had decided them to be rash. Yesterday in the office of their stationery-supplies company they felt they were melting with the heat. Suddenly a weekend in Lyme Regis by the sea was irresistible. The cutting remark John Freeman, one of their neighbours, had made about them last Friday at his barbecue had also influenced the decision.

They had only gone to be neighbourly. Rose Freeman was the street snoop and gossip, and they were wary of becoming involved with her on any level. And they hated standing around eating overcooked burgers and making small-talk with people they had nothing in common with. By nine thirty they thanked John for having them and made the excuse they had some work to do.

John imagined himself to be very funny, and instead of just saying goodnight and he was glad they had come, he'd had to make a joke about them leaving early as they were always up at the crack of dawn. He said their car, starting early every Saturday morning to go to Sainsbury's, woke him.

'Always on the dot of seven too.' He chortled. 'I bet you two even schedule having sex into your diary. What day is that? Sunday?'

His wife roared with laughter, too, and no doubt she would spitefully repeat her husband's remarks again and again.

Rob had shrugged it off, but it had stung that people were laughing at their predictability. He decided they must do something out of character every now and then. So, as he and Maureen had walked to the park earlier that morning with Harry, they had both agreed it was refreshing to do something spontaneous.

But just twenty minutes later when he'd looked down at the dead girl, Rob had wished he was on his way to Sainsbury's as usual, and tears had started in his eyes at the horror of the scene. Dried blood was caked on her head, face and arms, and her pretty cotton dress was pulled up, showing her white knickers. She couldn't have been more than thirteen, her life over almost before it had begun. Who could have done such an evil thing?

The police and the paramedics arrived simultaneously. But after checking the girl was indeed dead, the paramedics drove off. Rob heard one of the police say that the pathologist and the forensics team were on their way.

After giving the police their details, Rob and Maureen were relieved to be told they could go home, where they would be formally interviewed later. A shelter had been erected over the child's body and the crime scene cordoned off. Police were redirecting other dog-walkers, who were trying to see what was going on.

'Has a local child been reported missing?' Maureen asked a female officer. 'Her mother must be panic-stricken if she didn't come home last night.'

'I don't know,' the officer said, her tone a little frosty, as if she resented questions from the public. 'I haven't heard anything.'

As they left to go home Maureen turned to her husband. 'Have you seen the girl before?' He usually had a good memory for faces.

'Her hair was across her face and there was so much blood I couldn't say.' Rob's voice shook, and she could see he was close to breaking down. 'Well, it's put paid to our weekend. Even if the police weren't calling for a statement, my heart wouldn't be in it.'

Maureen slipped her hand through his arm. She'd only seen the body from a distance, and that was more than enough for her. Rob was far more sensitive than she was, and the shock of finding the girl was likely to give him nightmares.

3

'So could this girl be Chloë Church?' Detective Inspector Jim Marshall asked Ian Dowling, his sergeant. They'd just sent the Willises home and were looking down at the child lying crumpled on the ground.

Her father had rung the station at about nine thirty the previous evening to report his daughter missing. Although she was only two hours late coming home, he said, it wasn't like her. He had already checked the playground and the other places she met her friends, without success, and he'd been told she'd gone home ages before.

Church had rung the police station again at six that morning to say she still hadn't come home. An hour later Mrs Willis had called to say she and her husband had found a dead child.

Giles Patterson, the pathologist, had just arrived to join Marshall and Dowling, and was preparing to do his initial examination.

Dowling sighed. 'She fits the description of Chloë, thirteen, fair hair, blue eyes and a white dress with red poppies.' He always dreaded child deaths. With three children of his own, he tended to get emotional, imagining it was one of them. He looked down at the girl, who had literally been pounded to death with a stone or brick. How could anyone have done that to a child?

Marshall sighed in agreement with his sergeant. He was fifty, divorced and had no children. But having none of his own didn't prevent him sharing the pain and grief parents felt at losing a child. Or being angry that some brute had taken a young life.

'To me this looks like malice,' Patterson offered, kneeling at the girl's side. 'Someone with a powerful grudge. Maybe against her parents. Though God knows how anyone could hate enough to attack an innocent child to get at her parents.'

'I see what you mean,' Dowling said thoughtfully. 'The wounds inflicted are like the attacker couldn't stop because he was in such a rage. I've heard of children being attacked as a lesson to their parents.'

'That should be one line of inquiry, though we'll have to be very tactful with the parents. Suggesting it could be someone with a grievance against them is likely to upset them even more. We'll have to get them in to identify the girl after we've got her cleaned up. Not that anything can mitigate the shock and horror of seeing your child dead,' Marshall said, his voice husky with emotion. 'Finding the killer is the only thing that helps, so we must get him quickly. It's a shame the ground is so dry – there are no footprints.'

Jim Marshall had been in the force for almost thirty years. Just recently, on nights when he was home alone, he'd begun to think he had made a grave mistake in thinking his career was the most important thing in life. When Sandra, his wife, was leaving him, she'd turned at the door and looked at him sadly. 'I have to go, Jim. There's no room for anything in your life but your job. You can't even chat to someone without analysing the hidden meaning in what they're saying. You don't trust anyone any more, especially me.'

He'd argued with her that he was right not to trust her, as she'd been having an affair for months, and now she was leaving him for that man.

'Where were you when I was seeing doctors about infertility?' she snapped back. 'What about all those cold, lonely nights when you went off to have a drink with your police buddies and never thought about me? You're married to your job. I'm only good for the odd home-cooked meal, a laundry service, and sex when you're in the mood. Is it any wonder I fell for a man who puts me first?'

Sandra was right, of course. After he'd stopped being bitter, he came to see that, and hoped she was happy at last. She deserved to be.

Now, when he looked in the mirror, he couldn't see any trace of the young man with thick dark hair, smooth olive skin and the eagerness for life that

Sandra had once loved about him. Now he saw grey hair at his temples, bags under his brown eyes, the sagging cheeks and neck. He rarely had time to cycle, swim or play tennis, the things he enjoyed. He realized, too, that he'd probably left it too late to find an independent, fun-loving, warm lady in her forties. That was the lady he dreamt about.

Occasionally he went to a club that was well known for attracting a clientele of more mature women. But he couldn't bear the peculiar brand of desperation he encountered there, not just in the women but the men too. Most had escaped unhappy marriages, but they couldn't wait to get into another.

'I've found a hair on her dress,' Patterson called. 'It's brown, so definitely not hers, but of course it could have come from another child, or her parents. Judging by her body temperature, I'd give a rough guess that she was killed between eleven and thirteen hours ago. Struck with a stone, with force – there are small pieces of it in her hair too. She tried to fight her killer. There are defensive wounds on her hands as she raised them to protect her head.'

'Was she raped?'

The pathologist pursed his lips. 'It doesn't appear so, but I need to get her back for a more thorough examination and to confirm time of death.'

'Any sign of the murder weapon?' Marshall asked Dowling.

'Not so far, sir.' PC Gibson, his face pitted with acne, had only recently joined the force and had answered from his position about fifteen yards away. 'But I'm looking very carefully.'

As the sun rose in the cloudless sky, so did the temperature. The police hurried to see that all photographs were taken, then the child's body removed and taken to the mortuary. Two officers were posted to guard the cordoned-off crime scene, and several others were doing a fingertip search around it.

At three in the afternoon Maureen and Rob had moved to the swing seat in their garden for tea and cake. Harry sat between them, looking from one to the other as if he sensed they were distressed. 'I wonder how the police go about starting an investigation,' Maureen said thoughtfully, stroking the dog's head to reassure him. 'I wanted to ask the sergeant this morning, but I lost my nerve. I mean, do they start with interviewing the family and friends of the child, or do they look through police files to find someone local who has a predilection for violence towards young girls?'

'They say most children are murdered by a close relative,' Rob said glumly. 'What could that child have done to make the killer do this?'

Maureen shuddered. 'Do you think he raped her?' she asked.

'I couldn't say, and I don't want to know, dearest,' Rob replied. 'Let's not talk about it any more.'

Maureen half smiled. She liked it when Rob called her 'dearest'. He was her one and only love. She'd been twenty-three when she met him and, before him, she'd had little success with the opposite sex. She was five foot six with lank brown hair and small grey eyes, and she knew she was plain. As her mother had rather unkindly pointed out, it wasn't so much that she was plain, more that she made no effort with her appearance or with people. She went on to say Maureen needed to lose half a stone and stop wearing such old-fashioned clothes – only frumps wore pleated skirts and twinsets. Even during her time at Nottingham University, when she had made more of an effort with her appearance – with trips to the hairdresser and wearing make-up for the dances at the weekend – she hadn't notched up more than half a dozen drunken fumbles.

Rob was two years older than her. He'd had a couple of short-lived relationships while he was at Durham University, but the moment they met – eighteen years ago in Cheltenham Library, where Maureen worked – it had been like a firework going off.

Mostly Maureen barely looked at the people she helped find books for, but Rob was different: he had milk-chocolate eyes that crinkled up when he smiled at her. His dark suit was a bit shiny with wear and the collar of his striped shirt was frayed, but somehow she knew this was carelessness with his wardrobe, which she found endearing. He was looking for Charles Dickens's *American Notes*, a little-known travelogue that the author had written while on a tour of the United States. Maureen was a devotee of Dickens, but she hadn't read that one, and as she searched for a copy for him, he informed her that he didn't think Dickens liked America much.

'Can you imagine?' he said, in his quiet but deep voice. 'He was as popular as the Beatles – crowds mobbed him wherever he went.'

Maureen knew then that he was the man for her. She didn't care what he did for a living or where he lived. He was the one. Later he was to admit it was the same for him, but he was scared to ask her if they could meet for a drink after she finished work. When he overcame that fear, to his delight, she smiled and agreed that would be lovely.

Back in those days she still wore sensible shoes, her hair fixed up in a bun, no make-up. She had resigned herself to being a spinster, yet Rob, who seemed to think she was perfect just as she was, made her feel beautiful and special. He loved libraries, saying they were 'cathedrals of learning'. He teased her about liking the silence rule because she wasn't much of a talker. Yet he understood she wasn't shy, only that forced chit-chat seemed phoney to her.

At the time of their meeting, Rob had recently joined a national book and stationery company in Cheltenham, but Maureen soon found he was ambitious and was a lot more outgoing than she was. Just after they married, he was made a regional manager. The shiny suit and frayed shirt were thrown away.

Five years ago in 2004 he was made redundant, and his pay-off was enough to set up their own stationery company, which they could run together. That was the point at which Maureen had decided to upgrade her image. She realized Rob would want her to attend trade fairs and company meetings with him, and she saw that the dull, shapeless dresses she'd worn as a librarian would no longer do. She had her hair cut in a shorter, more fashionable style, complete with blonde highlights, and started wearing make-up. Rob claimed she looked gorgeous, and although she knew that wasn't true, she liked what she saw in the mirror. She looked younger and felt more confident. When she popped back into the library one day to see her old colleagues, they barely recognized her with her new hairstyle, her smart slacks and vibrant pink jacket. Her new image changed their social life too. All at once their neighbours began to invite them to parties and barbecues.

Maureen was forty-one now and they'd been married for sixteen years. The fireworks had been replaced by warmth and tenderness.

Pinewood, the small housing estate where they lived, was on the outskirts of Cheltenham. It was built in the 1980s and advertised by the building company as luxury homes for discerning people. With six roads all named after trees, ten houses in each arranged in a horseshoe pattern, it was an attractive and desirable place to live. A wood had been cut down to make way for the houses, but a few pines, oaks and sycamores were left behind the garden fences. Beyond those trees, common land was dotted with bushes and brambles, and that was where Rob had found the dead girl.

Twenty years on from being built, Pinewood was dated. The luxury promised stopped at a downstairs cloakroom, integral garage and a fitted kitchen complete with a built-in dishwasher. The present owners often complained the houses were poorly insulated, and the kitchens too small.

Maureen and Rob had bought number four Willow Close just before their wedding in 1993. A downturn in the property market a year later meant they and many of their neighbours went into negative equity. As a result some people living on the estate had either neglected their homes or had them re-possessed by the mortgage companies. But the estate had risen since then and, once again, every front garden was manicured.

John and Rose Freeman, the nosy couple at number one, were constantly remarking that the value of their house was climbing steadily. Rob and Maureen had sniggered: they hoped the rising prices meant John and Rose would move away and they could be free of the gossips. So, when Rob and Maureen's doorbell rang at mid-morning, they guessed it would be the gossiping duo on a fact-finding mission.

Rob suggested they ignore the bell.

'You know they'll just keep coming back,' Maureen sighed. 'Besides, it might be that young couple who've moved in next door. I saw them through the bedroom window earlier and they looked nice. I wouldn't want them to think we were standoffish.'

Rob made a despairing gesture with his hands. 'On your head be it.' Maureen went indoors to open the front door.

It was John and Rose, their eyes sparkling in anticipation of being the first to be privy to breaking news. It looked as if Rose had dressed up to go hunting for it. She'd put up her bleach-blonde hair with a sparkly bulldog-type clip, and wore full make-up, with a navy and white spotted sun dress. She even had on high heels. At any other time Maureen would have told her she looked nice. But Rose's sharp features were almost quivering with pent-up excitement. To Maureen that was obscene.

Rose fired straight into it. 'We hear you found the girl's body. We can't believe someone could be murdered so close to our homes.'

Rob came to the door too. Maureen knew this was to draw her away if their neighbours became too pushy.

Maureen merely nodded. She hoped by saying nothing they would go away.

'We can see how deeply shocked you are. It must have been a horrible thing to stumble on,' John said, his voice silky in an effort to sound sincere.

'How had she been killed? Was she fully dressed?' Rose asked, pretending to be devastated by dabbing her completely dry eyes with a tissue.

'I heard it was Mike Church's daughter,' John said. 'Is that true?'

Rob and Maureen were caught on the wrong foot. They hadn't been told that. They had always got on very well with Mike and Ruth Church, who lived at number ten across the Close. Rob certainly hadn't recognized the dead girl as being their Chloë.

'If it is Chloë I didn't realize,' Rob said wearily, hoping against hope they were wrong.

'Angela who works for you is the sister of Ruth Church,' Rose added. She had the glimmer in her eye that had prompted Maureen once to call her the Huntress. 'Can't you ring her, Rob, and check if it is Chloë? You could offer all our condolences.'

Maureen and Rob looked at each other in horror. It was a terrible shock to hear the dead girl could be Mike and Ruth's daughter. Chloë was such a sunny-natured girl and such a credit to her parents, but to learn she was also Angela's niece and, as such, almost family made it even worse.

'Go away,' Rob said sharply. 'You've only called hoping to get some juicy gossip. A child is dead, for God's sake! How could you?'

'Well, pardon me!' Rose said indignantly. 'We only wanted to offer our help.'

'The best way to help a grieving family is not to talk about them,' Rob snapped, and slammed the front door in their faces. 'Vultures,' he hissed. 'They'll feed on this for weeks now.'

'Do you think it really is Chloë?' Maureen's eyes filled with tears. Any child's murder was appalling, but doubly so when they knew and liked her – and to think she was Angela's niece. Angela was not just an employee, but a trusted, loyal friend. Maureen remembered now that Angela had brought a pretty little girl into the office a couple of years ago. She had an engaging smile and good manners.

But now she wondered why Angela hadn't explained who she was. It would have been so easy to say, 'You must already know Chloë. Her mum is my sister and she lives just across the road from you.' Maybe Angela had thought she would be overstepping the mark between employer and employee. But if that was so, what did it say about her and Rob? *Were* they seen as standoffish?

'This is going to destroy Mike and Ruth,' Maureen murmured. 'That child was the centre of their life.'

Rob wiped his damp eyes. 'Let's just hope Rose and John got it wrong. It might not be Chloë.' His voice had a sort of plea in it.

'You know better than that. They wouldn't have called round until they were pretty certain who the child was,' Maureen said, and the tears she'd tried to hold back spilt over. She and Rob had wanted children, but it just hadn't happened. Most of the time Maureen reminded herself that she had everything she wanted, Rob, a lovely home and a dog she adored. But when she heard about children being killed or hurt, it brought back the sorrow at not having her own child, which she had tried to bury.

Rob took her in his arms and rocked her silently. He understood. He felt much the same as his wife. Whenever he saw children who looked neglected, he felt bitter that their parents didn't appreciate how lucky they were to have them.

4

Mike Church held his sobbing wife tightly, tears streaming down his cheeks. Having to identify Chloë's body was the worst possible thing any parent could be asked to do. He had prayed silently, as they were driven to the police station, that it would turn out to be a mistake, and that she'd be returned to them unharmed.

But, of course, it was her, lying there as if she were asleep. Although the abrasions on her face and head had been cleaned, Mike heard Ruth's sharp intake of breath and his stomach heaved, guessing at the damage that lay hidden beneath the white sheet. So often in the past they'd marvelled at how pretty and talented their daughter was, joking that maybe she'd been switched at the hospital, and their plain, ordinary child was with another couple.

Chloë was blonde like her mother, but Ruth's features had never been as delicate or her skin so translucent. Now at thirty-eight Ruth was a stone heavier than when they had met, there were lines around her eyes and she had the start of a double chin. As for Mike he'd often been taken for a farmer, with his red hair and ruddy complexion. The only feature Chloë had inherited from him was her speedwell blue eyes.

Ruth had said on the way home from the police station that it was impossible for her to comprehend that she would never hold Chloë again. Mike had just clasped his wife tighter, but he was filled with anger that he would never kiss his daughter again, watch her opening Christmas presents or hear her groaning at his inability to dance with any grace.

Now Chloë would never attain her dream of making it to the West End as a star in a musical. Instead her parents could only listen to a tape they had made a few months ago of her singing. But as that had brought tears to their eyes when she was alive, they couldn't imagine what it would do to them now.

Three years before Chloë had arrived, they'd had a baby boy, who was stillborn. It had floored them. The pain was unbearable. Even when Chloë was on the way, they were fearful it might happen again. But, happily, she was a healthy seven-pounder, and they chose to think then that their share of heartache and tragedy was behind them. But to love and care for her for thirteen years, then have her die so brutally was beyond belief.

They had shared so many dreams with her. She was a talented dancer and singer and had already starred in three amateur productions. They were looking into a *Fame*-style drama school where she could keep up her dancing along with learning acting skills. Only a few days ago she'd had a letter asking her to come for an audition at the end of the month. The school was in London's Waterloo.

Now they felt as if they had nothing to live for. Mike had his own computer and electronics company, and Ruth was the school nurse at the local comprehensive. They both had other interests, but their daughter was the jewel in their crown. And now she had been snatched from them.

'Who could've done it?' Ruth whimpered against his shoulder. 'Everyone liked her.'

'I don't think killers have any feelings about their victims. Thank God she wasn't –' He stopped, unable to say 'raped'.

It was four thirty now, and since returning from the identification this morning, the police had been at their house for four hours. So many questions, most of which seemed completely irrelevant. They had gone through Chloë's bedroom with a fine-tooth comb, and among all the soft toys, photographs, and singing and dancing memorabilia, they hadn't found anything. Nothing shed any light on why she'd been attacked or by whom.

They asked Mike and Ruth so many questions about their neighbours and Chloë's friends. Neither believed any of their neighbours would harm their

daughter, and although a couple of local men sometimes acted inappropriately when they drank too
much at parties, they certainly didn't think either was
a killer. There was also one man in Elm Close, the
road beside Willow Close, who was known to hit his
wife and kids. Everyone had heard the screams coming from their house, but as distasteful and horrible
as his violence was, to their knowledge he had only
ever turned on his own family. They named those
men, though, because, as the police said, it was their
duty to pass on any information. If they were innocent, and could prove where they were at the time of
the killing, they had nothing to fear.

As for Chloë's friends, it was impossible to imagine
any of those sweet and funny kids attacking her.

'Over the years we've had virtually every single
child in her class here for sleepovers, tea or just playing,' Ruth had said to the police. 'We've met all their
parents too. Nothing strange or creepy about any of
them. Several have said how nice it is that I let all the
children come to our house. But my husband and I
had always taken the view it was better to have them
here than hanging around on street corners getting
into mischief.'

Remembering some of the more probing questions
about his relationship with their daughter, Mike felt
a pang of fear. While he knew most murdered children were killed by a family member, it was terrible

that anyone could even think he might be capable of hurting Chloë.

Mike hugged Ruth close again, remembering how noisy it had been sometimes with their daughter's friends playing here. They would never hear that again, and he wondered how they would ever get through this. He had always thought of himself as a lucky man. It had hit him hard when their first baby was stillborn, but even then, he was able to take the pragmatic view that such things happened for a good reason, and maybe he had had a serious defect. He grieved with Ruth, supported and loved her, and they managed to revert to their old optimistic selves once Chloë was on the way.

Born to middle-class parents and brought up in Cheltenham, Mike had had the best of educations and a secure, loving home life. He had accepted he wasn't much in the looks department, only five eight, but he'd had many friends who were girls. A couple he'd met at the youth club would often go to the pictures or a gig with him. One of them, Lizzie Bracknell, had come to their wedding and was now Chloë's godmother. She had developed a strong bond with Ruth and Chloë. Mike knew she would be devastated when she learnt what had happened.

He had chosen to go to Cardiff University because it was far enough from home to live in hall, yet close enough for him to spend the odd weekend with his parents. He did business studies and computer science as he sensed that, before long, computers would change the world, and when that came about, he wanted to be in on it.

People often said how astute he had been, and still was, and he laughed it off. But his success wasn't through luck: he'd worked hard for it, constantly keeping an eye on world markets, and adapting his company's products to meet the challenges, hopefully keeping one step ahead of the game.

He'd met Ruth during his final year at Cardiff. It was at a disco that was well known for being popular with nurses. While sipping a pint of lager he'd watched her dancing with a friend and couldn't take his eyes off her. She was small, perhaps five foot four, slim, with shoulder-length blonde hair, and a smile that could have lit up Cardiff. He sensed right then that she was 'the one', and he was so convinced of it that he put down his drink and asked her to dance.

She wasn't Welsh, as he'd expected, but from Gloucester, the next town to his home, Cheltenham. She teased him, saying that made him a posh boy. She had done her nursing training in Cardiff and intended to stay at the Royal Infirmary for at least another year. Looking back, Mike was amazed he got a good degree later that year, as all he could think about was Ruth when he should have been studying.

She was fun, warm, kind and sexy. A happy girl

who loved her work and life. He told her he loved her after only two weeks and she laughed, her blue eyes shining and a dimple showing on her right cheek. 'Tell me that again in another month and maybe I'll take you seriously,' she said.

It was so cold that winter of '90, squally winds and icy rain. Yet somehow the weather didn't seem to matter to them. They had both liked nights out with a crowd of friends before they met, but more and more they wanted to be alone.

He waited for exactly one month to pass and told her he loved her again.

Ruth threw her arms around him and said she loved him too.

They took a cheap holiday in Lanzarote that Easter, and although the hotel was basic, and the bed creaked, they made love all night. By day it was hot and sunny, and they lay by the pool planning their future life together.

'A detached house with a big garden and four kids,' Ruth said. 'In Cheltenham – it's much classier than Gloucester. We'll invite our neighbours to our dinner parties, and they'll all be terribly envious of us.'

They got a link-detached house, and one child. But it was in Cheltenham, and they often had dinner parties. Mike thought the neighbours were probably a bit jealous of them, as Ruth was so pretty and he was extremely successful.

Ironically, they had recently been planning to find a bigger house, one of the lovely Regency ones in central Cheltenham. They thought that once Chloë was at the stage school in London she wouldn't have much in common with her old friends in Pinewood, so it would be an ideal time to move.

Both he and Ruth were thirty-eight now. Not too old to have another child, but Mike knew that was unthinkable. Nothing and no one could ever replace Chloë.

'What happens now?' Ruth said brokenly. 'One of the policemen said she had to have a post-mortem.'

Mike had no idea what to say. Ruth was a trained nurse, so she understood what post-mortems were for and what they entailed. But this was her child. How could any mother bear the thought of such invasive procedures on her child's young body?

'Let's take each day as it comes,' he suggested, even though it was a meaningless cliché. 'I'll make us each a drink, and maybe we could go and lie down for a while. I know you didn't sleep at all last night.'

5

Trudy Singer at number six came into her kitchen from the integral garage and dumped her heavy shopping bags on the floor. She was sweating profusely, and her sleeveless pink T-shirt, with black leggings, merely accentuated the rolls of fat round her middle. She swept back her hair from her forehead to mop her brow and fanned her armpits with a letter left on the kitchen work surface.

'Amy!' she called, to her thirteen-year-old. 'Rose Freeman just told me Chloë Church has been killed. Had you heard?'

Amy came thundering down the stairs and into the kitchen. 'Did you say Chloë's been killed? Was she run over?' she asked breathlessly.

Amy was very overweight, like her mother. She had her father's dark hair and height but not his handsome features. Her small eyes and mouth, plus puffy cheeks, gave her an odd doll-like appearance.

Trudy was so shaken by the news that she hadn't thought to soften it to her daughter. Now, when she saw her stricken face, she felt ashamed.

Chloë and Amy had been friends since they were

four-year-olds. So many shared parties and sleepovers, and now that sweet girl was dead. Trudy splashed her face with water and took a long drink, giving herself time to think.

'No, love, it's said she was murdered. But I can't believe it. Surely Rose has got it wrong – she's always gossiping and getting the wrong end of the stick. You were playing with Chloë yesterday, weren't you?'

'Not really. I just saw her at the park. Oh, Mum, how awful.' Amy ran to her mother and flung her arms around her.

'There, there,' Trudy said, patting her daughter's back for comfort. 'Yes, it is terrible if it's true, but don't get too upset, love, until it's confirmed. Though Heaven knows why anyone would say such a thing if it wasn't true.'

Trudy had never been any good at dealing with emotional stuff. Even as she held Amy, she was eyeing the laden shopping bags and dying to put it all away. She'd suffered with postnatal depression when Amy was born, and she was sure that was what had stopped her being the cuddly mother she'd have liked to be.

'I've got frozen stuff in the bags that I must put in the freezer,' she said eventually, gently prising Amy's arms from round her. 'Will you help me put the rest of the stuff away?'

She noted how pale her daughter had become. As always, when she felt guilty, her way of dealing with it was to offer food. 'As soon as we're done here, we'll go and sit in the garden. I bought us both a cream slice, your favourite.'

Thirty minutes later Trudy and Amy were lying on sun-loungers in the garden. 'Is Daddy coming home today?' Amy asked.

Trudy had changed into a sun dress with spaghetti straps, the skirt pulled up to tan her legs. Amy was still in jeans and a T-shirt: she hated putting on anything revealing, insisting she was too fat.

Trudy knew her daughter was overweight, but she'd been like that at the same age. In those days they'd called it puppy fat and it had dropped off by the time she was sixteen. But she knew she wasn't a good role model to Amy as she now weighed nearly thirteen stone and she was only five foot five. Crisps, cake and sweets were her downfall.

She glanced at Amy and saw she was squeezing the cake, then licking off the cream oozing out of the sides. She wanted to shout at her to eat it properly, but under the circumstances she thought she'd better ignore it.

'I'm not sure if your dad's coming home. He hasn't phoned,' Trudy said. 'He told me yesterday he still had a great deal more work to do in Brighton and it would make sense to stay there, rather than drive all the way home and then have to go back again early on Monday. With this hot weather the traffic will be bad.'

'Could we go to the seaside tomorrow, then?' Amy asked.

Trudy lay back and closed her eyes. She often wondered why Amy never seemed able to hold a real conversation but fired out questions usually unrelated to the subject in hand. Surely the average child would express disappointment that her father wasn't coming home, ask where he'd be staying, or if he had made any friends there. Yet she just moved on to ask about going to the seaside. 'Maybe. We'll see. Now I'm going to have a snooze.'

As much as she wanted to sleep, Trudy kept thinking about Amy's reactions. Girls of her age were usually drama queens: they cried, they screamed and were inconsolable over much less than a murder. They were also prone to talking endlessly about something that disturbed them or was sensational. Amy hadn't reacted much at all. In fact, she hadn't mentioned Chloë's death since Trudy had told her about the murder.

Why didn't she ask how Mike and Ruth were? She'd spent so much time in their house that they were like relatives. She didn't even wonder who would be her friend, now Chloë wasn't around. Even odder, she hadn't used the phone to call other girls in her class and tell them what had happened. Was she holding back on a normal response because she had learnt from her mother to suppress her feelings?

Trudy's problem was guilt. About her weight, looks, extravagance, being a poor wife and mother, anything. She never admitted to the crushing guilt that cast a shadow over everything in her life. She was aware, however, that by blaming herself for absolutely everything, it affected Amy and Roger too.

Her mother used to say, 'If you become a doormat, everyone will wipe their feet on you.' And she supposed she had: Amy and Roger behaved as if she was their personal servant.

She suspected Roger had another woman in Brighton. But she didn't feel able to blame him for it. After all, she wasn't keen on sex, didn't drink and was always tired. She listened to other women talking about exciting meals they'd cooked, rooms they'd decorated, naughty underwear they'd bought. It seemed to Trudy that every other woman in the world had a way of putting a bit of oomph into their marriage, except her.

They had the same meals each week, chops, sausages, pasta and chicken. She couldn't think beyond that. Maybe if Roger exploded and said he was sick of having sausages every Tuesday she'd have found the will to change things, but he just ate what she put in front of him and didn't remark on it.

Maybe that was why she'd stopped caring about her appearance too. Even back in the day when she was so fussy about her hair, nails and clothes, he never said she looked nice. Now her hair had an inch of grey roots, and she just fastened it back in one lank bunch. She'd stopped wearing make-up and doing her nails, and wore comfortable, drab clothes to hide her fat.

Yet at seventeen Trudy Brown had been pretty, with shiny chestnut hair, a radiant complexion and a good figure. She'd met Roger at a dance, and after six months of courting he told her that if she really loved him she'd let him make love to her. She felt she had to, so she let him do it on the sofa when her parents were out for the evening. Soon after, she realized she was pregnant.

Roger was twenty, apprenticed to a mechanic, with only a few more months of his apprenticeship to serve. He had big ideas of starting his own garage. He hadn't reckoned on having a wife and baby to support. But Trudy's father gave him a stern talking-to and promised him that if he did the right thing by his daughter he would give him the deposit for a house.

Trudy was unaware of the inducement her father had offered. When Roger bought the house in Willow Close, she was impressed and excited as it seemed to her proof that he really loved her. It was only after Amy was born that he had blurted out the truth in an argument, and a part of her had died.

At the time she'd said she would never have married

him if she'd known. But that was just bravado: she knew deep down she had wanted him on any terms and, besides, any decent man should be providing for his wife and baby.

By the time Amy was a year old, Roger was earning a good wage. Trudy liked her home in Willow Close so she tried to be the perfect wife. She never argued with him, never complained. Whatever he wanted to do was fine with her. Within twenty minutes of him arriving home, his dinner was on the table. His freshly washed and ironed shirts hung ready for him in the wardrobe.

Sometimes she'd hear a small voice in the back of her head that claimed it took two to make a happy marriage. He had guilt-tripped her into sex, and he should have taken precautions. If he'd done that they might never have married. If he would only be more loving towards her, encourage her to be adventurous, and take a real interest in her and Amy, it might be different.

But always a more strident voice drowned out the small one and claimed it was all her fault. She had been stupid to let him have his way with her. She wallowed in self-pity, wondering why any man would want her.

These days, he wasn't a working mechanic: he owned four garages in different towns, and his role was like the ring-master, hiring, firing, doing the accounts and making sure each of his premises made big profits. Now and then he would prove to his staff that he knew motors inside out, by rolling up his sleeves and changing a carburettor or a clutch.

His businesses were the ideal excuse to miss parents' evenings, sports days, even Amy's birthday parties. For the last year or so he'd been claiming the Brighton garage was struggling. A failing garage was a good excuse to go there regularly. Although he often left the accounts books at home, she knew she wouldn't understand them even if she tried to check them. As Roger often pointed out, she was thick.

She had confided her predicament to Janice Wyatt, at number two. Janice was glamorous and something of a mystery woman. She wore long, flowing dresses and dyed her hair with henna. Her house was full of treasures from India and Africa, yet she never seemed to want to talk about her travels, or her personal life.

It was nearly Christmas when Trudy had run into Janice while walking back from the local shop. She insisted Trudy come into her house for a drink and it seemed churlish not to accept, even though she hardly ever drank alcohol. Janice insisted on giving her a glass of Baileys with some brandy in it to warm her up. Sitting on a long, low couch, with wool-embroidered and mirrored cushions all around her, she felt as if she'd been transported to the kasbah. There were intricate, handcrafted lantern lights over the beautifully carved coffee-table and the smell of an exotic perfume wafting around.

One glass of the delicious drink was enough to loosen Trudy's tongue, and before she could stop herself, she'd blurted out the whole sorry tale of her marriage.

Janice was a good listener. She didn't interrupt or look bored. When Trudy finished, Janice sighed deeply. 'It makes me so sad that people stay in toxic marriages. We should only share a life with someone we can't bear to live without,' she said. 'I'm not saying you should run away just now. Talk to Roger, quietly and firmly, without shouting or hysterics. Tell him you're unhappy, and you suspect he has someone else. He may be glad to admit he's been wanting out.'

'What if he insists he's happy with how things are?'

'You tell him you know that's not true. Stick up for yourself, Trudy. Say you'll be fair if he is, and you'll never stop him seeing Amy. But you need to stay in the house because of her.'

With a couple of stiff drinks inside her, Trudy really intended to tackle Roger. But as soon as she sobered up, she felt he'd ask for a divorce, and she knew she couldn't bear that. She couldn't imagine a life without her husband. Maybe it wasn't romantic-fiction love, but she was proud that he'd done so well, and he was handsome. Tall, slender, thick dark hair and bright blue eyes that everyone remarked on. His skin never lost its tan, because he played golf in all weathers, and he was fit because he ran four or five miles most days too.

Trudy liked other women remarking on his looks: it made her feel less of a loser. Besides, if he left, she'd have to get a job, and she wasn't trained for anything. She couldn't face working in a supermarket. Plus, there was Amy. Since she'd got into her teens she often sank into black moods when she barely spoke. She'd really ramp it up if her father was gone.

It was all very well for Janice to say she must talk about it to Roger. But how? He never even asked her what she'd done all day, or how Amy was getting on at school. When she tried to make conversation he always had work to do in his office upstairs, or there was something he wanted to watch on TV. When she thought about it, they hadn't had a real conversation since before Amy was born.

The doorbell ringing brought Trudy suddenly back to the here and now. 'Who on earth can that be?' she asked Amy. 'One of your friends?'

Amy was reading a magazine, and shook her head. 'Doubt it. They'll all be down the park.'

Trudy heaved herself off the sun-lounger, smoothed down her dress and slipped on her sandals. As she got to the hall, she could see two policemen through the opaque glass door.

'Good afternoon, Mrs Singer,' the taller of the two

men said, as she opened the door. 'I'm sure you've already heard the tragic news that a child's body was discovered earlier this morning near here.'

'Yes. They said it was Chloë Church, but I was hoping it was some awful mistake as she's my daughter's friend.'

'No mistake, I'm afraid, Mrs Singer, and it's your daughter Amy we wish to speak to.'

Trudy opened the door wider. 'Do come in. She's out in the garden. I'll call her.'

'If you would, but I'm afraid we must ask you both to accompany us to the police station for a formal interview.'

'Why us?' Trudy frowned.

'We have information that Amy was with Chloë yesterday. In cases like this, speed in interviewing people who had contact with the victim just prior to the crime is of vital importance. She'll need an adult sitting in on the interview. There's nothing to worry about. Just come with us now.'

As Trudy went to get Amy, she remembered something her mother often said: 'When people say there's nothing to worry about, there usually is.'

6

Alfie glanced out of the window and saw that the police were not driving away as he'd expected after speaking to him and Dee. They were going to the Singers at number six.

Alfie Strong's name was apt: a craggy face that could have been moulded by fists, tall, broad shoulders and muscular arms. He had a history of being a hard case in south London in his twenties, but now at forty-seven he had a small beer paunch instead of an iron six-pack. Yet he still looked capable of tearing someone's head off their shoulders.

His south London accent, icy blue eyes and surprisingly gentlemanly ways made him intriguing to most women. He looked back into the room at his wife, still shocked by her reaction to the news that Chloë Church was dead. She had poured herself a large gin and tonic as soon as the police left the house and was now sitting on the sofa smoking a cigarette, with a face like a bag of wasps.

When the police had called, Alfie had expected her to be as upset as he was. Instead she showed indignation that they had dared to ask where she and Alfie had been between six and ten thirty the previous evening. While Alfie could barely speak for fear of breaking down at the thought of Mike and Rose's agony, Dee just sat there, not a shred of emotion. She was not even interested enough to ask any questions. He knew his wife had a cold heart, but surely a child's death would thaw even the iciest.

Alfie was trying to find the right words to tell Dee what he thought of her reaction earlier when she spoke out: 'It'll be Mike what done it.' Her mean little mouth was even tighter-lipped than usual. 'There's always been something about him.'

Alfie was so appalled at that vile remark he could only stare at her. Again and again he'd wondered why she always thought the worst of everyone. What could have made her so spiteful?

She was the same age as him, but she could pass for thirty-five with her trim figure, shoulder-length platinum-blonde hair and youthful clothes. Today she wore pink shorts and a pink and white striped halter-neck top. Down at the pub other men eyed her up and told him he was lucky, but Alfie didn't feel he was.

While he'd known she was no angel when he married her, some of the things she'd done in the past had shocked him. And shocking Alfie Strong wasn't an easy thing to do. Yet over the fifteen years of their marriage, instead of growing kinder, softer and less judgemental she had gone the opposite way. Harder, more devious and quite often terrifying.

'Mike adored his daughter,' he said, stifling the desire to slap her face. 'You really shouldn't say things like that, Dee. Aren't you capable of understanding how terrible it is to lose a child?'

'Of course I am.' She tossed her head in defiance. 'But that Mike, he's so . . .' She paused, not knowing how to explain herself. It wasn't what he said, just the way he looked at her, as if she was something he'd scraped off his shoes. Most men flirted with her, tried to kiss her if the opportunity arose, but not Mike.

'Intelligent. That's the word,' Alfie said. 'And he sees you for what you are. Dumb, common and cruel.'

'What? I can't believe you'd say such a thing,' she exploded, leaping up to stand in front of him, her hands on her narrow hips.

Alfie saw the malevolence in her eyes and knew she'd find a way to get him back for speaking out. But he didn't care any longer. A sweet, polite and well-loved child from this estate being killed brought many things into sharp focus, including that he didn't like his wife, let alone love her.

'Aah, come on, Dee, you *are* common and cruel, and too dumb to realize everyone can see it. Do you ever have a kind thought about anyone? You've let your old mother rot in that nursing home you talked me into paying for, and never go to see her. You didn't want children, because it would ruin your body, and you haven't got one friend, because other women know you're poison.'

She slapped his face. It stung a little. 'You bastard,' she hissed at him. 'I'm going to make you very sorry.'

'Not as sorry as I am already for not realizing you wouldn't change for the better after marriage. I blame myself that I actually thought your past was exciting. It wasn't. It was cruel and sordid,' he snarled back. 'We'll get a divorce, and you can go and find some other patsy to bleed dry.'

'You needn't think I'm leaving this house,' she said, smirking with triumph because she knew what the house meant to him.

'We'll see about that,' he said grimly. 'I bought this house before I met you and it's still in my name only. You've never done a day's honest work since we got married. No court would let you take it, so you may as well get out now.'

'I'm going nowhere,' she said, flouncing out of the sitting room and up the stairs.

Alfie didn't bother to chase after her. Instead he poured himself a large Scotch. Their entire marriage, except for the first three months, had been a battle-ground. As always, after one of their spats, he wished he'd thought harder before proposing to her. She was pretty, he'd admit to that, but it was like being given a beautiful box of chocolates, all tied up with silk ribbon, but once opened, you find it's filled with something rotten.

She had boasted soon after they met that she'd tricked lots of men into giving her money and expensive jewellery. He knew, too, that she'd worked as a call-girl in London. But none of that bothered him. After all, he'd been to prison a couple of times and committed a lot of crimes he'd got away with. He had also met many women with chequered pasts who took pride in robbing rich, corrupt men, but at the same time helped out old friends and lovers. Not Dee. She had preyed on weak men, had lied, stolen, and aided and abetted many vicious crimes. He knew he should have chucked her out years ago. But Dee had one weapon in her armoury that laid him low. It seemed to stop his brain noting that with her it was all take, never any give. She was dynamite in bed.

She boasted to other people that she got him to do what she wanted with his cock. That shamed him now, because back when he was under her thrall, he believed loving him made her so good at sex. How dumb was that? Much of it was an act.

Alfie had several friends who had married hookers, and all of them were happy. Their wives were great mothers, excellent cooks, warm, kind, fun-loving women. But most of them had gone into prostitution because they had a couple of kids, and it was well-nigh impossible for a single mother to get a job.

They did what they could to put food on the table and shoes on those children's feet.

Dee claimed she wanted a child before they got married, and when she didn't get pregnant, she seemed convincingly sad. But eighteen months into their marriage Alfie had stumbled upon some birth-control pills, and he knew then that she'd lied to him. She'd never wanted children.

He thought back to the questions from the police. Dee had been very quick to say she'd been sunbathing in the garden until six, when she came indoors to have a shower, mix a gin and tonic, then later cooked their supper. She'd added that Alfie was with her the whole time.

That wasn't strictly true. She had been sunbathing in the afternoon, but she went out about five, and didn't come back till seven thirty. Even stranger, she came in through the garage and put her dress into the washing-machine. Alfie knew this because, although he'd been watching the news on the TV, he had seen her go past the door in her underwear. When he asked why, she said she'd fallen over in the street and got dog mess on her dress. She'd taken it off and put it on to wash.

This made Alfie wonder whether she could have killed Chloë. But why?

7

Trudy and Amy Singer were ushered into an interview room at the police station by PC Holt, who told them Detective Inspector Marshall would be with them soon. She offered them a drink. Trudy said she'd like coffee and Amy asked for orange squash.

The policewoman came back with the drinks seconds before DI Marshall and a Detective Constable Morris came in and introduced themselves.

'We just wanted to talk to you, Amy, about your friend Chloë,' Marshall said. 'As we understand it, you were her best friend. Is that right?'

'Yes,' Amy said. 'We've been friends since we were little.'

'So you've always played together? Perhaps at thirteen you don't call it that any more. Is it "hanging out"?'

Amy nodded.

'Is that usually at your house, or Chloë's?'

'Mostly at Chloë's.'

'Do you walk home from school together?'

'Yes, most days.'

'You broke up at school yesterday for the summer holidays, didn't you? Did you come home together?'

'No. I had to get a book from my teacher, after the bell went. She wanted me to read it during the holidays, so Chloë went on home without me.'

'It was a lovely warm afternoon. What did you do when you got home?'

'I made her a sandwich, and she sat in the garden with me for a bit,' Trudy volunteered.

'Could you let your daughter answer, please,' DI Marshall said gently.

Trudy blushed.

'And later, what then?'

'I went down the park.'

'To be clear. When you say the park, I take it you mean the lower part of the common land, which has a children's playground with swings?' Marshall asked.

'Yes. We all call it the park.'

'What time did you go there?'

Amy looked at her mother. 'I think it was about half past five.'

Trudy nodded confirmation.

'Did you call for Chloë on the way?'

'No. I knew she would've gone already.'

'So was she there when you arrived?'

'Yes, but she was sitting on one of the swings, talking to Jason Longham and Wayne Maudland.'

'Did you go and join her?'

Amy shook her head. 'No, I just walked away. I got the feeling she didn't want me interrupting.'

'So who did you talk to, or hang out with?'

'Susie Bagham, Mark Pople. I didn't really talk to them. I was just around.'

Jim Marshall sensed Amy was one of those kids who hung around the periphery, never really getting close to the inner circle. He noticed her mother appeared to be the nervy sort, sitting on the edge of her seat, not even reaching out a calming hand to her daughter. He wanted to know about the father.

'What time does your dad get home from work?' he asked.

The girl and her mother exchanged glances. 'He's not coming home tonight,' Amy said. 'He's at his garage in Brighton.'

'I expect you miss him when he's away. Does he have to stay away a lot?'

Amy hesitated. Marshall sensed this meant she wasn't very close to him. 'I miss him, but he's away for a night or two most weeks, so I've got used to it.'

'When I was a boy if my father wasn't coming home, I always stayed out later than I was supposed to, because my mum didn't carry on like Dad did. Do you do that?'

'Not really. It's Mum that always tells me what time to come home.'

Marshall looked at Amy thoughtfully. She wasn't at ease: she kept glancing at her mother as if for reassurance. Not that she got any – Mrs Singer was staring into space, seemingly oblivious to what was being said.

'So, Amy, what time did you get in yesterday evening?'

'I can't remember,' she said, looking again to her mother. 'Do you remember, Mum?'

'About seven thirty, I think. I was upstairs watching the TV in my bedroom, but I heard you call out.'

'Did you come down to see her?' Marshall asked Trudy.

'No, I fell asleep and when I woke it was dark. I got up, and Amy was in bed fast asleep. I went downstairs to check the door was locked, and the windows closed. It was just after half ten.'

Marshall wondered why she hadn't come out of her bedroom to ask if Amy wanted a cup of tea or something to eat. Dozing in a chair was one thing, his own mother had done that, but she'd always sprung up the moment he walked in, often boxing his ears if he was late back. He had the impression that Amy was alone or ignored a great deal. 'Did you see anyone else in the park, a stranger, someone older perhaps, not someone from your school?'

'There were a few mums with little kids when I first got there. And some people with their dogs. But they were all strangers to me. I don't know them,' she said thoughtfully. 'Oh, yes, and the man we call Tex, he was there. He's a bit simple and wears a cowboy hat.'

'Did you speak to him?' Marshall asked. He knew the man she meant. He also knew some kids were quite cruel to him, calling him names and winding him up so he'd chase them.

'No. He was sitting on the grass smoking. Then I saw him walking up the hill, the bit where all the brambles grow.'

'Did he come back down before you went home?'

'No – well, if he did, I didn't notice him. There were a couple of older boys arrived on their scrambler bikes, and they drove up the way Tex had gone.'

'Do you know the names of those boys?' he asked.

She shook her head. 'I've only seen them a few times. Someone said they come from Gloucester. But I don't know if that's true.'

'Now, Amy,' Marshall said, leaning forward across the desk towards her in a more conspiratorial way, 'I know you've been best friends with Chloë for years, so you must know everything about her. Did she ever tell you about boys she liked, perhaps an older one?'

'She liked Jason Longham, but there was another boy at the dance school she goes to. His name's Dean – she's always on about him.'

'Where does Jason live?'

'In Elm Close, the road next to ours. Chloë once said she can see into his bedroom from hers.'

'What about Dean?'

'I think he lives in one of the big posh houses in Montpelier. His dad is a doctor. Chloë said her parents were planning to buy a house there too.'

'Chloë was good at singing and dancing. Do you feel a bit left out that you don't do those things too?'

He'd guessed that she didn't do singing and dancing. He wanted to see her reaction to this question.

She opened her mouth to speak but closed it immediately. Marshall sensed she was going to agree, but had then thought better of it.

'No. I thought she was great. I was proud to be her best friend,' she said hurriedly, but her blush gave away her fib.

Marshall glanced at Mrs Singer. She looked very bored, as if she wasn't listening to what was being said. Again, he had the feeling she was rarely interested in her daughter. 'Well, Mrs Singer, can you add anything to what Amy's told us?'

She almost jumped with surprise at her name being said. 'Like what?' she asked.

'In my experience mothers often know things about their children's friends and family that their child is unaware of. What do you know about the Churches?'

'They're nice people,' she said. 'Ruth is a nurse, and she'll always help anyone in the close if they've got a medical problem. I've run to her a few times when Amy's cut herself or I was worried about something. All the children like her – she's a bit of an earth-mother.'

'What about Mr Church?'

'He's very clever – I never really know what to say to him. But he's kind and very welcoming.'

'What was Amy wearing when she went to the park yesterday?'

The woman half closed her eyes as if trying to picture her daughter. 'I can't remember,' she said, after a few seconds.

'Oh, Mum, I was still wearing my school uniform dress,' Amy said. She gave Marshall a little grin. 'Mum doesn't remember things very well.'

'What colour was the dress?' Marshall asked.

'Green and white stripes,' Amy said.

'We'll need it for tests,' Marshall said. 'We'll collect it when we run you home.'

'Surely you don't think my Amy killed Chloë.' Suddenly Trudy Singer seemed wide awake.

'We test the clothing of anyone who came in close contact with the victim,' Marshall said. 'It's just routine.'

Amy was frowning. Marshall wondered what she was thinking about. 'Are you going to question Tex?' she asked suddenly. 'Only I've seen him get really angry with people. He's not all there.'

Marshall looked reprovingly at her. 'That's not

a nice way to describe anyone, or that he's simple. "Learning difficulties" is kinder,' he said sharply. 'Did you see him get angry with Chloë?'

'No.' Amy hung her head, her cheeks red. 'But a few weeks ago he punched David Saunders, a boy from my school. He had to have stitches above his eye.'

Marshall nodded. 'Yes, we're aware of that. We know, too, that Saunders had been provoking Tex by throwing stones at him and shouting insults.'

'Can we go now?' Trudy asked. 'We haven't had our tea yet.'

Marshall looked hard at her. With the weight she was carrying it wouldn't hurt her to go without her tea. 'Yes, you can. One of the officers will take you back and collect Amy's dress.'

Trudy and Amy got up to leave, but once they were out in the corridor Amy clutched at her mother's arm. 'Why does he want my school dress? Does he think I killed Chloë?'

Trudy looked at her daughter despairingly. She had the look of a frightened rabbit caught in headlights. 'They just want to check Chloë's blood isn't on it, and of course he doesn't think you killed her. The police always act scary – it's to make you blurt out things you shouldn't.'

'Like me saying Tex isn't all there?'

'No, not that. Lying about things. They check out what a person has said, and if they find it was a lie, they come down on them like a ton of bricks. Did you tell any lies?'

'No.' Amy shook her head, as if shocked her mother would ask such a thing. 'Why would I? I haven't done anything wrong.'

'Well, that's okay, then. Maybe we will go to the seaside tomorrow and forget all this sadness.'

8

Terry and Wilma Parkin drove away from Willow Close at seven on Saturday morning. Terry had woken Wilma an hour earlier to tell her he'd booked them a weekend in a hotel in the New Forest as a surprise. He had taken Monday off too. As he said, they must make the most of the hot weather. He asked her to pack quickly as he wanted to get on the road before the traffic became heavy.

Wilma was like a little mouse, so bland in every way, from her dull clothes to her hair always scraped into a bun, that people seldom remembered her. Even at her church, of which she was a fervent supporter, few people noticed her. Despite her rather pious nature, she was highly intelligent, spoke three European languages and was one of life's observers, quietly noticing everything about people she met.

Terry was her opposite. He stood out in a crowd: six foot three, thick dark hair, with just a touch of silver at his temples. He was well-built, but not flabby, his stomach as flat as an ironing board because he worked out daily in a gym he'd built in their garden. He was forty-eight, and had spent twenty-five years in the army. His time deployed in Afghanistan, Northern Ireland and the Baltics had given him mental as well as physical strength.

Wilma had often overheard people questioning why a man like Terry would pick a wife so different from himself. She had heard Terry's response three or four times, and he always quipped, 'Why would I want a wife like me?'

She knew that although Terry appeared brave, outspoken, daring and charismatic, he needed a woman he could trust implicitly: underneath the swaggering bravado, he was extremely insecure. His parents had been vile to him and he had four older brothers who had made him the scapegoat. He was beaten and half starved, and had never known a kind word or affectionate gesture in his entire childhood. But he'd had his escape planned. When he left school, he lodged with an old lady he knew, and spent the next two years labouring on building sites. He built up his muscles, learnt how to get along with other men, and was ready for the second stage in his life: to join the army. He would become a leader so no one could ever put him down again.

He succeeded and rose quickly to sergeant. The men under him respected and admired him because he never expected anyone to do anything he couldn't or wouldn't do himself. The officers held him in high regard: they knew he could keep a cool head in the most dangerous situations, and he trained his men well.

On retiring from the army he went to work for British Telecom. He was surprised to find he enjoyed the job – after so many years of giving orders and watching his men's backs it was good to relax in a mundane job with no surprises. His workmates looked up to him, because of his army career, the hours were good and the pay wasn't bad. The bonus of the job was that he could escape Wilma's often suffocating godliness.

The first thing she asked when he told her they were going away was 'But what about church on Sunday?'

In his head he said, 'Fuck church', but to her he smiled and said they had churches in the New Forest too. She looked worried about that. But then she worried about everything. He often wondered how she'd survived back in the days when he was deployed in trouble spots.

She was worried on Friday night when she went out to water the flowers in the front garden at dusk because she saw Mike from number ten going down towards the park, looking agitated. She came in suggesting Terry ought to go and talk to him. Terry snapped at her, saying he wasn't going to poke his nose into someone else's business.

As they were driving to the New Forest, they heard

on the radio that a child's body had been found on waste ground in Cheltenham. She said, 'Could that be why Mike looked worried? Was Chloë missing?'

Terry was thrown by the news too. From Mike's behaviour the previous evening, it was possible the child could be Chloë, but he didn't want Wilma wittering on about it all weekend, so he turned the radio off, said it was extremely unlikely, and could she please embrace a weekend away without going on about home and their neighbours?

Brian Alcott at number nine stood behind the lowered venetian blinds in the bedroom, looking up and down the street. He had been scared all day by the police presence, and he hadn't answered the door when a couple of uniforms knocked. He knew it was customary for them to call at every house during a murder inquiry, but he needed to get his story, and the house, straight before he let them in to take a statement.

May was panicking, but his wife was prone to that. She'd spent some time quietly taking the boxes through the door into the integral garage and loading up the van they kept there. She wanted him to drive it away now to the salon in Bromsgrove. But, he thought, it would look suspicious because everyone in the close assumed they were away for the weekend. Besides, the police would stop him immediately.

With hindsight, it might have been better if he and

May had joined the other neighbours in the street this morning when the news broke about the dead kid. At the time they'd still been in bed, but that woman Rose had such a loud voice they heard her broadcasting that Rob and Maureen had found a body in the woods at the back of their house. He and May should have driven away then, just saying they were off to the Midlands.

At that time they hadn't known the victim was Chloë Church. That had come later. From the upstairs window he had watched the two policemen go to the front door of number ten, then heard Ruth scream in anguish. That was when they knew it was Chloë.

Even though their houses were linked only by the garage, and Brian had the windows closed, he'd heard Ruth crying all day. He watched the couple, grey-faced, their backs bent with grief, being escorted out to a police car, presumably to identify their daughter.

He and May had never had much to do with Mike and Ruth, but Chloë was a happy, sunny-natured kid, who always spoke to them. To feel they had to hide in the house and not go next door to offer their condolences, or ask if they needed anything, was a kind of torture. But they'd made the decision to pretend they were away, and they'd even heard Alfie Strong tell the police that they owned some sunbed salons in the Midlands and went there most weekends.

'How much longer are you going to stare out of that window?' May's voice behind him was sharp with reproach. 'Why should I be the one to do everything?'

Brian turned to face his wife. She was right, of course. But then she was about most things. At forty-two she was still as slender and attractive as she'd been when they'd met fifteen years ago. In a summery pale green dress, her dark hair in a glossy bob to her shoulders and a tan that suggested the South of France, she looked good.

May worked at staying fit, with daily exercises, a yoga class and swimming when she could fit it in. She had been a hairdresser until she married Brian, but happily relinquished the burden of long hours and small return for the sunbed business. It required nothing more than a reliable manager at each of the eight salons, someone who could clean well, and bank the takings. May enjoyed the regular Saturday drop-ins at each branch to check the cleanliness and the accounts book. She dressed up for it, knowing her staff were impressed by her designer clothes and shoes, her perfect hair and nails. The majority were single mothers, dependent on a job with flexible hours, the freedom to bring their children to work in an emergency, or nip home if necessary. They also appreciated the cash bonus they received on top of their wages if the takings went over the target.

But she and Brian had another business, far more

lucrative than tanning salons, and they were terrified of it being exposed.

Gareth Price opened another bottle of Scotch and poured himself a large measure. The glass was smeared, the coffee-table littered with takeaway food cartons, a bottle of tomato sauce, five more glasses, a loaded ashtray and a pile of letters he needed to deal with. He had felt some shame when the police came earlier about Chloë, not just about the coffee-table but the whole house: there was dirt and clutter everywhere. The policewoman looked askance at the washing-up piled in the sink, and Gareth knew he'd immediately gone to the top of her list of suspects.

The fact that he'd once been as close as an uncle to Chloë and was horrified to hear she'd been killed would never prevent them seeing him as a prime suspect. But fortunately he had an unbreakable alibi. He'd been in the Wheatsheaf from five thirty when it opened until closing time, so drunk by then someone had driven him home because he could barely stand, let alone walk. Besides, why would he kill a child? Didn't they know he'd lost his fourteen-year-old daughter to a road accident, thirteen years ago? The grief had broken up his marriage: Gloria had said she couldn't bear to see his face any more. She blamed him for forgetting to pick Clare up from her ballet lesson. Clare had started to walk home alone, in the

66

rain. The driver had said she darted out between two parked cars, right in front of him.

After that Gloria didn't want to live at number five, or with him anywhere: she said she couldn't deal with the memories. They had been the first people to move into the close when it was built, and were so happy. They'd loved the woodland beyond the garden fence, and the safety for a child to live in a road where she could ride her bike and push her dolls' pram. Ironic, perhaps, that she was killed by a car. Maybe if they'd lived in a street where traffic was an issue, she'd have learnt to be more careful.

Gloria left a year after Clare's death, in 1997. Gareth had bought her out of her share in the house, and thrown himself into his work to try to forget. He was a partner in Knight, Price and Franklin, a firm of architects, and was one of the two architects who had designed the Pinewood estate.

For a few years after Gloria left, he kept everything together, but one drink when he got home, just to un-wind, became two, then three and four.

He remained a partner even when the drinking began to get out of hand. He could still throw in some bright ideas at a meeting with a new client if he kept off the booze for a few days beforehand, got his hair trimmed and wore an ironed shirt. But Percy Knight and James Franklin eventually became wary of him when he failed to turn up to some meetings, so in 2005 they retired him at sixty on a full pension. They had all been friends from their university days and still cared about him, but he was now too much of a liability.

When Gareth was sober, he was only too aware of what his drinking was doing to him, and looking around him he could see his house was a disgrace. But he paid a man to keep the garden tidy, back and front, knowing full well his neighbours would be on the warpath if he let that slide too. He refused to believe he was a true alcoholic: he could lay off the booze for days when he chose to, and he rarely had a drink before four in the afternoon. But he knew that the state of his home showed he was on a slippery slope. Sometimes he felt it would be good to embrace that slope fully and slide into welcome oblivion.

Nina flopped on to a chair by the bedroom window. It had been a long, tiring day unpacking in their new home, and now that the bed was made, all she really wanted was to crawl into it.

But Conrad wanted to get a takeaway curry, so bedtime would be delayed.

'It strikes me we've moved into a rather odd community,' she said thoughtfully, as she watched Janice, their next-door neighbour, walk across the close with a dish in her hands to the people at number ten. She believed they were called Mike and Ruth.

'Why?' Conrad asked, as he put some sweaters into a drawer.

'Well, take Janice next door. She's carrying a pot of something across to Mike and Ruth. That's kind, but she's wearing a long pink sarong and she's got a flower in her hair. It's sweet of her to cook something for them, but it's a funny outfit to be wearing at eight in the evening when you live alone.'

'I don't think one pink sarong is evidence of an odd community,' Conrad said, with a wide grin. 'She might have a red-blooded man waiting indoors for her to come back.'

Nina ignored the last remark. Conrad liked to think everyone was having red-hot sex. 'It's not just her who's odd. I don't like John and Rose at all. They're really malicious. When they called round with that bottle of wine, I knew they only wanted to gossip and find stuff out about us. First, she went on about the murder, and who she thought could be a suspect. She favours Gareth at number five because apparently he's very strange. I heard her say he's an alcoholic. That doesn't make him a child-killer.' Nina sighed. 'She's one of those women who thinks the worst of everyone. She gets off on finding out people's secrets, and her husband is nearly as bad. You should've stayed in the room instead of disappearing into the garage.'

'Maybe if I had I'd have winkled out her secrets.'

Conrad laughed. 'But I agree, there is something re-pellent about her, and John is just a yes-man.'

'She even had the nerve to ask me if we were trying for a baby! You don't ask a complete stranger that.'

'Maybe she heard us trying to put the bed together earlier, and thought we were on the job,' Conrad sug-gested, his dark eyes twinkling with mischief. 'Let's put on a real display for them tonight. Headboard rattling, shrieks of tortured lust.'

Nina had to laugh. He was quite capable of staging that just for the fun of it. 'Don't you dare.' She wig-gled a reproachful finger at him. 'It's inappropriate with a child dead.'

'You're right, as always. So, there's a few oddballs, but there are still five houses left for normal people.'

'According to Rose, the people at number eight are contenders for the Swingers Club. Apparently the glamorous wife eats men for breakfast. There was a lot more dirt, but it went in one ear and out the other. Promise me you'll never be nice to her or John. That way we can keep them at bay.'

'Okay, but I like the idea of being surrounded by odd people.' Conrad chuckled. 'We might be able to give up television and become curtain twitchers. When I was eighteen I had a landlady who did that and knew everything about everyone in the road. Nothing was secret. She knew who was playing away, who was in debt, and who hit his wife on a Saturday night. She was incorrigible, and equally nosy about her tenants. I know she went in my room when I was out, and she must have found my saucy magazines because she started looking at me as if I was a sex maniac.'

'Which, of course, you aren't.' Nina raised one eyebrow questioningly. Conrad's enthusiasm for almost anything was uplifting. 'I'd quite like to find out a bit more about Janice next door. A woman living alone who puts a flower in her hair is intriguing.'

'Tomorrow you should knock on her door to see if you can borrow some sugar or tea. She's bound to invite you in, and you can suss her out.'

'I'm going to stay in bed all day tomorrow,' Nina said. 'Well, at least all morning. And I hope you'll be there with me.'

'Now that's an invitation I won't refuse.' He put his arms around her and kissed her tenderly. 'But I'm off now to get the curry.'

Janice Wyatt returned from the Churches' after delivering the lasagne she'd made. As she went through her front door, she called, 'I'm all yours now, duty done and time to party!'

She stepped into her sitting room. Freddy was lying on the couch wearing only his striped boxer shorts. He looked good, muscular and tanned, and claimed he was forty-five, but she suspected she should add on another ten years. But he was fun, generous, kind and a great lover, so she didn't care.

Janice went by the name of Beau to her men friends. She ought to call them clients, as they paid her, but she found that reality spoilt her enjoyment. Her thick curtains were drawn, the Moroccan lamps were turned on, scented candles lit, and as she approached Freddy, she let her sarong slip to the floor. Beneath it she wore a gauzy little pink number, with peepholes to reveal her nipples and her carefully waxed vulva.

'Umm,' he said appreciatively. 'Just put one foot up on the couch for a while so I can look at you.'

This was what Beau liked most: a man who grew hard just looking at her, who thought more about her pleasure than his own. It was astounding to her that she got paid for it too.

'Fantastic,' Freddy murmured, sometime later. She was now lying in his arms, her head on his muscular chest. 'Beau, you really are the best. I wish I could stay with you for ever.'

Beau put one finger on his lips to silence him. The only reason Freddy was allowed at her house when all the other men had to book a hotel room was because she knew he meant what he said. He was married to Francesca, who had become disabled after a riding accident. From what he'd told Beau, she was a real bitch, and he'd been on the verge of leaving her even before the accident. But when he saw her in hospital, he felt it was wrong to bail out at a time when she was so vulnerable.

He had hoped the accident would make her less confrontational, and grateful that he had stayed with her. But the reverse was true: it had made her even nastier. She insulted everyone, especially Freddy, and threw everything – plates, glasses, knives and some-times even a bed pan – at him and the people he employed to care for her.

Freddy had inherited wealth, and in theory he could walk away and continue to pay for her round-the-clock care, but he knew she'd stir up a storm that would destroy his and his family's good name. He told Beau that once he'd even imagined hiring someone to kill her, making it look like a burglary gone wrong. But it was clear he just wasn't capable of doing that.

So he stayed, having as little contact with Francesca as possible, and finding happiness elsewhere.

Mostly Janice was perfectly happy with that. But he had the knack of touching her heart, along with every other part of her body, and she too wished Francesca dead.

9

Detective Inspector Jim Marshall sat at his desk on Sunday morning, head in hands. He was totally dejected. It had been twenty-four hours since Chloë Church's body had been found but he still hadn't got any real leads. Was it possible for the killer to be so clever and forensically aware that he'd managed to kill a young girl in broad daylight, without leaving any evidence? No footprints, no cigarette ends, no bloodstained clothing, no fingerprints. It looked as if the first blow was to the side of her head, as Chloë hadn't got her killer's DNA beneath her fingernails. It suggested the killer came up behind her and almost knocked her out with the first blow, leaving her unable to fight back. She'd only got a couple of wounds on her hands as if she'd instinctively tried to protect her head once on the ground. Yet no one had heard a scream or seen anyone running away. But the killer must have been covered with blood and surely someone would have spotted that.

Early on in Marshall's police career, there had been

a murder of an elderly woman in a wood, with a similarly puzzling lack of evidence. It turned out that two young men were involved, and one carried a small rucksack in which they had two identical changes of clothes to the ones they were wearing. They attacked, killed and robbed the woman of money she'd just got out of a bank, and the gold jewellery she wore, then changed their clothes, put the bloodstained ones into the rucksack and carried on with their walk.

The young men were caught some weeks later because one had blurted out what he'd done to his girlfriend. She reported him later when she discovered he was seeing another girl. It transpired the two men had burnt their clothes in a garden incinerator, where, fortunately, a few scraps were found, complete with bloodstains, and a leather strap from the rucksack. The police also found a brooch belonging to the old lady in one of their drawers. It seemed they hadn't considered it valuable enough to sell, but it had a nice big thumbprint on it.

But even mulling over that murder didn't help Marshall with this one. Those killers had set out to rob the lady, knowing she always walked through the small wood from her daughter's house to hers each Friday evening around six. They claimed at their trial that they hadn't meant to kill her, but carrying a change of clothing proved it was premeditated.

Chloë either trusted whoever she'd gone up that

path with, or the killer had either followed her or lain in wait. Yet the latter seemed impossible, as how could anyone know she'd walk up that path at that time?

When a child was killed the first people to be questioned and investigated were always family members, close friends and neighbours. There was usually a motive. It might be jealousy, anger, or fear that the child was going to reveal something.

It was far less common for someone to kill a child they had no connection with, and no motive to do so. Most people would call those people psychopaths. They killed for the buzz it gave them.

Yet Marshall was not convinced this was the work of a psychopath. For one thing a psychopath planned what they were going to do, and invariably took the chosen weapon with them. There was usually some sort of sexual compulsion. His gut reaction was that this killing had been done by someone who lived close to Chloë.

All these hours later he still thought the keyword for this murder was 'malice'. It had been a messy, frenzied attack, but with no suggestion of anything sexual. Whoever committed it had either hated Chloë or what she stood for. Was that because she was a pretty and much-loved only child, or because the killer resented her parents?

It had been committed in an area where at any moment a dog-walker, a couple or another child could have come by. Children had said there were boys on scrambling bikes: surely the noise they had made would have been enough to frighten off any prospective murderer.

As for suspects, Marshall was one hundred per cent sure that neither parent could have done it. Their grief was so transparent and awful – no one could pretend that. So he set about looking at their neighbours.

The Freemans at number one had no real alibi, he thought. They said they were having a drink together before eating their dinner and watering the garden when the murder happened. They were a nosy, irritating couple and clearly not liked much by their neighbours, but his gut reaction was that they weren't capable of murder.

Janice Wyatt was spending the night with a boy-friend in the Cotswolds and that alibi checked out. Similarly, the Willises hadn't done it as they found the body, they were distraught, and he doubted anyone could fake that kind of emotion. Gareth Price had a strong alibi from the Wheatsheaf.

Mrs Singer and her daughter Amy were a curious duo. The mother kept apologizing for everything, and Marshall felt she wasn't a particularly good mother. She didn't know for sure when Amy had gone out, or when she returned. Another neighbour had said Amy was out in the street wearing her pyjamas at eight thirty. How hard could it be to keep tabs on one child?

The mother claimed she'd been watching TV in her bedroom all evening, but there was no proof of that. He had the idea she liked Amy even less than she liked herself, but however sad or peculiar that was, it wasn't enough to suspect her of murdering someone else's child. Amy had given the female police officer her school uniform dress without any hesitation, and there wasn't a trace of blood on it: she hadn't been anywhere near the crime scene. Yet something about the mother and daughter was a bit off. He hoped that when Mr Singer came back from Brighton and was interviewed, he'd get a different perspective on the family.

He also needed to interview Terry and Wilma Parkin. It was a bit suspicious that they'd shot off for a weekend break so early on Saturday morning. As for Brian and May Alcott, he felt certain that they had been in their home when the police officers called but hadn't opened the door.

In a murder inquiry it was common for past crimes to be uncovered, and his instinct told him that both couples might be hiding something and he was determined to root it out.

Dee Strong was another candidate for suspicion. Despite being very attractive, he thought she was cruel – he could almost smell it on her. She had insinuated herself towards him, like a snake seeking its prey, and it had made his blood run cold. He wanted to know a great deal more about her. It was possible Chloë had discovered something, something so potentially damaging to her that she had followed Chloë up that path, and attacked her.

Yet Alfie, her husband, seemed a decent sort, even though he had a police record and had been in prison twice. He'd kept his nose clean since he was thirty and built up his own business, installing replacement windows, which looked completely above board.

Marshall knew from previous cases that liking or disliking someone didn't mean a thing. He had liked some people who turned out to be evil. Likewise he'd hated others and would gladly have sent them down, but it transpired they were innocent.

Tomorrow he would cast his net wider and talk to residents in the other streets on the Pinewood estate. There would also be a television plea for information. He silently prayed it would bring forth something. But for now he had to find Tex.

Marshall had known Tex, or Duncan Simmonds, to give him his real name, for at least fifteen years. He stood out in people's memory because he wore a cowboy hat, a fringed, western-style shirt, jeans and cowboy boots. Marshall had never seen him wearing a coat, not even in the depths of winter. People always described Tex as big, but in fact he was five foot five and skinny. It was amazing what western dress could do for a man.

Around half the officers at the station believed Tex was Chloë's killer, based on nothing more than that he was a strange character with learning difficulties. Marshall had interviewed him so many times, suspected of being a Peeping Tom, snatching a handbag, defecating in the street, frightening an old lady and robbery, to name just a few examples of people's prejudice. Yet Marshall had found him to have a gentle nature, and a surprisingly strong sense of right and wrong. In years gone by, he would have spent his life in a psychiatric hospital, possibly being allowed to work in the gardens because he was no threat to anyone. But the government had made these hospitals spit out all those poor souls with mental-health problems into the community, when what they needed most was protection and understanding.

Now he'd have to go and question the man. He'd be frightened, and when he felt cornered, he had been known to lash out: that was why he had punched the boy who had been throwing stones at him. Those stones were not pebbles, as reported, but half-bricks, and the 'boy' was seventeen, six foot three and a weight trainer, with shoulders like a barn door. He'd deserved that punch from Tex. Yet that, to some of the officers in this station, would be enough evidence that he could easily batter a child to death.

Marshall didn't agree with that. He knew children could taunt Tex, call him names, sometimes throw things at him, and Tex would retaliate by chasing them. But there had never been one report of him catching hold of a child, not even grabbing their shoulders or an arm. When questioned, children said that it was a game: they liked him to chase them.

Marshall drove to Pearl Street alone, parking at the end and walking back to Hudson House. In the previous century the terrace of ten large, attractive early-Victorian houses, close to the town centre, was home to bankers, solicitors, accountants and other professionals. They had enough room on their four floors for a sizeable family and a maid or two. But in the early 1900s, as new houses with modern facilities and bigger gardens were built in pleasant tree-lined avenues away from the busy town, those people moved out. The First World War, the Depression in the 1930s and then the Second World War had all taken their toll on the once smart address. A fire in one and bomb damage in another left gaps in the terrace, and the remaining houses became like rabbit warrens with as many as five or six families living in one.

In the 1970s the council had finally made a compulsory purchase offer for the remaining houses. Some were pulled down and offices were built, but the two at the end of the terrace were knocked into one, and the place was earmarked as a hostel for people being discharged from psychiatric wards. A full-time supervisor would keep an eye on things.

They called it Hudson House after Rowland Hudson, a councillor who had been enthusiastic about patients being released into the community.

But now, in 2009, Hudson House was a hostel for ex-prisoners, drug addicts and a few men like Tex. It was a seedy, grubby place and the so-called 'supervisor', Stan Mangham, spent more time in a nearby betting shop or watching TV than taking an interest in his charges. Around a year ago one of the newer, younger residents had died of a head injury. It was reported he'd come back to the hostel at nine thirty in the evening, lurching as if he was drunk, blood running down his head. Another resident said Stan didn't even come out of his office to look at the wound but shouted at the injured man to get to bed and sleep it off.

At the post-mortem it was found he had no alcohol or drugs in his blood. He'd been beaten over the head with a blunt instrument, presumably for his unemployment benefit, which he'd received that morning.

Marshall felt Stan should have been taken to task for failing in a duty of care, but maybe because no one in authority saw the men at the hostel being of any value, he was left to continue in his post.

Hudson House looked even dirtier and more battered than it had last time Marshall was there. The light grey hall and stairs carpet was black with dirt and strewn with bits of paper and cigarette butts. The paintwork on banisters, doors and skirting boards was so grubby that he cringed at the thought he might accidentally touch them.

'What now?' Stan asked, looking around the door of his office and recognizing Marshall. He was as lacking in cleanliness as the hostel. Overweight, he wore a greasy navy T-shirt and stained grey tracksuit trousers, and what little hair he had left was lank and uncombed.

'I want to have a word with Tex,' Marshall said. 'I'll just go up.'

'What's he done?'

It was tempting to ask what it had got to do with him, but Marshall resisted. Stan was quite capable of ringing the local papers claiming he had a scoop. 'Nothing. He just happened to be near to an incident I'm investigating. Worth talking to him in case he saw something. I'll go on up to his room.'

Tex's room was on the first floor. While it was one of the biggest in the house, its position meant it could be very noisy when the drunks came home.

'Nothing to worry about, Tex,' Marshall said, as Tex opened the door and looked alarmed. He seemed small and very ordinary without his hat. His greying hair was sparse, and his face pale. But he had memorable eyes, pale blue-green, like bird's eggs. 'I'm sure you remember me. DI Marshall. Just a friendly visit to see if you saw anything in the park on Friday evening. May I come in?'

Tex looked puzzled but beckoned him in.

Marshall cared enough about this forty-year-old man, who was blamed for so much, to find out more about him. It transpired that when he was eight, his middle-class parents had paid for him to go into a privately owned boarding school for children with learning difficulties. Even then he'd been cowboy mad, arriving at the school in a small Stetson a relative had given him. Six months later his parents sold their house and disappeared. It was thought by neighbours they'd gone to either Goa or Thailand. But all efforts to find them failed.

The school was very fair: they kept young Duncan there for well over a year, without receiving any payment. But eventually, when it was clear his parents had planned to dump their son, the school arranged for him to be moved to a vastly inferior council-owned children's home.

Marshall felt deeply for that small boy. It had had to be explained to him that his parents couldn't be found. Did he imagine they'd died, or did he sense the truth that he'd been abandoned because he was too much of a burden and they didn't love him?

If it hadn't been for one assistant at the home, who had clearly grown fond of Duncan, he might have ended up with an even sadder life, thieving to buy drugs, which would eventually kill him. But that one man kept in touch with him when he'd had to leave school at sixteen and visited to teach him how to cope on his own.

That man's care had paid off: Tex's room was very neat and tidy, his bed made, a red blanket tucked over it. The work surface, which held the sink, a microwave and his small television, was so clean it was almost like an operating theatre.

He had kept away from drugs and he didn't steal. He lived frugally on the benefits he was able to claim.

Marshall sat down on the bed. Tex perched on an upright chair by his small table. He looked frightened.

'You aren't in any trouble,' Marshall assured him. 'Do you know the park behind the houses of the Pinewood estate?' he asked.

Tex nodded. 'I goes there lots. Last time was Friday,' he said. 'I like it there. It gets so hot in here in summer. I like to walk.'

The room was very warm, and Marshall guessed the windows didn't open more than a crack. In previous chats Tex had talked about walking in the evenings so he could sleep better at night. Marshall often saw him a long way from Pearl Street, marching along purposefully. He didn't drink, and he'd said before he didn't like going into pubs. Marshall suspected that he'd been bullied in the past so steered clear.

'It was Friday I wanted to ask you about. Did you see a pretty blonde girl there, about thirteen? She was wearing a white dress.'

Tex frowned. 'Yes. She was on the swings when I got there.'

'You know her, then?'

'She usually waves to me. I don't know her name.'

'Who was she with?'

He shrugged. 'Two boys, I think. They was talking. But I don't think she saw me cos she didn't wave.'

'Do you know the boys?'

'No, but I've seen 'em afore. I think they go to school with the blonde girl.'

'Do you ever see her with anyone else?'

'Mostly she's with another girl, a fat one with brown hair. But I didn't see her on Friday.'

'So what time was this?'

Tex shrugged and shook his head. 'Don't know. I ain't got a watch cos I don't tell the time too good. But it was early evening, just getting cooler.'

'Did you see a blonde woman at all? She's nice-looking and probably in her thirties.'

Tex shook his head. 'Maybe if I saw a picture of her I might know, but I can't remember anyone like that.'

'So what did you do, then?'

'I sat on the grass for a while. I was watching a man trying to train his dog to stay when the man walked away. It was funny cos the dog didn't run after him, but he kind of wriggled along on his belly. He made me laugh.'

'How long did you stay in the park for?'

'Maybe an hour, I don't know. I dropped off to sleep for a bit. When I woke, I was going to walk up the hill and go right round the estate. There's a road at the back and it's a different way to go home. But I started to walk and these two boys on motorbikes came. One of them tried to run me over once before so I hid in some bushes till they'd gone past, and then I went home the way I came in case they came back.'

'Would you come with me and show me where you hid and how far up the path it was? We could go in my car – it's not a police one.'

It occurred to Marshall that Tex hadn't asked why he wanted to know about the girl. This wasn't in any way suspicious to him. He certainly showed no sign of anxiety. Maybe he'd leave it till tomorrow: today being Sunday and a big police presence at the murder site, there would be a lot of people around. He'd go tomorrow – he didn't want anyone to think Tex was a suspect – and walk him up to the spot where Chloë had died and see how he reacted to that. The officers were still combing the surrounding area where the body was found for evidence. He just hoped the fine weather would last long enough to find anything that might be out there.

IO

Monday, 20 July, Day Three

'So what's going on?' Roger Singer said, as he walked through his front door and found his wife lying on the sofa in her dressing-gown, with red swollen eyes. He guessed she'd been blubbering for hours.

As for Amy, she was hunched in the armchair wearing pyjamas and also red-eyed but shovelling popcorn into her mouth as if she were dying of starvation.

It was just after midnight, and the drive back from Brighton had seemed endless to Roger. He was already pissed off that he'd been begged to come home when he'd had a meal booked at the Seahorse, his favourite seafood restaurant. Carrie had been sulky too, once again saying she knew he was never going to leave Trudy.

But that was one thing he was completely honest about. He was desperate to get away from Trudy, to be with a sexy, fun woman, who never talked about what she'd seen in the supermarket or her varicose veins, and never asked pitifully if he still loved her.

'I already told you. Chloë Church was murdered

on Friday night. Amy and I were taken to the police station to give statements as if we were criminals.'

'I understood perfectly that Chloë was dead – you were so hysterical I couldn't fail to get that. But you could have told me the rest on the phone without dragging me home.'

'Don't you care what we've been through?' Trudy was crying harder now. 'I needed you here.'

Roger rolled his eyes in despair. Trudy always made everything about her. Any normal mother would be saying how terrible it must be for Mike and Ruth to be told their daughter had been killed. Surely that made going to the police station to be questioned absolutely nothing. Most people would be glad to go to make themselves feel they were helping in some small way.

'What did you need me for that couldn't wait till I got back this evening? Me being here now won't bring the poor kid back. I appreciate her death is awful – she was a lovely kid. But it will push all my work back and I'll lose money. So what good has it done dragging me here tonight?'

'I needed you – we needed you,' she sobbed out. 'Do you know what it's like to be questioned by the police?'

Roger sighed, sat on the arm of the sofa and put one hand on his wife's shoulder. 'Of course they had to question you and Amy. She spent half her life with

Chloë. If there's anyone who would know if she was being pestered, followed or anything, it's Amy.'

'You should've been here. You're her father.'

'For God's sake, Trudy,' he sighed, 'I work to keep you two and this house going. My work means I must go to my garages. Why can't you just grow a spine and deal with things yourself without all this maudlin self-pity?'

He got up and went over to the wall cabinet where they kept the drinks and poured himself a large whisky. He looked back at his daughter, who was now tucking into a family-sized bag of crisps.

Trudy sobbed even louder at his lack of sympathy. 'I'm scared they think our Amy did it.'

'Don't be ridiculous,' Roger snapped, glancing back at his wife and wincing at her bloated red face. 'As if a big soft lump like her could ever kill anyone. Why do you let her keep on eating like that, Trudy? She's obese. If you don't curb her now, she'll be thirty stone before she's twenty.'

That was the cue for Amy to make a hiccuping sob. 'That's a horrible thing to say, Daddy. Chloë was my best friend. And I'm not obese, it's just puppy fat.'

Roger walked into the kitchen, ran the cold tap and splashed water on to his face and wrists. He felt exasperated. He knew he ought to be kinder to them, especially to Amy, who was only a kid. But he felt wound up just looking at them. The drive home had been never-ending, huge tailbacks from Brighton to the M25. Instead of the two and a half hours it normally took him, it had been six. And for what? A lot of hysterical bleating.

Everything about Trudy irritated him. She was so limited, a carbon copy of her mother, who only ever removed her apron when she went to church, who thought making the perfect Victoria sponge was evidence of her being the perfect wife.

Trudy thought food was the antidote to everything. Right from when they were first married, she'd start to make him something to eat in the middle of a row, as if that solved the disagreement. She'd sooner have a cake or a bar of chocolate than make love. If he was angry, she thought a bacon sandwich would cheer him; if he was tired, she'd dish up soup. Back in the days they'd gone out at weekends as a family she always made a lavish picnic, even when he said he wanted to go to a restaurant.

He wanted sophistication, not sitting in a field of cow pats eating corned-beef sandwiches. He wanted a pretty, slender wife who wore high heels and sexy dresses, preferably one who read books, who could discuss stories in the news, and wanted to go to rock concerts. Carrie was like that, but she liked fast cars, too, and holidays in the West Indies, and bought her clothes in Bond Street. She loved sex too.

He went back into the sitting room. Amy was just

going up to bed. 'Night, Daddy,' she said, in a small voice, one hand on the door. 'I'm glad you're home again.'

'Give Daddy a kiss, then?' he said, going over to her, sorry that he'd been rattled enough to talk about her weight in front of her.

She stood on tiptoe to kiss his cheek and he hugged her. 'I'm glad to be home. Sorry I was grumpy. It was a long journey tonight.'

'Would you like me to make you a mushroom omelette?' Trudy asked, from behind him, her voice wavering.

Roger was still at the door with his back to her. He closed his eyes in frustration. Hadn't she worked out yet how much it annoyed him?

His plan, before her phone call on Sunday afternoon, was to leave Brighton around four on Monday, today, to come home, and tell her he was leaving her. He had it straight in his head: she could stay in this house, and he'd do up the flat above his garage in Brighton and move there. He'd even thought if she got hysterical, he would take his things and drive straight back to Brighton.

Now he was forced to stay the night, and under the circumstances, he couldn't tell her he was leaving her.

'No. I don't want any food,' he said, as he turned back to her. 'If I did, Trudy, I'm quite capable of making it myself. Now go to bed. I need to unwind, and I'll sleep in the spare room, so I don't disturb you.'

Just after six in the morning Brian Alcott was in his garage, sitting in his van, the remote to open the garage door in his hand. He had weighed up the pros and cons of when he should drive to Bromsgrove, but still wasn't sure. He'd wanted to go all day yesterday, but the police kept coming and going and he was too scared to just drive out, in case they stopped him. At six in the morning everyone should be fast asleep. But the Churches next door were unlikely to be and they might look out of the window at the sound of the engine.

Brian was a worry-guts. Whatever needed to be done, he'd look at every possible scenario, weighing them all up, and usually it was May who told him what to do. But last night she'd told him in no uncertain terms what he had to do today. She would be savage if he went upstairs and asked her opinion again.

The engine was less likely to be noticed later in the day, but then people would be out mowing lawns or washing cars, and they'd see him.

Fear of his wife's anger decided it. He might as well go now and get it over with. If anyone did spot him, he could say he and May had come back late the previous night.

So he pressed the remote and the door opened almost silently. He turned on the ignition, put the van into gear and drove out on to the drive. He pressed the remote again, the door came down behind him and he set off.

The sun was up, with the promise of another hot day, but no one was about, not even a dog-walker. As Brian reached the road beyond the Pinewood estate, he breathed a sigh of relief. He hoped there were no CCTV cameras between here and the motorway.

There was little traffic on the M5, and it took less than forty minutes to reach the salon in Bromsgrove. It was in a small side-street, one of half a dozen lock-up shops, and although some had a flat above, the people who lived in them were used to Brian and May coming at odd times to do maintenance work.

Brian unlocked the salon door, then carried all the boxes inside. This was his favourite salon because of the rooms upstairs. One was furnished as a sitting room, complete with comfy sofas and a television, where Tania, their trusty manager, could relax.

Brian and May often came here on Saturdays after their inspections. They'd have some fish and chips from the shop two doors down, and once Tania had left for the day, they'd see people about their second business.

Brian didn't normally store the goods in this salon – at least, not for more than a couple of days. It was all about fast turnover. He'd bring them here, ring his regulars and they'd come to collect them and pay him. But the recent good weather had skewed things. People had gone away or just didn't want any. So Brian had a bit of a glut, which was why he'd taken it home to store, thinking he might be able to sell it on to some customers in Bristol. But while he was thinking about contacting them, the murder had happened.

May said he was disorganized, along with being unable to make snap decisions. She was probably right.

He carried all the goods up to the storeroom and stacked them up. Then, locking the door, he left, relieved it was done.

The journey home was even quicker. With the lack of traffic, the sun shining and Barbra Streisand on his stereo, Brian felt very calm.

May woke up as he went into the bedroom with a cup of tea for her.

'All done,' he said. 'No more worries.'

She rubbed her eyes sleepily and took the tea from him. 'Don't you think it's time we knocked it on the head, Brian? I was thinking about us last night and I reckon we ought to sell the salons too. Start again somewhere new.'

Brian knew what she meant. It was only a matter of time before someone twigged what they were doing and talked, so he nodded. 'We could invest the money in property and rent it out.'

'I was thinking more along the lines of opening a hairdressing and beauty salon here in Cheltenham,' she said. 'A really classy place, with a couple of sunbeds too. I'd rent chairs to the hairdressers and beauticians – that keeps them working harder. I'd quite enjoy going back to work too.'

'But what would I do?' Brian looked doubtful.

'You could still get into property.' She gave a little laugh. 'Have you forgotten you used to be a builder? Buy one house, do it up and flog it, then another.'

Brian wasn't keen to go back to humping bags of concrete, plumbing in bathrooms and crawling around rewiring, even if he had been good at it. He'd thought those days were over and he'd got used to wearing nice clothes, lunching out with May and generally having a very comfortable life.

She saw the lack of enthusiasm written on his face. 'We've got away with things for a long time now and made a lot of money,' she reminded him. 'The police presence in the street isn't going to stop until they find the killer. Have you even thought what you're going to tell them when they want to know where you were on Friday evening?'

'I'll say I was with you.'

'But you can't, Brian. I was at my exercise class, if you remember. Then I had a drink with a couple of the girls. You didn't come home till after ten, and you never told me where you were.'

'Pete picked me up and we went for a curry,' Brian said. 'I did tell you on Saturday morning when all that rumpus about Chloë was going on.'

She nodded, clearly remembering that.

'But if you tell the police about Pete, they'll go and check it with him. They'll look him up and find he's done time and might think you two are up to something together.'

'What if I said I didn't go out, just stayed in alone?'

'Pete might have been seen picking you up.'

'He picked me up from the bottom of the road. He didn't want Alfie next door to clock him.'

'Shit, Brian, this is going from bad to worse.' May sighed. She tossed back the bedclothes and got up. 'You were out on Friday with an alibi you can't admit to the police. We pretended we weren't here all weekend so the police couldn't interview us or find the stuff. If I was a policeman, I'd be really suspicious.'

'Cheer me up, why don't you?' Brian snapped at her. 'If you're so fucking clever let me know what you think I should tell the police.'

She thought for a minute. 'Admit you went down the road, say you were planning to go for a walk. Keep fit and all that. But you got just round the corner and you really didn't feel like it, so you came home.'

'What if someone was out on the street and they say they didn't see me?'

'Just shrug and say they probably weren't looking.

No one goes out the front of the house in the evenings, do they? When did you last see anyone out there?'

'Ruth and Mike were on Friday by all accounts, and loads of people have been watering their gardens in the evenings since it got hot. As for Dee, she's a nosy-parker and so is Rose from number one. Either of them could've been peeping round the curtains.'

'You'll just have to take a chance on that,' May said. 'You didn't kill the girl, did you?' She smirked at his horrified expression. 'Of course you didn't. You aren't organized enough for that. So let's have some breakfast now.'

'Brian and May are up to something,' Dee said to Alfie. She was perched on the arm of the sofa under their window, looking out.

'Those two are too bloody dull to be getting up to anything,' he replied, without looking up from the *Sun* newspaper.

'That's where you're wrong,' she said. 'I know they were at home all weekend, cos they left the back windows open upstairs. And I heard them talking while I hung some washing out. They just didn't want to speak to the police.'

'Well, neither did I,' Alfie said. 'But I learnt a long time ago that they always come back if you don't answer the door. And they get more suspicious of you.'

'But he went out in his van at six this morning. I heard him,' Dee went on. 'So I guess they didn't answer the door before because they had something in that van they didn't want the police to see. Now what could that have been?'

'You tell me, darlin',' Alfie said, grinning at her. 'Becoming quite the Mrs Sherlock Holmes these days.'

He thought Dee looked sexy this morning. She

wore a tiny pair of leopard-print shorts and a black cropped top, which showed her tanned midriff. He had a strong compulsion to get up out of his chair, bend her over the sofa, pull those shorts down and fuck her. But to do that would be to put himself back in her debt. So he controlled the urge.

'I'll find out, you just wait,' she said, and her grin was wolfish. 'Don't I always?'

Alfie had to admit she was good at sniffing out any kind of illicit activities, and she had a real nose for perversion. Since they'd married, he had found to his cost that she was also sadistic, deviant and had no scruples.

When he first met her, she was working in a hotel in London's Mayfair. She told him she was the events manager. By the time Alfie had discovered the 'events' were just a scam between her and Rudi the hotel manager, he was in too deep with her to walk away.

Rudi was a charming Italian who had ice in his veins and was as warped as she was. The wealthy business-men who stayed at the hotel often asked Rudi to find them a girl for the night. He could sense those who wanted more than straight sex, and that was where Dee came in. She was young and beautiful, and if she was offered enough money, she was up for anything.

But that was only part of it. Rudi had hidden cameras in the rooms they used, and he would film the action. Later, once he had researched a guest's background and what he had to lose, he would send a photograph to the man's office, and demand money to destroy the film.

Rudi was smart: he had a box number for the men to reply to and send a cheque. Should any of them call the police or send someone round to the hotel, he would deny any involvement and say it must have been another guest who had stayed at the same time and managed to rig up a camera.

But no one ever did take it further. The money he asked for was never so much that they couldn't afford it, and they clearly thought paying him off was a smarter move than risking exposure. Dee, of course, received half of the money.

Rudi must have realized that before long she would play him at his own game and rip him off. So he quit his job at the hotel and gave her a big payoff, thus buying her silence.

When Dee tearfully told Alfie she'd lost her job, he comforted her, then asked her to marry him and move to Cheltenham. The year before, he'd moved his replacement-windows company to Gloucester as business premises were much cheaper there, and he'd bought the house on the Pinewood estate in Cheltenham. At that time, he didn't have the slightest suspicion of what Dee had been up to at the hotel. He was a classic 'love is blind' candidate.

However, within three months of their lavish

wedding and expensive honeymoon in Barbados, Alfie started to see Dee wasn't the sweet, kind, generous woman he had taken her for. As long as he was buying her expensive presents, taking her out to restaurants and for weekends away in good hotels, she was sexy, loving and fun. But one word of recrimination about her spending, a suggestion that she iron his shirts or prepare dinner, and the playful kitten unsheathed her claws and turned into a hellcat.

He remembered ruefully the time he'd suggested she become the receptionist at his company. 'Me? Work in a two-bit replacement-windows company?' she said disdainfully. 'On a trading estate? You've got to be joking.'

He often wondered how she had managed to hide this side of her from him for so long, but she was a good actress and a very plausible liar. Almost every aspect of her past she presented to people was false. Alfie found out the truth only when he tracked down Rudi, the former hotel manager – by then he had taken over the running of a string of massage parlours. Alfie had to rough him up to get the truth, and it all came out – he even saw some of the videos Dee had starred in.

Alfie wanted a divorce, but he knew she would fight him tooth and nail and get half of everything he had. Plus, she knew a couple of dodgy deals he'd done and wouldn't think twice about grassing him up.

'So.' Alfie put down his newspaper and grinned at his wife. 'Tell me what you think Brian and May might be up to.'

'The sunbed salons are a front for something else. Drugs, maybe. Or prostitution.'

Alfie wanted to laugh. They were far too inhibited for either business but he agreed with Dee for now. If he argued, she'd only get mad with him. What was he doing with a woman he couldn't stand up to? If any of his old mates in south London could see him now, they'd laugh at him.

12

Later on Monday morning DI Marshall glanced sideways at Tex as he drove him to the children's playground by the Pinewood estate. He noted that the man showed no sign of tension or nervousness, the opposite, in fact: he seemed happy to be having an outing in a car, the way a child would.

'As we walk through the park, I want you to try to remember who you saw on Friday, where they were, what they were doing,' Marshall said, once they had arrived. 'Can you do that for me? It's important.'

'Yes, sir,' Tex said, frowning a little as if in concentration. 'I'm good at remembering.'

As they got out of the car, Tex put on his Stetson and they walked towards the playground. All the grass was very brown and dry now. Marshall hoped for rain soon as his own garden was crying out for it, but he'd like it to wait a few more days so he could be sure they'd found all the remaining evidence here.

'Did you come in this way?' Marshall asked. The children's playground was to their left.

Tex nodded. 'The blonde girl was on that swing,' he said, pointing to the frame that held six. Two had been swung up and over the top rail so they couldn't be used. 'She was on the middle one,' Tex went on. 'The two boys was either side of her talking. They was smoking too. But not her.'

Surprised that Tex recalled such details. 'Who else was here?'

'Not many people, I expect they'd all gone home for their tea. There was a woman with her little boy on the seesaw – she was pressing it up and down cos no one was on the other end. There was a couple of small kids on the roundabout too. That's all.'

They were walking beyond the playground area now. 'Who was out here?' Marshall asked.

Tex thought for a while. 'There was a man with an Alsatian dog throwing a ball for it, and a lady with some little kids, sitting on a blanket. They was right over the other side, looked like they'd got a picnic.' Tex pointed into the distance, where a man was now throwing a Frisbee for his dog. 'There was a man running. He had a bare chest and shorts. He was going that way.' Tex pointed to the way Marshall intended to take him, up the slope to where Chloë was killed.

'How old was that man, do you think? Can you describe him?'

'He was young and fit, maybe twenty. About as tall as me, dark cropped hair. Muscular.'

Marshall was impressed by Tex's memory and that he took in so much about people. He was already intending to send some officers up there later today to question everyone to find out if they were there on Friday evening. But he wanted to know more about the runner. People weren't normally suspicious of runners, so it might have been good cover for a man intent on killing. 'So where did you go on Friday?'

'Over there.' Tex pointed to a spot some twenty yards from where they stood. 'I sat down on the grass. I like watching people. Soon after I sat down the man with the dog came. His dog was called Sam – I heard him call him.'

'Anyone else?'

'The blonde girl's friend come. She's fat with brown hair, but she were with two other kids about the same age as her. They came from down the bottom.' He pointed through the park to a gate. 'But I didn't pay them much attention cos I was watching the dog.'

'Then what?'

'I don't remember anything else till the boys with the motorbikes come. I'd lain down, and dropped off. But the bikes woke me – they was revving them up, showing off, like, to the other kids. They did some wheelies, and the blonde girl was laughing. I started to go up the slope, but then, like I said before, I heard the bikers coming so I hid in the bushes till they'd gone past. I was too scared to go on that way, in case they come back. So I come back down the slope and went out the way I came.'

'The blonde girl, Chloë, was she still on the swings when you left?'

'Not on the swings. She walked up the slope – I saw her go past while I was hid.'

'Alone, or with someone?'

'Alone. But I think she liked one of the motorbike boys.'

'What about her friend? Where was she?'

'I dunno, I didn't see her. Maybe she'd gone home.'

'Do you know anything about the motorbike boys? Their names, where they live?'

'Nope, only that they're mean. But I've seen 'em scare kids too. The blonde girl could tell you who the kids they scared are – she was there one time when they was doing it. She ran over to 'em and told 'em to stop.'

Marshall sensed that Tex had absolutely no idea Chloë was dead. 'Did they stop?'

'Yup! Guess they was surprised at her being so brave. Most people are like me, scared to say anything in case they does something worse.'

Marshall was touched by Tex's honesty. 'Is there anyone in here now that you recognize from last Friday?'

Tex looked around carefully. 'No. The teenagers mostly come early evening. During the day it's old people and mums with little kids. People with dogs come anytime, though.'

Marshall made a mental note to come back alone around six. 'Let's walk up there now, Tex,' he suggested, pointing up the slope. 'Show me where you hid in the bushes. If you remember anyone else you saw on Friday, just tell me.'

They had only gone some fifty or sixty yards when Tex pointed to a large clump of brambles to the right of the slope. 'I hid behind there,' he said.

Marshall went round the bush. The grass and weeds were trampled but then the police had been all over the entire area. He picked up a cigarette butt and put it in an evidence bag to get it checked.

He and Tex moved on. 'Did you see or hear anyone else come this way?' Marshall asked, as they continued up the slope.

'Not that I remember,' Tex said. 'But someone could've come up or down while I was hiding. I wouldn't have heard them over the bikes' noise.'

Not for the first time, it seemed to Marshall that Tex had better powers of observation than many of his officers.

The spot where Chloë had been killed was about three hundred yards further on. As they went round a slight bend and the taped-off crime scene, with two officers guarding it, came into view, Tex stopped in his tracks and looked questioningly at Marshall.

'The blonde girl you spoke of, Chloë Church, was killed here on Friday evening,' Marshall said.

Tex was suddenly rigid, his horrified expression proof he had known nothing of Chloë's death and could not have had a hand in it. 'Why? What had she done?' Tex's voice shook and his eyes filled. 'She was nice – she always waved to me.'

Even from twenty feet outside the cordon, Chloë's blood was still clearly visible on the grass. It was dark brown and dried hard from the sun, a few flies buzzing around it.

'We don't know why she was killed. Have you any ideas? Or have you ever met or seen anyone around here who you thought was odd or suspicious?' Marshall asked.

Tex shook his head mournfully. He looked pale now, clearly badly shaken. 'She were nice.'

'Okay, then, I'll drive you back to Pearl Street. I'm sorry, Tex, that I had to bring you here.'

'You thought it was me what done it.'

It was a statement, not a question, and Marshall felt ashamed. 'No, not me. I just brought you here because I hoped you might have seen something that would lead us to the killer.'

On arriving back at the station, Marshall told his team firmly that Tex was not the killer and instructed them to make finding the two youths on scramble bikes and the running man a priority. He also wanted four of them to patrol the park, not just to question people about whether they'd been there on Friday, but to warn them to be careful and watch out for anyone who looked or behaved suspiciously.

He did the television appeal for information in the afternoon. He hadn't asked Mr and Mrs Church to join him – they were too distraught. But he planned to do a re-enactment in the next couple of days. They would find a girl similar in size and age to Chloë to be filmed in the park on the swing, then walking up the slope. He hoped the boys she was talking to at the time would take part. They were in the clear: the officers who had tracked them down said they'd left the park around six o'clock, which was before Chloë was killed, and called into the fish and chip shop on the way home. The owner had confirmed he'd served them, and both boys' mothers confirmed they were back indoors by seven.

Everyone on the other roads on the Pinewood estate had been questioned now. Some of the women had been alone at home at the time and there were a couple of men who had no alibi, but according to the team who interviewed them, none of them were suspicious.

A few of his men were working their way through sex offenders in Cheltenham and the surrounding area. Marshall did not think that paedophiles, who by their nature were secretive and had the patience to groom children, would suddenly savagely attack a child in broad daylight and in a public place. But it was good practice to check everyone on the register from time to time, if for no other reason than to let them know they were on the police radar. Besides, some of those loathsome men might have heard something useful on the grapevine. Most would have grassed up their own grandmother to get on the right side of the law.

But if that failed to turn up any leads, Marshall knew he'd have to widen the search area, and do a house-to-house investigation, possibly all over Cheltenham. Yet he was still sticking by his original hunch that the killer was very local, someone who knew the park, scrubland and woods around the Pinewood estate very well. He also felt the killer must have been well known to Chloë. Even though she was a confident, outgoing girl, she was sensible and would never have gone off with a stranger.

Marshall had only the last two couples in Willow Close left to question, and from what the neighbours had said about them being quiet, reserved people, he didn't bear much hope they'd be the killers. But he'd go and see them now so he could tick them off the list.

Wilma Parkin slid their emptied suitcase under their bed and smiled at her husband, who was folding a sweater and putting it away.

'Oh, Terry, it was such a lovely weekend. I wish we could've stayed all week. I love the New Forest.'

'Maybe we can go again in a month or so,' he replied. 'By then I'll be able to ask for the Monday off again, like this time.'

He was glad Wilma seemed so happy about the long weekend, but he was relieved to be going back to work in the morning. Three whole days with Wilma was more than enough. He loved her for her gentle sweetness, but so much placidity made him feel stifled and irritated.

It had been the same when he was in the army: he'd looked forward to his leave, but once he was home, he wanted out. Now he was happiest at work. The other engineers were a fun bunch, lots of laughing, taking the rise out of each other, and the women in the office joined in too. Some of them were very bawdy, shockingly so sometimes, and there was always a bit of intrigue about who was having a dabble with whom. He thought he was the only one of the engineers who had never had an affair with one of the office girls.

Martin, his twenty-eight-year-old son, was just as dull and self-righteous as his mother. On the rare occasions he agreed to join Terry at the pub he could make a half of lager last a couple of hours, then go home. Terry was proud that Martin had done so well, a first-class degree at Bristol University, and now lecturing on history and geography there. He was much too self-effacing to boast that he was good at his job, but Wilma had an old friend at the university who said he brought his subjects to life, and his lectures were some of the best-attended.

It was good to hear that his son's students thought him a great lecturer, but even if he was Terry's son, he failed to see how that could be. His wife Sandra was as sweet and kind as Wilma, but also as dowdy, and the couple had chosen to buy a bungalow in a road full of old people. Terry was astounded that he'd produced a son who had slipped into staid middle-age while still in his twenties.

Once, when he'd had a few too many drinks, Terry asked his son why he hadn't gone for a woman with more fire. Martin looked puzzled. 'I wanted a wife like Mum,' he said, totally surprised that his father wasn't a hundred per cent behind his daughter-in-law. 'I can't imagine anything worse than being married to someone flighty or quarrelsome. Sandra is such a good housekeeper, and a fantastic cook, and she makes all her own clothes too.'

Terry thought her clothes looked homemade – at times she resembled a Plymouth Brethren woman, long, full skirts, baggy cardigans and sensible shoes. She didn't wear make-up or colour her hair. Terry just hoped she was good in bed, but he doubted she was. He suspected Martin wouldn't even know what that was because Sandra had been his first girlfriend at the age of twenty-one. Terry didn't have to imagine what seven years of boring shags would be like. He'd lived through more than twenty years of them.

'What shall we do now? It's only three, too early to start preparing dinner,' Wilma said, as she sat down on the dressing-table stool to brush her hair and fix it up again. She had pretty hair, a pale reddish gold – he thought they called it strawberry blonde. Years ago he had begged her to wear it loose, but she refused. Her parents were extremely religious, and they'd given her the idea that it was sinful for a married woman to flaunt herself. Hence the plain, drab clothes and hair always twisted up in a bun.

She was upset to learn when they returned home that the murdered girl they'd heard about on the news was Chloë Church, who lived three doors down from them. She had sat crying in the kitchen for some time, but Terry ignored her as he always did when she cried. It wasn't that he didn't feel bad that a kid in their street had been murdered, but Wilma was inclined to hysterics if he reacted to her tears. Besides, she'd annoyed him the previous day by saying they must find a church so she could attend communion. He refused to drive her to one and she began wailing.

'Missing one Sunday won't hurt. I paid a lot to stay here and I've been looking forward to a slap-up breakfast. After that we can have a nice walk in the forest,' he said firmly. 'And stop crying and putting on that sour face.'

She had stopped crying but the sour face remained. She was silent during breakfast, irritating him further by eating barely anything. He hated it when she did the martyr bit.

Now, though, she was asking what they were going to do with the remainder of the day, which was a good sign.

'How about you leave your hair down and get in bed with me?' he said hopefully.

Her face was quite lined because she never used face cream, and it stiffened in disapproval at his words. 'Oh, Terry, I can't do that in broad daylight.'

Terry didn't bother to argue or beg, he just turned away and went downstairs as if unconcerned by her response. But he was angry. He was often angered by her puritanical outlook, but he could never bring himself to show it to her. He could feel that anger rising now, like a volcano that was likely to erupt and make him do something he'd regret. Usually when he felt this way, he went to a massage parlour and relieved the tension. But he couldn't go there now: the one he used didn't open till seven. Another four hours.

As he reached the bottom of the stairs the bell rang. He pulled the door open. 'Yes?' he said, to the two men standing there.

'Mr Parkin? Police, we'd like a word with you and your wife.'

Terry's heart plummeted as they flashed their warrant cards. 'What's this about?' he asked.

'Chloë Church from number ten was murdered on Friday evening, as I'm sure you know. We just want to establish where you and your wife were between six thirty and eight thirty that day. May we come in?'

Terry's stomach flipped, as it always did when the police started asking questions. 'Come in,' he said, though he didn't want them in his house. 'Cup of tea or coffee?' he added, as they stepped into the hall.

'No, thank you,' the older of the two men replied. 'I'm DS Allen and this is DC Pople.'

'Come in the kitchen,' Terry said.

They walked right into the room, but stood, declining to sit down, which made it awkward for him to shut the door so Wilma couldn't come in.

'We went to the New Forest for the weekend,' Terry volunteered. 'Didn't do anything much on Friday evening. I watered the garden and did a few jobs out there as the weather was so good.'

'And Mrs Parkin? Was she helping you in the garden? Or making dinner perhaps.'

'We ate early, about five. I finish work at four on Fridays, you see, and the missis goes to a Bible study group.'

'What time did she go out?' DS Allen asked.

Terry blew out his cheeks while he thought about it. 'Six, I think. She said she'd walk there as I was busy. She got a lift home, though, and that was almost nine. I'd just come indoors and expected her to be there. She came in a few minutes later. She said she'd been chatting to the vicar.'

'So you were in the garden all that time?' Allen asked. 'From six till nine?'

'Us gardeners lose track of time.' Terry grinned. 'Are you a gardener?'

'No,' Allen said, looking out of the kitchen window. 'I live in a flat. But looking at yours makes me wish I had one.'

Terry beamed. His garden was his pride and joy, and he'd packed so many bushes and plants into it that it was impossible to see any soil between them. He liked the voluptuous look, flowers that billowed into one another, and he was good at putting colours together that complemented each other.

Allen wrote down the name of the vicar and the address where the Bible study group met. For once Terry was glad Wilma was religious: her alibi appeared to have stopped him being questioned further.

'Do you need to speak to my wife?' he asked.

Allen shook his head as he put his notebook back into his pocket. 'I don't think that will be necessary.'

Wilma came downstairs as he shut the door after the two detectives. 'What did they want?' she asked.

'Just to ask where we both were on Friday night.'

'Because of Chloë Church being killed?'

Terry nodded.

'Are they questioning everyone?' She looked at him oddly, perhaps remembering other times the police had pulled him in for questioning.

'Absolutely everyone. We were last, I think, as we were away. Let's hope they catch the killer soon.'

13

Tuesday, 21 July, Day Four

'Trudy, it's over. I want a divorce.'

Trudy could only stare, mouth agape, at her husband's words. He had arrived unexpectedly at eight in the morning when she was still in bed. He'd only left the day before. She'd come down when she heard him in the kitchen. Now he said he was leaving her and wanted a divorce.

'You can't leave me,' she said weakly. 'I won't be able to cope without you.'

Even as she made that statement, she knew it would anger him. But it was the way she felt. As if she would wither and die, like a plant without water.

'It's that attitude that makes me desperate to get out of this marriage,' he said, his voice rasping with bitterness. 'Of course you can manage. What is there to do? A bit of cleaning, cooking and laundry, and maybe mow the grass. Hardly a challenge.'

'I meant being without you,' she whimpered. 'You are my love, my life.'

She saw him close his eyes in exasperation.

'I am not. That's the stuff of cheap romantic fiction. We are not suited, Trudy. We never have been. I want fun, action, adventure. To you that's a trip to Tesco. Sorry it didn't work out but let me remind you that I've worked my socks off to get this standard of living. You've done nothing. You can't even choose wallpaper without agonizing over it for weeks. In the end it's always me who decides. I'm sick of it, Trudy. I'd rather come home to a woman who'd dyed her hair purple and painted the lounge shocking pink, because she was creative, than be married to a spineless slob who thinks of nothing but food.'

Predictably Trudy began to wail. Crying was her speciality, loud and snotty and enough to turn Roger's stomach.

'If you think that'll change my mind, think again. I'm going now.'

As he went out into the hall, his bag in his hand, Amy came racing down the stairs. Her face was flushed, eyes watery. Clearly, she'd been listening.

'Don't go, Daddy,' she begged. 'Or let me come with you.'

'I am going, Amy, and, no, you can't come. Stay with your mum and take care of her.'

'She should be looking after me!' Amy sobbed. 'It's not fair.'

'I'm sorry I'm letting you down,' Roger softened his voice as he spoke to his daughter. After all, none of this was her fault. 'But your mum and I haven't been happy together for a long time. I'll pay all the bills and I'll ring you now and then. But I'm not coming back.'

He opened the front door then, lifted a heavy box of files into his arms with a bag of clothes balanced on top, and marched out to his car.

In a fit of temper, Amy slammed the door behind him, then turned to her mother. 'This is all your fault!' she shouted at her. 'I hate you!'

Wilma Parkin was dusting the sitting room and heard the rumpus next door because she had her windows open.

She had seen Roger come home, and until the row started she had supposed he had come home to give his wife and daughter some support. She imagined Amy was taking the death of her friend hard.

She could hardly believe the cruel things he'd said to Trudy. If Terry said such things to her she would never get over it. It was true Trudy was a bit feeble and lacking in personality but, as a religious woman, Wilma believed marriage was for life. Even if your husband or wife didn't turn out quite as expected, you had to stay and make the best of it.

But her fear now was for Amy. She had always spent more time in the Churches' home than her own, which suggested the child found her own home a toxic place. Her only friend, pretty Chloë, was dead, and now her father was walking out on her too. That was never right.

Wilma had no doubt there was another woman. Just to look at handsome, suave Roger was to know he had a mistress tucked away somewhere. He and Trudy were opposites. He was outgoing, she a home bird. He cared about his appearance while Trudy seemed unaware of hers.

It was hard to like Trudy: she talked about food, cleaning materials, what she'd seen on TV and very little else. But that was possibly because her life was so narrow. Terry got on well with Roger. They often chatted about cars, sport and travel. Terry said he sympathized with Roger being married to a woman like a suet pudding.

Wilma hated it when Terry said such things. But Wilma had despaired of Trudy too. She had suggested her neighbour join her church, to make some new friends, but Trudy had said Roger wouldn't like it if she got religious. So all she had left was trying to shine at domestic tasks, and Roger threw that back in her face as worthless. He didn't take much interest in his daughter either.

What would happen to Amy? Her only friend dead, her father walking out, and a mother who claimed she couldn't cope. Thirteen was a very impressionable age, and the people who were supposed to love her had proved they cared little for her welfare. What was that going to do to the child?

'Con, have you noticed anything weird about this road?'

Conrad looked up from his newspaper. He'd come home for lunch today as Nina had been given a few days off from the florist's to get the house straight. She'd made a great tuna and pasta dish, and he wished he could come home for lunch more often.

'What – apart from them all being swingers?' he said, with a chuckle. Since they'd moved in, Nina seemed to have been looking out of the window a great deal. But, then, their old rented flat had looked on to a concrete backyard that held nothing but the dustbins.

'You're a perve. You've still got swingers on the brain. No, it's the lack of kids. As far as I can make out there's only one child living here, the podgy one at number six – I think she's called Amy. Obviously there was Chloë, but she's not with us any more.'

'What's so weird about that? Maybe no one else could have kids, didn't want them or are too old now.'

Nina looked a bit troubled. 'When we first came to look at this house, the first thing I thought was that it would be a great place to raise a family. I bet loads of people have thought the same, so why didn't they buy a house here?'

'If you remember, the estate agent told us it's rare for a house to come up for sale here.'

'Maybe they've all eaten their kids or buried them in their gard–' Nina broke off, suddenly aware that it wasn't a joking matter. 'Forget I said that.'

'I'm wondering why it's taking them so long to crack this case and make an arrest,' Conrad said, suddenly serious. 'She wasn't killed in a really secluded place. It was broad daylight and a beautiful warm evening. Someone must have seen something.'

'Perhaps it was done by someone no one would suspect. You know, like hiding in plain sight,' Nina said. 'Look how long it took to catch the Yorkshire Ripper. He'd been questioned loads of times too. Even Fred West in Gloucester took for ever to catch. Now it seems impossible that those men got away with killing for so long.'

She wasn't going to admit it, but she was scared at the thought of a killer on the loose.

'So who would be someone that no one would suspect? A priest, a policeman? Why kill a young girl anyway?' Conrad said, his normal jovial manner replaced by sadness.

Nina knew crimes against children always upset Conrad. One of the reasons he chose to work with children in care was because of his own background. His father had died when he was six, and his mother married again less than a year later, possibly lured by the promises the very wealthy Lawrence Lovell had made to her.

Conrad said that the ink was barely dry on the wedding certificate before his new stepfather, whom he always had to address as 'sir', told Conrad in no uncertain terms that he was expected to stay out of sight, and would see his mother for just an hour a day when he came home from school.

Conrad's new domain was called the nursery, a cheerless room at the top of Mr Lovell's big house in Cirencester. Dawn, one of two maids, brought him his meals, cleaned the room, and saw that he had clean clothes and polished shoes to go to school. Had it not been for her, Conrad thought he would have wasted away. He missed his father dreadfully, and the time allotted for him to be with his mother was so short. He didn't understand why she went along with it.

There were only a few worn books in the nursery, some with missing pages, a clockwork train set that was broken, and a few board games. Dawn smuggled in books from her home, and coloured pencils and paper so he could draw.

By the time Conrad was eight, he had realized his mother feared her new husband. He often saw bruises where she'd been gripped hard on her arms, and black eyes, which she always claimed were the result of walking into a door. She begged Conrad to do exactly as he was told, or Sir would beat him. She didn't need to add he would beat her too – that much was obvious.

After he had dared to go downstairs one evening to see his mother when Sir was out, one of the servants must have told on him: he was caned so hard on his backside the skin was broken. He was almost eleven then, and shortly after he was sent away to school.

As it turned out, Manor Court School in Shropshire became his saviour. It was nothing like the cosy little school he'd been attending until his father's death, but a posh boarding place. He was certain Sir had chosen it as he expected it to be grim like in *Tom Brown's Schooldays*. Perhaps he'd been to a school like that himself. Thankfully, it was far better than Conrad could have hoped for. If it hadn't been for worrying about his mother, and missing her, he could have been really happy there.

The teachers were strict but fair. Bullies were rooted out and punished. But best of all was Conrad's teacher, the inspiring Mr Worthing. Perhaps he sensed that Conrad needed special attention, as he went out of his way to encourage him, lending him books he believed he needed to read, always praising his work and gently stretching his ability. He said that a good education was the passport to success in life.

When Conrad was told he was to stay at school during the holidays, he was pleased, at least for himself.

Two of his friends had to stay, too, as their parents were abroad. But as time went by, alarm bells for his mother kept ringing in his head. The letters she wrote each week were stilted and cool, clearly being checked by her husband. Conrad couldn't write back angrily, or even consolingly: to do so would endanger her. He had visions of her fading away like a Victorian lady, too scared to seek help because she knew her husband would punish her.

Conrad eventually told Mr Worthing his fears for his mother, and the teacher offered to go and see her in the next holiday, which was Easter.

But the week before school broke up for the Easter holidays, his mother committed suicide with a cocktail of barbiturates and painkillers.

There was no letter for Conrad. He was certain she must have written one, but his stepfather had destroyed it.

Conrad was just fourteen. Mr Worthing escorted him to his mother's funeral, then brought him back to Manor Court. His stepfather never spoke to Conrad at the funeral, he didn't even look at him, but he paid the school fees until he was sixteen. Conrad knew that wasn't an act of kindness, only a cover-up to make himself look noble.

Nina remembered that when Conrad had told her this story he'd finished by saying, 'I wanted to kill him, as he killed my mother. But Fate stepped in just a few months after Mum died. He had a massive stroke, which left him paralysed, unable to even feed himself. I went to the nursing home where he was, stood at the end of his bed, told him what a bastard he'd been, and how pathetic he looked now. Then I laughed at him. It wasn't much of a revenge, but he knew what I'd said, and it made me feel a bit better.'

Nina had put her arms around her husband and held him tight after that disclosure. He never looked for sympathy for his miserable childhood. Instead he did his best to emulate Mr Worthing, who, with encouragement and understanding, had made Conrad stand on his own two feet and know his own worth.

'I can't imagine why anyone would kill a child,' Nina said. 'But I've got a creepy feeling it's someone living in this close. So who could it be?'

'Child murders give me the screaming ab-dabs. As newcomers, we can't possibly make any judgements about our neighbours. And I wouldn't want to. Anyhow, it's time for me to get back to work.'

Nina kissed him lingeringly. She loved him so much and knew he'd turned around the lives of many children who had come into his care.

'I shall have to come back for lunch more often,' Conrad said, rubbing his nose affectionately against hers. 'But as a reward for being so lovely to your old man, I think I'll take you out for a meal tomorrow night. Let's get dressed up and forget about all the unpacking and sorting still waiting to be done.'

'That sounds like Heaven,' Nina said. 'Now and then I'm reminded why I married you.'

14

Wednesday, 22 July, Day Five

Terry Parkin pulled over to the side of the road when he saw who was ringing him. 'Thanks for calling back, Sid,' he said. 'I need you to ship the goods out of the lockup.'

Terry rolled his eyes impatiently as Sid made the delaying excuses he'd half expected. 'I'm sorry to hear your wife isn't too good, but as you've probably heard, a kid in my street was murdered last Friday and the police are crawling all over the place. If they find out I've got a lockup they'll want to look in it. They'll do fingerprint and DNA tests, and that will implicate you, just as much as me. So, if you want to stay in the clear you've got to take the stuff now.'

Sid began to whine: he had problems with his van, he'd got a hernia, and his wife would be on his back if he told her he had to take stuff to London.

'Sid, this is serious,' Terry said sternly. 'You got me into this, and you're the one with the contact in London. I can't even come with you as I think the police are keeping an eye on me and all the other men around here because of this kid. Now don't let me down. I've done my part, and now you must do yours. We've got a lot of money riding on this.'

As Terry spoke, he pictured Sid. He was a small man, only five foot six, but he was all muscle with the tenacity of a pit bull terrier. They both came from Bristol, but they had met for the first time waiting in line to apply to join the army when they were eighteen. They went for a drink afterwards, and as Sid often told people, 'I felt like Terry was my long-lost brother.'

They joined the Royal Engineers, in different battalions, but they remained firm friends, writing the odd letter to each other when they were in basic training, and meeting up later on when they were on a tour in Northern Ireland. They always tried to get together when they were both on leave in Bristol, and occasionally had drunken nights out when they'd sworn a lifetime of allegiance to one another.

Terry remembered how shocked he was when Sid told him he'd applied to join the bomb-disposal squad. That to him seemed like planning suicide, but at the same time he was proud of him.

Terry married Wilma around that time, and Sid was here, there and everywhere round the world, so their friendship went on the back-burner for over three years. But one bitterly cold Saturday night in Bristol he ran into Sid again. He was with three of his army mates and it was one of them, a chap called Lawrence, who told Terry that in Belfast Sid had calmly defused a bomb big enough to take out half a street. He'd become something of a regimental legend.

Terry and Sid renewed their friendship after that chance meeting. Later Sid married Julie, and Terry was his best man. Several years on Terry retired from the army to work for BT and bought their house in Willow Close, but he still kept in touch with Sid, wherever he was.

A couple of years later Sid left the army and bought a house in Gloucester. He said he felt his luck might run out and he didn't want to think of his two children growing up without a father. Like Terry, he had a good army pension, and he did a few building jobs on the side.

To anyone who didn't know what Sid had done in the army they might have assumed from his appearance and his moaning that he was a two-bit thug with a very lazy streak. But Terry knew better.

'So when will you do it?' Terry asked. 'This evening would be good.'

There was a long pause. He could imagine his old friend weighing up everything.

'It'll have to be tomorrow. I'll meet you at your lockup at seven – make sure the police aren't following you. With luck and clear roads I should be on my way back by eleven. I'll give you a bell on the way. We can arrange then where to meet.'

Terry liked that he didn't say 'pay-out' but that was what he meant. 'Be careful,' he said, from force of habit.

15

Thursday, 23 July, Day Six

'Give us a twirl!' Conrad said, as Nina came down the stairs wearing a cream dress he didn't think he'd seen before and high heels. She'd put her hair up too.

Nina laughed and obediently twirled. 'Before you ask, yes, it's a new dress from the boutique by Petals. But you did say dress up and I haven't unpacked all my clothes yet.'

'You don't have to make excuses for looking lovely,' he said. 'But just remember we've booked an Indian meal so don't spill any on the dress.'

Nina smiled. She knew he was remembering dinner at another Indian restaurant not long after they'd first met. She'd picked up one of the small serving dishes of curry and it was so hot she dropped it, and it slopped on to her lap. She was mortified at being so clumsy and ruining a very new pair of cream trousers. 'I now always do a test run on dishes to check how hot they are,' she said. 'But you can shout. Look how often you've spilt food down a jacket.'

'*Touché*,' Conrad said. 'And we'd better get going.'

As they drove from their house out into the road, a silver Mercedes shot out of the garage of number seven, narrowly missing crashing into their Golf.

'Arsehole!' Conrad exclaimed, as he blasted his horn. 'What is it with men driving Mercedes? They seem to think the roads belong to them.'

'He did mouth an apology,' Nina said. 'But what could be so important for him to drive like that?'

'Shall we follow him?'

Nina knew her husband's way of getting back at thoughtless drivers was to overtake them, then drive slowly in front to teach them a lesson. It was like a game to him, and Nina had seen him do it so often she didn't bother to complain any longer.

'As long as it doesn't go on too long,' she warned him. 'I'm hungry.'

Conrad kept right on their neighbour's tail for about a mile, waiting for the opportunity to overtake. Then, without indicating, the man suddenly swerved sharply to the right into a narrow lane.

'Bloody hell!' Conrad was forced to slam on his brakes again. 'The man must have a death wish. I'm going to have it out with him.'

'Oh, don't, Con, you'll just start bad feeling,' Nina begged him. 'He's a neighbour, and things are bad enough in the close without any further trouble.' Not knowing who had killed Chloë was getting to her – she was a bit suspicious of everyone.

'I'm not going to hit him. I just want to see what he's up to. That lane is a dead end, so why is he going down it?' Conrad replied. He parked up and opened the car door.

Nina watched as he strode across the road and went into the lane, where he began to creep forward cautiously. It made her want to laugh because although he hadn't got an aggressive bone in his body he made up for it with inquisitiveness. As for her, she couldn't care less why her neighbour was speeding to go to this lane, but her husband was something of a student of human behaviour, and he liked to have answers to puzzles.

He had now gone so far into the lane that she couldn't see him any more. The minutes ticked past, five and then ten. Just as she was growing anxious about him, he reappeared, ran across the road, leapt into the car and drove off fast.

'Well?'

He was too busy looking in the mirror to answer immediately, but once convinced he was safe, he reached out and squeezed her knee. 'Very suspicious,' he said. 'There's nothing in that lane but a few back gates on the left-hand side belonging to the houses in the next road. On the right are the grounds of a nursing home, plus the garage our chap was making for. Another tough-looking bloke was there, waiting for him to open the garage. I guess our neighbour was speeding because he was late for the meet. Anyway, he unlocked the garage, and they started to load up the other man's van with wooden boxes. They looked quite heavy. I didn't dare get closer to hear what they were talking about because there was nothing to hide behind. But I could tell by the way they were behaving that it was something dodgy.'

Nina smiled. Conrad was so used to naughty kids, he was inclined to be suspicious of everything. 'How were they behaving?'

'Furtive, keeping an eye out. They weren't shifting second-hand furniture, or boxes of household goods. I'd say it was some kind of contraband. What comes in wooden boxes?'

'Gold nuggets! Fresh-caught fish, engine parts. I don't know, Con. What do you think it was?'

'I dunno. Is he the bloke Rose mentioned that's ex-army? If he is, it could be guns or ammunition.'

Nina felt he had a point. After all, a child had been killed. But she wasn't going to agree with him or he'd never get off the subject and they were supposed to be having a night out. 'Oh, Con. You've been watching too many thrillers,' she said. 'His name is Terry Parkin and, yes, he is ex-army. Well, I think he's the man Rose told me about. Apparently his wife Wilma is holier than thou, a devout church-goer. Maybe the wooden boxes are full of Bibles being shipped to missionaries in Africa.'

Conrad laughed. 'Shipping Bibles could be a great smokescreen. They could be stuffed with drugs. But they wouldn't put them in wooden boxes, would they?'

'Oh, Con!' She laughed. 'What an imagination you've got!'

'I can't help the imagination, but my whole working life has been spent with bad lads, so I know when someone's up to something.'

'Okay, let's change the subject. This is getting worrying,' Nina said. 'Now what do you fancy to eat tonight? Something very hot? Or mild?'

'Curry alone won't stop me wanting to be a detective.' Conrad smiled. 'But for now I'll button it.' He squeezed her leg affectionately, his way of having the last word.

Later that evening Nina lay awake long after Conrad was sound asleep. He hadn't mentioned their neighbour and his mysterious wooden boxes again, but she had a feeling it wasn't because he'd forgotten about it.

Meeting Conrad was the best thing that had ever happened to her. She could honestly say it had been love at first sight, and she had thought her parents would love him too. But she ought to have known better: they were staid, unimaginative people, who were nervous about anything or anyone out of the ordinary. And, of course, Conrad wasn't ordinary, with his dark curls, his irreverent manner and his strong social conscience.

Nina had been born when her mother was forty-two and her father forty-eight, a shock to their systems. She had known from an early age that they saw her as a living wedge that would push them apart. They had grown accustomed to their cosy, sedate life together, and they didn't like the change a baby brought with it.

Nina felt they both loved her, but in a somewhat detached way. A noisy, excitable little girl who couldn't sit still for long and was always asking questions was too much for them.

Looking back Nina could see she'd always rebelled against their endless rules. She recalled doing things like swimming in the local river, purely because they'd told her not to. She'd made friends with kids they didn't approve of; she'd caught the bus into town when they thought she was playing in the garden. As she got older, she'd knocked off school just for the hell of it.

The crunch came when she was sixteen. She'd wanted to share a flat with her friend Sophie, whom her parents were sniffy about because she lived on a council estate. When Nina couldn't get their approval, she went ahead and moved in with Sophie anyway.

Two such young girls away from home for the first time, with no set boundaries and no one to monitor what they got up to, was a recipe for disaster. Nina had only recently started work as a trainee florist, Sophie as an office junior, and after paying their rent they had little money left over. But their little flat soon became Party Central, a magnet for all young people in Cirencester. Things got out of hand one night: the flat was trashed, and neighbours called the police. Both girls were taken home to their parents, but not before a telling-off from police officers.

Nina's parents were furious with her. They paid the landlord for the damage caused, but she had to reimburse them out of her wages and was grounded indefinitely.

Nina knew she'd been silly and feckless. She wanted to make amends, but her parents were so nasty that she made up her mind to leave again as soon as the debt was paid. She paid them back quickly by getting a job as a waitress in the evenings, and she saved enough for a little nest egg too. When she was seventeen, she'd had enough of her parents' silent treatment, heavy sighs and unspoken disappointment. So she told them she was leaving and this time she would never come back.

'You don't want a daughter,' she said accusingly. 'A dog would have suited you better. So I'll be off now.'

She left them her address, she sent birthday and Christmas cards, but they never responded. Then when she met Conrad, she thought she would try one last time with them, telling them she had met the man she wanted to marry.

They did write back then, a cold 'Bring him to tea on Sunday.'

Conrad did his best to charm them, but they could not see beyond his too long hair, his work with delinquent boys and his leftie leanings.

'He's not our sort!' her mother had sniffed as Nina tried to kiss her goodbye.

'He's my sort,' Nina said. 'But you and Dad aren't.'

On the drive home, Conrad had put his hand on her knee. 'Looks like we're both orphans now.' As always summing up the situation succinctly with a touch of humour.

Nina smiled. He was all she wanted, and if her parents weren't prepared to get to know him, she had no intention of seeing them again. It had surprised her how good it felt to sever the connection with them. She didn't feel sad, only free. But she often wondered what they would think of the events in this road. Murder, and suspected arms dealings.

Nina understood Conrad's curiosity. She was now curious too. What if it was guns or ammunition in those boxes? Their neighbour was home when they got back from the restaurant, the Mercedes back on the couple's drive. So where had the other man taken the wooden boxes?

16

Friday, 24 July, Day Seven

As Nina turned into the close Rose almost pounced on her. 'Glad I caught you,' she said, her sharp features even sharper than usual. She was clearly on a mission. 'It's the re-enactment tonight of the events leading up to when Chloë was killed. I thought you and Conrad might not know but would want to be there. It's at six thirty in the park.'

Nina was tired. It had been a hectic day: she'd made up a dozen bridal bouquets, plus what seemed like half a million buttonholes and corsages. The bus was so crowded she'd had to stand all the way home, and all she wanted now was a glass of chilled wine and a shower.

'We did know about it,' she said, trying not to let her voice give away her irritation at her neighbour. 'But we decided, as we didn't live here then and didn't know Chloë, there was no reason for us to go.'

'Oh, but it's a community thing . . . to support Mike and Ruth.'

'To me it feels more like rubber-necking at a car

crash than support. And a distraction to those who were in the park the night of the murder and who might be shy of telling the police what they know,' Nina said. 'Now, if you'll excuse me, I need to get in and take my shoes off. I've been on my feet all day.'

As Nina turned on to the front path, Rose spoke again: 'I hope you're going to mow your lawn soon. If you leave it much longer it'll be hard to cut.'

Nina turned back to Rose, incensed by being told what to do. 'Some of us have work to go to, and our lawn is our business, not yours,' she said. 'Now fuck off, Rose. I'm hot, tired and grumpy.'

She heard Rose gasp indignantly, and Nina guessed she was standing there with her hands on her hips plotting revenge. But Nina didn't look back, just opened her front door and swept in.

An hour later Nina had showered and changed, and was sitting on her patio with a glass of wine, waiting for Conrad to come home, when Janice from next door beckoned to her over the fence. Nina liked Janice: the couple of times they'd chatted she found her to be a vibrant, intelligent and interesting woman. She thought they could become good friends, so she bounded over to the fence.

'Sorry to behave like a spy,' Janice said, with a wide grin. 'I didn't want to alert the eyes and ears of Willow Close that we were talking. We ought to rig up a signal, a little flag or something.'

'Great idea,' Nina agreed, giggling. Rose and John's house was on the other side of Janice's. 'Are they in their garden?' she whispered. She couldn't tell as Janice had quite a high fence on that side and it was covered with honeysuckle and jasmine. On Nina's side it was much lower, and they were speaking through a gap in the foliage. 'I had a bit of a run-in with her earlier.'

Janice smirked. 'John is out there, but down the bottom of their garden in the place they call the Dell. It's just a bench behind a bit of trellis — no one else would give it a grand name. I heard the conversation you had with her. I loved that you told her to fuck off. She's in her kitchen now making a spell so all your hair falls out.'

Nina pulled a pretend-scared face. 'Perhaps I was a bit hasty. Should I apologize?'

'Don't you dare,' Janice said. 'When I first moved in, she was like an Exocet missile trained on me to make me do her bidding. I lost it with her one night when she knocked on the door while I was entertaining a friend. She said she loved the music I was playing and wanted to know what it was.'

'Really?' Nina sniggered. 'Why couldn't she wait till the next day to ask you?'

'That's just it. She knew I had a man friend here because his car was on the drive. She wanted to put her nib in and look at him. And possibly find me half undressed.'

'Were you?'

'No, we hadn't got that far. But I slammed the door shut in her face and the next day I went round to hers and said that my visitors and music were none of her business and to stay away from my house. Of course, John came out and said I shouldn't speak to his wife like that. I said it was a wonder anyone ever spoke to her as she was such a nosy-parker. I said I felt sorry for him and stalked off.'

'That was brave,' Nina said admiringly. 'So it worked? She leaves you alone now?'

'More or less. She tries to court my affections now and then by offering me some home-baked cake. I thank her but tell her I don't eat cake. I don't want to get back in her clutches.'

'Are you going to this re-enactment tonight?'

Janice shook her head. 'I wasn't here that evening and, as you so rightly said, it's like rubber-necking at a car crash. But I can't think why the police haven't found who did it yet. It's been a week. They're up and down the road often enough, and all around the rest of the estate. I spoke to that head honcho Detective Inspector Marshall yesterday. He said it was a baffling case. I said he ought to enrol Rose, she could sniff out anything.'

'Did he agree?'

'He kind of rolled his eyes as if he'd already had a basinful of her. Well, I'd better clear off now. I just heard Conrad's car and you'll be wanting to eat.'

'We must have a drink together soon,' Nina said. She heard Conrad open the front door and call her name. 'Let me know a good time.'

They had just finished their meal close to seven that evening when, through the open windows, they heard something going on out in the street.

'Who is Rose picking on now?' Conrad joked. Nina had told him what had happened earlier.

'She can't be here. She was going to the re-enactment,' Nina said.

They went over to the window and saw the noise was coming from straight across the close at number eight, Alfie and Dee's. Alfie had the bedroom window open and he was throwing his wife's clothes down. 'You treacherous bitch,' he bellowed. 'I've always suspected you had a lump of stone instead of a heart, but this takes the bloody biscuit. Get out of here and don't come back.'

Dee was standing on the lawn dressed in her customary shorts, red this time, and a red and white halter-neck top. 'You bastard!' she yelled up at him. 'You can't do this!'

'Oh yes I can, and I am!' Alfie yelled back. 'You've gone too far this time. And here's a suitcase to pack your stuff in.' He lobbed a large blue suitcase down, which nearly hit Dee.

'My God!' Nina exclaimed. 'I wonder what she's done!'

The couple next door to Alfie were looking on from their doorstep. Living so close, they possibly knew what this was about, but even from across the street it was possible to see the woman, the religious one, was rigid with anxiety.

'Rose and John will be sorry they went to the re-enactment and missed this,' Conrad said. 'They'd be over there sticking their oar in.'

Conrad had got the gen on Dee at the pub within forty-eight hours of moving in. It was said she was a first-class schemer and a dangerous enemy. Janice said she couldn't abide the woman and felt sorry for Alfie, so all this told Nina and Conrad not to offer her any help.

Dee opened the case and started pushing her clothes into it. 'I want my shoes and make-up,' she shouted. 'And give me some money too.'

Even from a distance they could see her face and neck were as red as her shorts, yet she still shouted at Alfie that he'd pay for this. Nina shuddered. There was something scary about the woman, and as Alfie, her husband, seemed such a kind and helpful man her sympathies were all with him.

Alfie came to the window again and threw down four pairs of shoes, all high heels. Then he hurled out what looked like a cosmetics bag. Finally he threw down an envelope. 'There's a hundred quid in there. That's all you're getting and it's a hundred quid more than you came into this marriage with.'

'That won't keep me even for a week,' she roared back. 'You always were a tight bastard.'

'Get back on the street and sell your snatch like you used to,' he responded. 'You're a bit old now but some men like their meat well aged.' With that he closed the window.

Conrad looked at Nina with raised eyebrows. 'Looks like wife-swapping's too tame for this road. I can't believe what Alfie just said.'

'What now? Do you think she'll go quietly?' Nina said thoughtfully.

Neither of them expected her to, but to their surprise she did. She gathered up the last of her things and called a taxi. It was there within five minutes and she went off in it.

They had another glass of wine each and Nina asked Conrad what he thought had caused such drama.

'I'd say she betrayed him in some way,' Conrad said thoughtfully. 'We haven't known any of our neighbours long enough to judge them, but I'd say Alfie's old-school. Betrayal is the only thing I can imagine making him react like that. And I don't mean her having an affair necessarily. I'd dearly love to know what she had on him.'

*

DI Marshall walked back from the park with Mike and Ruth soon after eight. The street was quiet, and they had no idea of the drama that had played out there an hour earlier.

'I'm impressed at how you managed to hold it together,' Marshall said to them both, as they entered Willow Close. Ruth had been close to breaking down for the whole of the re-enactment, but now she looked ready to collapse, only Mike's supporting arm around her waist holding her up. 'My men told me several members of the public gave them information. I don't know yet if any of it is helpful to our investigation, but I'm hopeful we might get a lead.'

'The girl looked so much like our Chloë,' Ruth said, in a shaky voice. 'I almost went over to hug her.' She was finding it difficult to hold herself together. People were kind, offering sympathy and asking if there was anything they could do to help. But she wanted to scream at them, 'You don't know what it's like. You haven't had your only child killed. I'm dead inside now, and I don't think anything will bring me back to life.'

She didn't say these things, of course, but she would wake in the middle of the night and ask, 'Why?' She and Mike were good people: they worked hard, were generous and warm-hearted. Why had they been singled out for tragedy?

Once again Ruth forced herself to smile at DI

Marshall to show her appreciation for his kindness to her and Mike. 'It was touching that the two boys on the swings seemed so troubled by the re-enactment. I didn't recognize Jason Longham until he came and spoke to me. He used to play at our house a lot when he was six or seven. A really nice boy.'

'Yes, he's been extremely helpful with information on the two boys on the scrambler bikes,' Marshall said. They had reached number ten now and the inspector took a step back as Mike opened the door. 'I'm terribly sorry you had to deal with those questions this afternoon,' he said, referring to what had happened earlier in the day with Dee and Alfie. 'It must have been intolerable to find a neighbour would play on your grief for some sick purpose,' he said.

Mike looked back at the policeman, and his eyes were dark with pure rage. 'If I ever see Dee again, I just might deck her,' he said. 'And hitting a woman would be a first for me.'

Mike Church wasn't the only man in the street wishing to deck Dee. Alfie Strong was downing a large whisky to try to stop himself shaking with fury at what Dee had done.

His day had begun quite normally. He'd come downstairs at seven thirty, walked around his garden in his dressing-gown doing the odd bit of dead-heading while he drank a cup of tea. He was out there for perhaps half an hour, then made Dee some tea and carried it upstairs. To his surprise she was already in the shower – normally it would be at least nine before she got out of bed.

'You're an early bird today,' he said, as she came out of the bathroom with the towel around her. 'Got a hair appointment?'

'No, just thought I'd get the shopping done at Tesco's early today and avoid the crowds. I might go into town after too.'

By the time Alfie had showered and shaved, she was already starting the Volvo and shot off down the road.

Alfie had made himself a couple of boiled eggs and toast, turning on the TV to watch the news. He was just taking his plate and mug into the kitchen when the bell rang. Through the glass door he could make out blue uniforms and, assuming they had a few more questions for him, opened the door to find four uniformed men.

The oldest, whom he hadn't seen before, spoke: 'I'm Sergeant Doubleday, and I have a warrant to search your house, Mr Strong.'

Alfie was stunned. He had done nothing wrong, and he hadn't got anything dodgy in the place. He guessed they'd discovered he had a criminal record and decided to shake him down.

'What on earth are you hoping to find?' he asked, as they came barging in.

They'd ignored him and proceeded to go through the house, pulling out drawers and opening cupboards, even yanking back carpet and going up into the attic. The search went on for over an hour, with Alfie getting more and more distressed. He soon found it was futile asking why they'd singled him out, or what they were looking for: they just carried on, ignoring his questions, grim-faced and silent.

Alfie was scared now. He knew there was nothing illegal or incriminating in the house, but he never put it past policemen to plant things. When he heard one of the men, who was in the garage, call out for the sergeant, his stomach churned.

'What's in this?' the sergeant asked Alfie, as he came out of the garage holding a small, grey wooden box.

'I've no idea,' Alfie said truthfully. 'I've never seen it before. Maybe it belongs to my wife. Show me what's in it.'

'We'll do that once we're at the police station,' the sergeant replied. 'We'll take you there now.'

On the drive to the station, Alfie realized that this was Dee's revenge for him saying he wanted a divorce and that she'd get nothing from him. She'd planned this since then, put something in that box, then rung the police this morning, probably without giving her name and from a callbox, to get them to search the house. No wonder she went out so early. But what was it? Drugs, maybe?

They took him down to the police station, put him in an interview room and left him there alone for over an hour.

When they returned, they asked all the same questions about what he was doing on the night of the murder. There were no different answers: the truth is easy to tell. He had just been working in the garden.

Finally Sergeant Doubleday opened the small grey box, and as he took out each item and laid it on the table, he studied Alfie's face for his reaction.

First out was a photograph of Chloë in a pink tutu. Alfie had taken it about a year ago, but the photo was crumpled as if it had been folded and taken out again and again to look at it.

'Why would you have a picture of a neighbour's child?' the sergeant asked.

'She had told me earlier that day she was going to be in a dancing show, then came running out while I was cleaning my car to show me the tutu,' Alfie said. 'She was bursting with excitement. I had a cheap camera in my car, so I took a snap of her.'

'But why?'

'Because I liked her. We always chatted. I chatted to her parents too.'

'Yes, but why have you got that picture hidden away in a box?'

'Last time I saw it was when I got the film developed. It was in a wallet with other photos of my wife and myself. I left the wallet in the kitchen or somewhere. I intended to give Chloë the picture of herself. But I forgot all about it.'

Alfie looked at the picture in despair. Its crumpled condition made him look like a liar. He knew it was Dee's work. But although she could be vindictive, he had never expected her to frame him as a pervert or a killer.

The next thing the sergeant pulled out of the box was a little pair of white knickers with tiny pink rosebuds on them.

Alfie's heart began to pound. He felt sick with fright and anger that his wife could do this to him.

'And why would you keep these? Where did you get them from?' the policeman asked.

'I've told you, I've never seen that box before. This is sick!'

Next came a multi-coloured bead bracelet, and a tiny teddy bear, no bigger than two inches.

Alfie knew this box was intended to look like a collection of trophies, the kind of thing the police on *CSI* often discovered, usually belonging to a serial killer. Dee loved those programmes.

'I promise you that, apart from the photo which I told you I took, I've never seen any of those things before,' he insisted. 'I liked Chloë. She was such a bright, happy child. But I didn't like her in a weird way. I'm quite certain there won't be any of my DNA on this stuff, but maybe you'd better check for my wife's. I hate to say it, but this looks like her work.'

They left him stewing in the interview room for nearly two more hours. Alfie was only too aware they would be studying his criminal record. But a bit of robbing, stealing cars and getting into a few fights when he was younger didn't mean he could kill a child. He was scared: he knew that corrupt officers were sometimes so desperate for a conviction that they would charge almost anyone who vaguely fitted their profile. Doctoring evidence, if necessary.

Just as he was beginning to despair, and ready to pound on the locked door to demand a solicitor, Detective Inspector Marshall came into the interview room with a young policewoman. 'Did your wife tell you she was going to drop in on Mr and Mrs Church yesterday?' Marshall asked, sitting down across the table and offering Alfie a cigarette.

Alfie was very surprised at the question but took the cigarette gratefully. Marshall took one too and lit them both. 'Well?' Marshall asked.

'No, she didn't. I'd have been staggered if she had told me that. She's hardly the most compassionate of women.'

Alfie noted that Marshall smirked.

'Well, she did call on them. Mrs Church said she was surprised and touched. She hadn't thought the woman had it in her to care about anyone but herself.'

'Too right,' Alfie muttered.

'Mrs Strong asked if she could use the bathroom while she was there, a strange request, I thought, when she only lived two doors away. But the Churches didn't see anything odd about it. As a result of further enquiries, it turns out those knickers were in the laundry basket in the bathroom. Understandably Mrs Church hadn't done any washing since Chloë was killed.'

Alfie felt relief flow through him like warm water. 'Dee took them? What a bitch!'

'It looks that way. The bear and the bracelet were on a small dish on the child's dressing-table. Mrs Church said she saw them earlier that day as she spends a lot of time in her daughter's room. Do you think your wife is capable of stealing them?'

'She'd steal the Crown Jewels if they weren't locked away. But that's low even for her,' Alfie growled. He wanted to throttle her.

'We intend to bring your wife in for questioning now,' Marshall said. 'I'm afraid we must hold you for a while longer while we check the box for fingerprints and DNA. But we'll take you home after that.'

'You'd better hold Dee here, then,' Alfie said, 'because I might just feel I've got to kill her.'

Marshall smiled. 'If that's the case, at least I'll be able to solve that murder quickly.'

Alfie let out a sigh of relief and chuckled. He liked people with a sense of humour.

17

Saturday, 25 July, Day Eight

Wearing boxer shorts, Conrad opened the bedroom curtains on Saturday morning to find it was raining so hard the water was cascading down the road like a river. He turned back to the bed where Nina was watching him. 'What is it?' he asked.

Nina smiled. 'A cat can look at a king,' she joked. 'Why are you so happy?'

'Because it's tipping down,' he said, perching on the edge of the bed.

'You're weird,' she said, but seeing that it was seven o'clock, she pushed back the covers.

'Well, aside from the grass going green again, maybe it'll calm down the neighbours. It's all become nasty. Funny, really, just a week here and we're kind of embroiled in all their business.'

Nina was always surprised, he knew, at how sensitive he was and intuitive about how things should be dealt with. 'Yes, maybe we'd best keep ourselves to ourselves until it's all over. I'm first for a shower. Will you make us some tea?'

Conrad agreed and went downstairs, but his mind was on the ugly scene the night before. After Alfie had thrown Dee's clothes out and she'd left in a taxi, the few neighbours who hadn't gone to the re-enactment in the park hung around by Alfie's house to chat. Conrad and Nina stayed indoors, but at eight thirty, others joined the group in the street, and as the noise level rose, they went up to their bedroom window to see what was going on.

At first their neighbours were just sharing their views on the re-enactment, debating whether it had revealed anything new. Rose and John were the most vocal: their view was that the lack of progress in the investigation was down to police laziness.

Few agreed with them, and as things grew a little more heated, their voices became louder. Then Brian Alcott reported on the Strongs' house being searched that morning, and that Alfie was taken away.

That created huge interest as most were unaware of it. To Conrad and Nina, it was shocking how quickly some of their neighbours suggested they'd always suspected Alfie was the killer. They even surmised that Dee had left him because of it.

At that point, Brian spoke up again and informed everyone that that wasn't true: the police had come back at two in the afternoon to take Dee in and soon after Alfie had come home.

'They wouldn't have let Alfie go if they'd thought

it was him. Besides, he's a good man and no way is he a child-killer. I wouldn't be surprised if Dee was, though. She's always struck me as capable of anything.'

That set everyone off. All talking at once, all with strong opinions, and those who had witnessed Alfie throwing Dee out earlier in the evening revelled in reporting on it, including all the bad language. It became full-on uproar as everyone shouted others down to get their point across.

Suddenly Alfie opened his bedroom window and stuck his head out. 'I've done nothing, you load of wankers. Now bugger off and put your own sad lives straight,' he roared, and slammed the window shut.

At that point Gareth Price from number five lurched drunkenly into the fray. 'The killer came through a bit of broken fence in my garden and got away over the fences. I've seen that kid from number six do it before now and the police didn't even check our fences,' he yelled indignantly.

Trudy Singer appeared then and, surprisingly, she seemed the worse for drink. 'You bastard,' she yelled at Gareth. That, too, seemed uncharacteristic, because it was said she was always quiet and docile. 'Fancy blaming my Amy when you're drunk all the time. I bet you see pink elephants out there too.'

'He isn't seeing things,' Rob and Maureen called, in Gareth's defence. 'We've found evidence of people going across our garden.'

'We have too,' Terry Parkin yelled. 'Trampled my petunias and asters. If I was to catch the sod that did it I'd trample on him too. The fucking police have got their heads up their arses. Surely the first thing they should've done was check the fences.'

'Terry, please don't use that awful language,' Maureen shot back at him. 'Gareth, if you thought the killer got through the fence, why didn't you inform the police? And you, Terry, you disappeared early on that Saturday morning, didn't you? Why was that? It looked suspicious to me.'

Conrad and Nina were still at their open window, thoroughly enjoying the fracas. 'She's accusing Terry of avoiding questioning? Does she really think he could be the killer?' Conrad said. 'My God, this is better than going to the pictures. Just wish we had some drinks and popcorn up here.'

Brian, encouraged by his wife May, said it might have been children from the next road as they'd had their flowerbeds trampled once or twice too. 'I can't see Amy coming down the road as far as us,' he pointed out. 'But the police should've checked the fences.'

Rose Freeman was in her element. Her sharp features seemed to become more rat-like as she egged everyone on to give voice to their complaints.

To Conrad it sounded like Rose was just spouting snippets of gossip, half-truths and innuendos collected over the week, which she now shamelessly lobbed like hand grenades into the mix. Soon absolutely everyone was shouting, even Rob and Maureen, who were usually quiet. Gareth's drunken voice boomed out, and Trudy Singer's shrill one, almost like a duet. To Conrad and Nina, much of it was incomprehensible, yet they sensed feelings of guilt were making some of the most vocal even more rabid.

'My Amy would never go into anyone's garden,' Trudy shrieked, at the top of her voice. 'How can you say such things, you people who've known her since she was a baby?'

Alfie opened his bedroom window again. 'Clear off or I'll turn on my hose and wash you all back into your own houses!' he yelled, red in the face with anger. 'You're all fucking tosspots.'

'Why did they take you to the police station, then, Alfie?' Rose shouted up at him, her voice loaded with malice, delighting that she'd managed to stir people up. 'I heard it was over some little girl's knickers you had.'

A shrill blast on a whistle made them all stop shouting and turn to see Mike Church stomping up the close towards the crowd. 'Have you got any idea what my wife and I are going through?' he roared. 'Isn't it bad enough that our daughter has been murdered, without all you lot, who we thought were friends, behaving like yobs at a football match? Go home.

And think yourselves lucky that you aren't standing in our shoes.'

Conrad was shamed. He immediately shut the window and looked at Nina with remorse. They had been enjoying the drama, forgetting in the heat of the moment that a little girl had been brutally murdered. They hadn't thought about her parents either. No one had.

But it was a new day now, and as he got back to the bedroom with two mugs of tea, Nina was just out the shower, a pink towel wrapped round her.

'Thank God it's a half-day today, but with ten lots of wedding flowers for collection or delivery, it's going to be mad at the shop.' She sighed.

'I thought I'd pick you up at one thirty. We could go and have some lunch, then buy a new sofa,' Conrad said. He needed something ordinary and safe to take away the awfulness of a child's death. 'It will be ages before we both get the same half-day again, and our old sofa is neither comfy nor beautiful.'

Nina beamed. 'And maybe stay out till it's dark so we don't have to see anyone!'

'Sounds like a plan. But I must get into the shower. It's no good me lecturing the boys on personal hygiene if I smell like a polecat.'

Dee Strong was still seething at eleven on Saturday morning, looking out of the window at the rain and wishing she was anywhere but Cheltenham. Last night she had got the taxi to take her to Langham's, a hotel in Montpelier, which, though clean and comfortable enough, was hardly the kind of place she felt she belonged in.

At least she could be glad she'd had the foresight to sew her savings-account book into the lining of her handbag some time ago: Alfie had turned her bag upside down and taken away their joint bank and credit cards. She'd been siphoning money out of the housekeeping and helping herself to some of the cash he'd left lying around for a few years in anticipation that a time like this might come. The hundred pounds he'd flung at her wouldn't have lasted a day. But she had some five thousand in her savings account.

On Monday she'd find a solicitor to get her a settlement, and she supposed she'd have to throw herself on the mercy of Social Security or she wouldn't be able to get legal aid. With hindsight, it had been a stupid idea to try to implicate Alfie as the murderer: she ought to have known they'd check that box for fingerprints, and that the Churches would say she'd been in their house.

If only she'd thought it through properly. Alfie would never let her back into his life now. As it was, she'd been charged with theft, falsifying evidence and wasting police time. She'd probably get a fine, but what worried her more was that the police now had her fingerprints and DNA. But what was done was done. She'd go to the hairdresser, and get herself dolled up tonight. Thankfully, there was always some other sucker out there looking for love and she knew the right places to find them. Sod Alfie!

Rob and Maureen Willis were cuddled up together on the sofa watching a vintage black and white movie. It felt quite decadent to be watching television in the afternoon – they were normally busy at weekends, with jobs in the house and garden. But the heavy rain meant the garden could be left, and after the rather shocking scenes out in the road last night they had no wish to be seen by anyone or to do any chores.

'We were always so happy living here,' Maureen said sadly. 'Maybe it's time we moved on. It seems all our neighbours are unpleasant characters. And Gareth ended up vomiting in the gutter.'

'It will all pass,' Rob said soothingly. 'But I must say the shine has gone off the place for me since we found little Chloë. However, no matter how drunk Gareth was last night, he was right. The killer could have escaped through the gardens. If he was covered with blood, he could even have hidden in one till it was dark. I'm surprised that neither we nor the police thought of it. Gareth's got that old shed in his garden and some sizeable bushes. That would make a great hiding place and he was unlikely to spot anyone. Maybe I should ring the police and suggest it.'

'Not now or they'll be round again and involve you. Let's enjoy the peace.'

As Rob and Maureen were getting cosy on the sofa, Trudy Singer was crying her heart out on hers. She had a bad hangover and although she couldn't remember exactly what the neighbours had been saying last night, she seemed to think they were pointing a finger at her and Amy.

She couldn't bear it. Roger coming back from Brighton to tell her their marriage was over was terrible. Her heart was broken. Seeing him walk out with clothes and files made it even more final. He had telephoned the next day and very coldly told her he'd just cancelled their joint account. He went on to say she must open her own account immediately and text him with the details so he could pay a monthly allowance for the housekeeping into it.

It really stung that he thought her first reaction would be to clean out that joint account. In all the years they'd been married she'd never taken advantage, always asking him if she needed something for herself. Anyone would think she was a gold-digger, like that Dee Strong.

Amy was playing up too, flouncing around the house, her face stony with sullen resentment. She kept going out without saying anything, she ate meals in silence, and in the evenings when Trudy told her to be home by half nine, she ignored her and came back as late as eleven. Last night she hadn't come home till long after that scene in the road was over. She wouldn't say where she'd been but she was dressed in black, like a Goth, with the white make-up they went in for, heavy black eyeliner and dark purple lipstick. She looked more like eighteen than thirteen.

Trudy knew she was playing up because of her father leaving, but what could she do? Lock her in her bedroom?

Gareth Price, next door to Trudy, was also feeling very alone, and for once sober. Unlike Trudy, however, he did remember what he'd said the previous night. Someone was coming in from the wooded area at the back through the broken slats in the fence. Sometimes they turned right and went into Rob and Maureen's garden, sometimes left to Trudy Singer's. Not just from the night the murder happened, it had started some time ago. It wasn't every night or even every week, and the tracks might be faint, but they were there. Whether this was someone going a sneaky way home, or a potential burglar, he had no idea. But he had mentioned it to a policeman the day after they questioned him, and suggested they get someone to come and investigate. But no one had.

He'd give the police one more chance, and if they didn't come today, he'd mend the fence. If they came in a few days' time, there would be little to see as by then he would have trampled on the ground around the hole and would probably have wiped off any DNA on the fence panels.

If Gareth was to be asked for his opinion on who killed Chloë, he'd say Alfie Strong. He had no grudge against the man – he liked him in fact – but he knew Alfie frequented massage parlours and had once told Gareth it was to relieve the pressure Dee subjected him to. He joked that if he didn't calm himself down, he'd kill her.

Gareth knew people often made remarks like that, and rarely acted on them. Visiting massage parlours didn't make anyone a paedophile or child-killer either. But Gareth had often seen Alfie talking and laughing with Chloë, and teenage girls were fond of teasing older men. It was possible Alfie had been tempted, had gone too far and Chloë had threatened to blow the whistle. For a strong, muscular man like Alfie, it wouldn't take much to kill a young girl. He probably hadn't meant to do it – maybe he didn't know his own strength – but it was done now. It would be so easy for him to get into his house across the gardens without being seen too. Gareth just hoped he was wrong.

Yet one thing this ghastly business had highlighted was that you didn't really know your neighbours, not until a disaster happened. Courage, cowardice, honest, dishonest, mean-spirited or generous, all was being revealed. And it took something as serious as a murdered child for him to look at himself and see how far he had fallen.

He knew now he needed help to stop drinking and get his life back on track. He had woken early that morning and looked out at the garden, reflecting that he was not too old to start a new relationship. He was solvent, with a decent house and a good pension, after all.

Today he was determined to find the closest A A group, get a haircut, clean the house and, if the rain stopped, mend that fence.

As the residents of Willow Close were either planning their weekend, avoiding their neighbours or sinking into misery, DI Jim Marshall was studying the evidence of the murder.

It was pitifully sketchy, time and place of death, the murder weapon a rock. But the re-enactment had brought forward a few more leads to follow up. The boys on the scrambler bikes had been found and questioned before the re-enactment. They claimed to have gone up the slope and driven out on the other side of the wooded areas before Chloë was killed. This was verified by a woman who lived in the street the track came out on to. She said she'd been angry at the noise the bikes made – apparently the boys had gone up and down several times before leaving. They'd also stopped at an off-licence to buy cigarettes. The shop owner remembered them as they'd given him some cheek.

However, the scrambler boys had come, as requested, to the re-enactment. It proved that such things really did work because as they took their part they suddenly remembered that as they were driving up the slope to leave the area they'd seen a man standing on the side of the track.

They said it wasn't Tex, this man was older, they thought maybe mid-forties to fifty, but he looked fit and muscular, wearing a denim shirt and jeans. He turned into the bushes as they drove up, which was why they didn't see his face.

Marshall recalled that a year ago there were reports of a flasher on that same waste ground. At the time they'd sent a few young female PCs up there in plain clothes but maybe he'd got wind of it as he was not seen again. However, the boys' description of the man was similar to the one they had on file.

One of the dog-walkers in the park also said she had seen a man standing on that slope a week before the murder, and as she'd felt a bit nervous of him, she hadn't gone that way since.

So this man had to be found. There was also the runner. No one at the re-enactment could shed any light on him. Not even which gate he'd used to leave the park.

As for Alfie Strong, he might seem to be a prime suspect, with his criminal record and his explosive temper, but Marshall thought the only thing he was really guilty of in this instance was being daft enough to marry that vicious schemer of a wife. She'd said plenty about him at the station, all of it unpleasant. He could imagine her taking a rock to the head of anyone who upset her. Although it was rare for a woman to attack a child it was not unheard of.

Then there was Terry Parkin. The man had done nothing to warrant suspicion, except taking his wife away for the weekend of the murder. But Rose Free-man said he had a bad temper and he used Diamonds, the massage parlour. Marshall wondered how she knew he went to that massage parlour. Perhaps it was her husband John who had dobbed him in. Weak men with domineering wives were prone to telling their partners such things. John might also be suspicious of the man because he was ex-army.

Marshall's phone rang, breaking his train of thought.

'Gareth Price, number five Willow Close,' the man's voice was deep and melodic. 'I did mention to one of your officers about the broken fence panel at the back of my garden and that I'd become aware someone had used it several times to come into my and my neighbours' gardens.'

'Really!' Marshall was surprised this information hadn't been passed on to him. 'I'll have to look into that, Mr Price.'

'You need to check it out quickly as I've bought the stuff to repair it. Once I've trampled around the site it won't tell you anything.'

Marshall realized this was the man who drank and had a very messy house. It was clear he meant 'Come and look at it now or never.'

'Okay, Mr Price, I'll come straight away, if that's convenient for you. Thank you for bringing this matter to my attention.'

After arranging that he would be there in the next half-hour, Marshall asked DS Dowling to come with him. 'Did you know that Gareth Price had informed someone about this broken fence panel?'

'No, sir, it didn't come to my ears.' Dowling frowned. 'I'm surprised the officers who interviewed him didn't automatically check his fence. I'm pretty certain they did on all the other houses.'

Marshall sighed. He had suspected that a few of the officers had not been as exacting as they should have been at the start of this investigation, which was very unusual for a child murder. Once they knew Gareth Price had such a strong, unbreakable alibi they perhaps didn't feel they had to search his place so thoroughly. Yet checking the fence so close to the murder scene was a priority. Why hadn't they done it?

'We really need a break. After we've been to Price's house I'll go and see Tex again and ask him if he's ever seen that man on the slope near the murder scene. He's observant, he might have. Worth a try.'

It was still raining hard when the police got to Gareth Price's house. 'If only we'd found this the same day as Chloë's body was found,' Marshall said quietly, as he squeezed behind a bush to look at the broken bit of fence. It was actually three damaged slats, but they'd been slid back into place so they didn't show. Sadly the heavy rain would have washed away any remaining forensics and footprints.

Marshall pulled back the slats and climbed through; it was a tight fit, but a big enough gap for an average-sized person. On the other side a little-used faint track led through the trees and undergrowth, yet even though the path beyond was less than twenty yards away from where he stood, the bushes and trees were so dense he could only see a tiny glimpse of it.

He felt a new surge of anger that his men hadn't examined this bit of fence. There was no excuse for failing to do that. Now it looked obvious as to why no one had seen a blood-soaked man that evening. He'd probably taken refuge in Price's garden and stayed hidden in the bushes until it was dark. After cleaning himself up at the tap in the garden, he could then have left by the side gate.

Marshall rang Forensics for them to send someone round. He doubted there would be any blood left now, or other forensic material, but you never knew what they would find in nooks and crannies. 'Hold fire on mending the fence,' he told Price. 'And I'm really sorry no one followed up on this before.'

Gareth Price merely shrugged. They'd have been quick enough to arrest him for the crime if he hadn't had such an unshakeable alibi. He wanted to point out that the murderer had to live in the close, someone who knew he drank so much he was unlikely to notice a man in his garden, but he said nothing. Let them work that one out for themselves.

18

'I understand the difficulties, and I don't want to suggest the police are not doing their utmost to apprehend the killer,' Mike Church said, in a tone that suggested whatever the difficulties were, he wanted them overcome. 'But Chloë was killed in broad daylight, on a warm evening when many people were around, just a short distance from our home. How hard can it be to find the killer? Or is he the Invisible Man?'

DI Marshall looked at Mike Church and saw not just grief in his eyes, but anger too. That anger had brought him rushing down to the police station, and the inspector felt ashamed he hadn't been able to find Chloë's killer yet.

'I can only reiterate what I told you at the reenactment,' Marshall said carefully. 'We're following several lines of inquiry, and we have done a door-to-door search in a huge radius of the crime scene. We have interviewed some two hundred people, checked CCTV cameras, and pulled in dozens of people who have previously committed offences against underage girls. Every policeman in Cheltenham wants this killer found. We are doing absolutely everything we can.'

Mike hung his head for a couple of seconds of silence, perhaps a little ashamed of blaming Marshall for not solving the crime quickly enough.

But then he lifted his head and Marshall saw tears in his eyes. 'Nothing is ever going to turn Ruth and me back into the people we were,' he said, his voice cracking with emotion. 'But to know who did this to our Chloë would help us to cope. Right now I'm scared stiff for Ruth. She sits in Chloë's room for hours, she isn't eating or sleeping. Sometimes she doesn't even speak.'

'I can imagine what it's doing to both of you,' Marshall said. 'But please believe me, Mike, when I say we're chasing up every last lead, and we will catch this man soon.'

Mike got to his feet, somewhat unsteadily. 'Thank you,' he said. 'I'd better go home now. Ruth will be worried about me.'

DI Marshall sat at his desk with his head in his hands for some minutes after Mike Church had gone. It was as if the man had sucked all the air out of the room, leaving him gasping. If he could have just one wish today, it would be that they would catch the killer. But no one was going to grant him a wish. It was all down to plain old police work, attention to detail. He'd make a start by going back to see Tex, and see if he'd heard anything on the grapevine.

'I'm sorry, Tex,' Marshall said, when the man opened his door furtively and immediately looked panicked. 'Nothing to worry about, I just wanted your help again. May I come in?'

Tex opened the door wider. He was wearing only jeans, his bare chest lily white and scrawny. Yet his room was as tidy as it had been on the previous visit – even his bed was made. 'I just finished shaving,' he said. 'I must get a shirt on.'

He opened his wardrobe and pulled out a navy blue one, with fringing along the yoke in western style.

'Do you have any shirts that aren't cowboy style?' Marshall asked, sitting down on one of the wooden upright chairs.

'I've got a white one,' Tex said, and gave a little smirk. 'But I keep that for funerals and other serious occasions.'

Marshall felt a pang of pity for a person who had just one smart shirt, reserved for difficult times. But he made no comment and went on to explain that he'd been told about the flasher at the re-enactment. He gave Tex the woman's description of the man. 'Have you ever seen someone like that?'

Tex frowned. 'Yup. Well, at least I saw a man like that near where the girl died. Not that day, but then

I never went up that far. It was about a week before. Course I can't be sure he was the flasher, cos he never done it to me.'

'So would you have any idea where he lives?'

'Somewhere on the other side of that slope where the bikers went. I saw him go down that way. But I don't know which road.'

'If I took you into the station would you help one of the officers with a photo-fit picture of him? Do you know what that is?'

Tex nodded. 'When you choose the eyes, then the nose and stuff. I don't think I looked at him long enough to remember, but I'll try. Why haven't you found this bad man yet?'

That question came to Marshall every minute of the day. There had been so much frantic investigating going on, more door-to-door questioning, checks made on people of interest, but nothing seemed to lead anywhere.

He'd never known a case quite like this before. The murder of a child was abhorrent to everyone. It raised a huge wave of sympathy for the parents, with so many people offering to help in any way they could. But a week on from when the child's body was found, there was now anger at the police as people thought they were sitting on their hands.

Journalists patrolled Willow Close, hoping to find someone who would reveal some new aspect of the case. They hung around the police station day and night waiting for something new to break. Television and radio stations made much of every snippet of news. Each time anyone was brought to the station for questioning, there was speculation about them.

Alfie Strong hadn't helped himself by threatening a journalist who tried to question him as he was leaving. That spawned a few inches in the press suggesting he could be the killer. Marshall thought his vindictive wife must be delighted at that. But speculation and rumour were frightening as they could lead to mob rule. Someone had rung the station last night and reported ugly scenes in Willow Close, but by the time officers got there, the people involved had dispersed.

He would have to be extremely careful taking Tex to the station: the last thing he wanted was for vigilantes to be going after him.

Tex wriggled right down into the back footwell, and Marshall put a blanket over him, then drove quickly through the station car park, past many journalists who tried to waylay him, to the gated underground entrance, which was always used for vulnerable witnesses and high-profile criminals.

'You can come out now, Tex,' he said, once they were safely inside. 'Now let's see what you can do with this photo-fit for me.'

*

The Spotted Dog was probably the scruffiest pub in Cheltenham, and renowned for its clientele of rugby players, horse-racing fans and local hard men. The regulars liked that it was an authentic boozer, which had never been gentrified. But Dee Strong didn't like it at all. It reminded her of the pubs her father used to leave her outside when she was a young girl. But she was here to find Jason Pickering, a man who had done many jobs for her in the past.

He was, as she expected, sitting in the corner with a pint. She took her gin and tonic with her and sat down opposite him.

His ugly face twisted into the semblance of a smile at seeing her, and Dee felt a little touch of nausea. Jason might be close to fifty, but he was strong and ruthless, six feet of sheer muscle and famous for having nerves of steel. But he needed all that to compensate for his face. There were many rumours about the two fearsome scars, one diagonally from his right eye, puckering his nose and cheek to his left ear, the other from his forehead down through his lips to his chin. He wouldn't say how he got them and people were generally too afraid to ask, but it was generally believed he'd been razored by a Russian gang leader when he'd tried to muscle into the gang's territory in London. That could, of course, be fiction: it was more likely to have been a teenage gang fight with razors and he'd got the worst of it. Either way the scars were probably not treated at the time, villains often reluctant to get medical help in case the police were called.

'So what brings you here?' he said.

Dee took a large swig of her drink, wishing she'd had something less noticeable to wear than tight white Capri pants and an equally tight shocking pink top. But Alfie hadn't dug to the back of the wardrobe and pulled out the sober clothes she wore when she wanted to be incognito. She took a deep breath and outlined what she wanted of Jason.

'Three hundred quid up front, and another three when it's done. Plus fringe benefits with me.' She added the last inducement with a sexy pout, knowing he'd always had the hots for her.

Jason looked at the sketch she'd drawn of the house's layout, then gave it back to her. ''Ow do you know the winder will be open?'

Even his speech made her nervous, a gravelly, rasping tone coupled with a Cockney accent. 'Because of the cat. It likes to go in and out that way. The side gate might be locked, but you can put your hand over and unlock it. Or climb over. It's a piece of cake to someone like you.'

She wished she hadn't had to call on Jason: he was a nasty piece of work. She hadn't wanted to give him so much money either, but he was the only man for the job, and in time she'd get a share of the insurance on the house.

'So next day meet up. Where? You double-cross me and you'll regret it.'

She knew he meant that. Her blood ran cold just thinking of what he might do to her. 'Your place. I'll come there at seven on Monday evening. I can't say Sunday as the police are bound to show up and take me in for more questioning, but they'll have to let me go as I'll make sure lots of people have seen me in the hotel. If I shouldn't turn up as promised, it'll be because they find some other excuse to hold me. But I'll ring you as soon as I'm released.'

'You'd better, doll,' he said, giving her that twisted leer-like smile. 'Wouldn't want to rearrange that pretty face.'

'So when will you do it?' Dee asked.

'Tonight. 'E's likely to go down the pub on a Saturday night, ain't 'e? Comes back three sheets to the wind, Bob's yer uncle.'

Dee didn't want to know more, she just wanted it done and that part of her life over. 'All being well I'll see you Monday,' she said, turning to go.

'Not so fast, money up front,' he said, holding out his hand.

'Oh, sorry,' she said sweetly. It had been worth a try to avoid handing money over, but she had withdrawn it just in case he insisted. She pulled the envelope out of her bag, handed it to him, and left.

*

At eight that evening Dee walked into the bar at her hotel wearing a dress she knew would be memorable. It was turquoise satin, with a plunging neckline back and front, the hem just above her knees, her golden tan enhanced by the colour. With four-inch-heeled strappy gold sandals, and her blonde hair a perfect up-do, washed and styled just that afternoon, she knew she was looking her best.

She ordered a double vodka and grapefruit and took it over to an empty table by the window. Aware all eyes, male and female, were on her, she took a paperback out of her handbag and began to read it.

While waiting for her drink at the bar she had already selected her partner for the evening, and she was now sitting at the table next to him. There wasn't much choice of men, just two who were alone. The rest were either with a friend, wife or girlfriend. One had a fat face the colour of beetroot – she wasn't prepared to spend an evening with him. But the other looked promising, slender, glasses, pale-faced but a well-cut grey suit and a good haircut. She thought he looked like a company salesman.

A waiter, a little round-shouldered man with a faint Italian accent, came over to her and handed her the dinner menu. 'I'll be back in a little while to take your order and I'll come for you when the meal is served,' he said.

He did the same for the man at the next table.

Dee studied her menu till the waiter had gone, then looked up to see her neighbour watching her. 'I never know what to order,' she said, smiling at him. 'I always get food envy when I see what other people are given. What are you having?'

'The chicken Kiev looks good to me,' he said.

'Well, maybe I'll have it too,' she said. 'Thank you for deciding for me.'

'Are you on your own, or waiting for someone?' he asked, just as she'd known he would.

'On my own, which is why I brought my book,' she said, patting it. 'Eating alone is the worst thing about travelling solo I find.'

'I find that too. Could I ask you to join me?'

'How lovely,' she said. 'I'm Dee.'

His name was Spencer, and when the waiter came back for their orders, he told him they'd like to share a table in the dining room. He ordered them both another drink, and came and sat with her.

She was careful to say little about herself, only that she lived in south-east London but was looking for a property in Cheltenham to move there. But she asked him a lot of questions, giving him her undivided attention. As she had expected he was a salesman, for a jewellery company based in Oxford. He said he was divorced but she didn't believe that as he had the well-groomed, well-fed look that married men mostly had. But, then, she wasn't interested in ensnaring him: her entire motivation was to make sure all the guests and the staff would remember her.

Already the married couples had noticed he'd joined her. No doubt over dinner she'd become the hot topic of their evening. The kind ones would hope it was the start of a romance for two lonely people. Others would say she had set out to trap a man with her low neckline and high shoes.

Just glancing around the room, Dee saw that at least eighty per cent of the guests were middle-aged. As they were barely speaking to one another, she guessed they were staid, dull people, who had thought a weekend in Cheltenham would enliven them. Yet they were watching her eagerly to see what unfolded.

She'd give them something to remember.

At ten that evening, the police in Bromsgrove got a call that the alarm at a tanning studio in Mild Street had gone off.

Mostly such calls were not a priority: the alarms were tripped by staff not setting them properly, kids banging on doors or windows. But a tanning studio was a big fire risk. If the electricity hadn't been turned off and the wiring was faulty, the place could go up within minutes, taking out the other businesses and flats in that street.

Tania Wells was the key holder on record. They called her number and she said she would go straight there. Meanwhile PC Peterson and his partner PC Ray were close to Mild Street and would go to the address too.

The police were already outside the salon when Tania arrived. 'I'm always careful locking up. I turn the sunbeds off at the mains,' she said, as she opened the door. 'It doesn't look as if anyone has broken in either.'

Peterson said he'd go round to the back of the building and check, while Tania and PC Ray went in.

Tania turned on the lights and suddenly the whole place was lit up like Blackpool Tower. She punched in the alarm code, and the racket stopped.

'What's upstairs?' PC Ray asked. She was small and dumpy and Tania, who was almost six foot tall with a model's figure, a leopard-print shift dress with shoestring straps, and curls tumbling over bare shoulders, made her feel inadequate.

'Just a bathroom and two other rooms. One is for stores. That's locked. The other is the staff room, for eating lunch and that. Mind you, the only staff is me.'

Peterson came in. 'Looks like someone intended to get in through the back upstairs window, as they've broken it,' he said. 'But they must've scarpered when the alarm went off.'

The three of them went upstairs, Tania explaining that she hadn't got a key for the storeroom.

'I'll have to force the door, then,' Peterson said,

clearly delighted to have an excuse to show off his strength to a pretty girl. 'They may have left something that could jeopardize the security of the building.'

PC Ray tried not to smile. It was evident to her that the broken window was the work of a teenager, not some real villain. They'd get in and find nothing more exciting than rolls of paper for cleaning the sun-beds, bottles of bleach and other cleaning materials.

But Peterson put his shoulder to the door, and it opened immediately, splintering the flimsy wood around the lock. He wasn't sure what he'd expected to see, but not a pile of cardboard boxes almost up to the ceiling. Ray darted forward and pulled back the flaps on one.

'Hell's bell's!' she exclaimed. 'It's cigarettes. Polish ones, if I'm not much mistaken.'

Tania looked perplexed. 'Why would they buy so many? They don't even smoke. And Polish ones!'

'Who is "they", Tania?' Ray said gently. 'Do you mean Mr and Mrs Alcott who own the salon?' She'd been given that information when they'd got the call about the alarm.

Tania was frowning. 'Yes, of course. They must've brought them here when the salon was shut.'

'They've been smuggled, to avoid tax.' Ray felt she had to explain to the poor girl. She opened another couple of boxes. They were all the same. 'Tens of thousands of pounds' worth.'

'But why would they do that?' Tania said, blue eyes wide with shock and bewilderment. Clearly, she wasn't the brightest light on the Christmas tree, and had no idea her employers had a racket going on right under her nose.

'The seedy, the needy and the greedy,' Ray said. Before she joined the force, she'd been a store detective and her boss had always said that shoplifters came under one of those categories. 'Now, you'd better toddle off home, Tania. It's very late. Someone will be in touch about taking your statement. I must insist you do not telephone the Alcotts and tell them about this. We will inform them ourselves. Meanwhile, we have to stay here to secure the building and we'll be taking these goods in with us.'

'So does this mean I won't have a job any more?' Tania asked, her big eyes wide and fearful.

'That depends on your employers,' Peterson chimed in. He was counting how many packages were in a box, then multiplying by the number of boxes. 'We'll have to keep the keys for the time being, and as it's Sunday tomorrow you wouldn't be opening anyway. Someone will be in touch with you.'

It wasn't until Peterson and Ray got back to the police station that they discovered the Alcotts lived in the same street as Chloë Church. There was a flurry of excitement in the station: on the face of it, a pure coincidence, but the two crimes could possibly be linked. The whole thing was handed over to a senior officer who said he would contact Cheltenham CID.

Marshall was at home, but the message was relayed to him and he immediately rang the number in Bromsgrove he'd been given.

He listened carefully, making notes. The first thing that occurred to him: the Alcotts hadn't answered their door a week ago. They might have been in the Midlands, as that busybody Rose had suggested, but on the other hand they could have been afraid of the police searching their home. Could Chloë have found out they were flogging cheap fags and threatened to tell someone?

From what he'd learnt about Chloë Church he couldn't imagine a well-brought-up girl like her poking her nose into a neighbour's business. Also Mr and Mrs Alcott seemed too pleasant and ordinary to be engaged in any criminal activity. But appearances were clearly deceptive.

Marshall's heart began to beat a fraction faster. He'd discounted Chloë being killed by a family member: those who lived close enough to have done it all had alibis and not one seemed capable of killing a child. One motive that so often appeared in murder cases was that the victim knew something damaging about the attacker. Was this the case?

Bromsgrove CID had said they would handle this

and come down to Cheltenham early in the morning to arrest the Alcotts. They pointed out that smuggling cigarettes into the country was tax evasion, a crime against the Crown rather than just an ordinary criminal act. It didn't warrant a middle-of-the-night arrest.

Marshall was relieved, and meanwhile he could order a search warrant to see what else they had in their house.

19

Sunday, 26 July, Day Nine

Jason Pickering turned into Willow Close at just after midnight. He'd planned his walking route meticulously from his home to the Pinewood estate, avoiding all roads with CCTV cameras. He had all he needed for the job in the pockets of his jacket, and he'd put his gloves on just before arriving at the close. He noted with pleasure that two of the streetlights weren't working, and as there was only a sliver of moon, it was very dark.

There were no lights on at number eight, the third house on the right, and the Volvo was on the drive. Dee had said her husband didn't take any notice of the drink-driving laws, so if the car was there, so was he.

Jason felt no guilt about what he was going to do. Guilt was something he'd left behind when his face was slashed twenty years ago. He'd changed his name, too, and learnt to live under the radar. There had been a time when he planned to save enough money for plastic surgery. But he'd grown to like being the man who could solve people's problems for a price. Those who used him were far too scared of him and so far over their heads that they would never grass on him.

He put his hand over the side gate and slid the bolt out. Then, moving as silently and gracefully as a cat, he went to the back of the house. As Dee had said, the transom window above the main casement was open, but first he crept to the French windows to check. The big room was in darkness, so he returned to the kitchen window. A plastic garden chair stood beside it, an ashtray beneath.

By standing on the chair it was simple to put his arm through the small window and unlatch the bigger one below. Luckily there was a clear work surface inside – so often he had to get over a sink piled high with dishes.

A few seconds later he was in. He crept to the hall and listened. He could hear loud snoring upstairs.

Pulling a small torch from his pocket he shone it into the lounge. There were a couple of newspapers on the sofa: he picked them up and placed them in a wicker waste-bin. Next, he poured the small bottle of petrol he'd brought with him over the papers and placed the bin at the bottom of the stairs where a denim jacket was hanging. There was a curtain at the window opposite the stairs – that would soon catch too.

He backed up towards the kitchen and flicked a lit match towards the bin. It caught immediately.

Turning, he was out of the window within seconds. He locked the side gate behind him and left the close to take a slightly different route home.

Dee had told him the smoke alarms didn't work: her husband had taken the batteries out because they kept going off when she was cooking. Looking back before leaving the close, he could make out just a faint orange glow from the hall window.

His job was done.

Conrad had woken to go to the bathroom. As he came back into the bedroom, he was awake enough to be puzzled by a light from outside. The streetlamp had stopped working a few days ago. Rose had told him she'd reported it to the council.

Peeping round the curtain, he expected to see a car's headlights, perhaps someone coming home in a taxi, but instead he saw a flickering orange light across the street in Alfie's house. He stared sleepily at it for a moment.

Then he realized what it was.

'Fire!' he exclaimed. Pulling on his jeans and a T-shirt, he shoved his feet into trainers, and as he ran across the road, he called 999 on his mobile.

He and Nina had seen Alfie come home just as they were going to bed. They'd been shocked at the way he swayed and wobbled as he locked his car. Clearly, he was completely plastered and shouldn't have been driving. Conrad had made a mental note to speak to him the next morning – he could have caused an accident.

Had he dropped a lit cigarette? Left something in a pan on the stove?

Guessing that it would be a waste of time to ring the doorbell, Conrad went round the back, climbed over the gate and looked through the kitchen window. The hall beyond was ablaze, and although he couldn't see the staircase from his position, he knew the flames must be licking up the stairs and cutting off Alfie's escape.

As he couldn't hear the fire engine coming, he felt he must act fast. He looked up at the back wall, spotted the drainpipe and saw a window open next to it. Without considering the danger he was putting himself in, spurred only by waking Alfie and getting him to a window for the fire brigade, Conrad shinned up the drainpipe.

He almost fell as he tried to reach the open window, but he caught hold of the sill and, for a moment or two, hung there, unable to get up or go down. He made a huge effort to push against the wall with his feet, then hauled himself up until he was bent over the sill, going head first inside.

He was in a spare room, and when he opened the door to the landing, a blast from the fire on the stairs knocked him right back. Knowing the bathroom was just next door, he pulled off the bedclothes, grabbed the sheet and rushed to soak it. He put it over his head and made for the front bedroom, shutting the door firmly behind him.

Alfie was lying on his back, still snoring loudly. Conrad slapped his face with the wet sheet, pulled off his covers and stuffed them along the bottom of the closed door. 'What?' Alfie said groggily, struggling to sit up.

'Your house is on fire,' Conrad said. 'Quick, get up and over to the window. The smoke's already bad in here.'

'How? Where?' Alfie said stupidly, still not moving.

'There's no time to talk. Just pull on your trousers.' Conrad yanked his arm and thrust the trousers lying on the floor into his hand.

Conrad opened the window and yelled for help. He still couldn't hear the fire engine, only the crackling of the fire out on the landing and he was beginning to panic that they'd both be trapped in the bedroom. The street was lit by the fire, and it could only be minutes before the front door caved in and the flames licked up the front of the house.

'Help! Fire! Help us!' he yelled again.

That seemed to bring Alfie back to life. He'd got his trousers and a shirt on now.

Lights were flicking on in the other houses in the close, and the first person to appear out of his door was Rob Willis from number four.

'It's Conrad from next door,' Conrad screamed. 'I saw the glow and climbed in an upstairs window. But the staircase is alight. I've rung the fire brigade but I'm worried the door won't hold the fire back. Have you got a ladder?'

The street was well lit now, and Conrad could hear crackling and spitting, louder now, from just beyond the bedroom door. The smoke was streaming in through the cracks around the door and making it hard to breathe. He wondered if he could jump onto the lawn below without breaking bones.

'Be right there!' Rob called back. He ran back into his house and a couple of seconds later his garage door opened and he emerged again, holding a ladder.

More people in their night clothes had come out now, and Conrad saw Gareth rush forward to help with the ladder. Nina appeared too, wearing just her nightie. Even though the glow of the fire made her look rosy, he could tell from her expression she was terrified for him.

As for Alfie he still looked vacant, and Conrad had to support him to stand at the window.

At last he heard the fire engine in the distance, but Rob and his companion still put the ladder up against the house.

'You first, Alfie,' Conrad roared at the older man, terrified now that they were both going to die of smoke inhalation before the fire engine got there. He thought Alfie was still drunk, as he didn't appear to understand what was happening. 'And hold on tightly as you go down.'

Getting Alfie out of the window was almost impossible. Conrad had to lift him on to the sill, lying on his stomach, with his feet outside so he could climb down, but the man was about fifteen stone, and being totally uncooperative. But Rob below must have seen the difficulty and came up the ladder, guiding Alfie's feet on to the rungs.

'I'm going down now. It won't hold us both,' Rob yelled back to Conrad.

'Move your feet and climb down,' Conrad entreated the older man, who was clinging to the windowsill as if it was a life-raft. 'If you don't, we'll both burn to death up here. Go!'

Alfie had just begun to move as the fire engine came, sirens blasting enough to wake the dead, quickly followed by a second.

Over the roaring of the fire Conrad heard a splitting sound and felt a sudden blast of heat. He didn't need to turn his head to know the fire had burnt through the bedroom door and would engulf him at any second now.

'Faster, Alfie!' he yelled. 'The fire is in the room now.'

Finally the older man moved down a rung, then another. Conrad got up on the windowsill and as he crouched there, waiting for Alfie to reach the bottom, the fire was licking across the bed, the heat from it blinding him and affecting his breathing. Then it reached him, scorching his back.

Self-preservation kicked in; he began to climb down, not caring if the ladder wouldn't take his weight too, or that he couldn't see. Someone was calling instructions to him, but they made no sense. Getting to Nina was his goal. Nothing else mattered.

'Conrad!' Nina screamed, as her husband fell the last six feet from the ladder to the lawn below, narrowly missing Alfie, who had slid the last few rungs and landed on the ground.

Fire had burnt away the back of Conrad's T-shirt, and he appeared to be unconscious, but mercifully the ambulance arrived.

The fire was too hot for Nina to get to Conrad, but the firefighters braved it and lifted him on to a stretcher face down.

Once they'd got him away from the blaze, Nina rushed to his side. 'How is he?' she asked a paramedic, crying now she could see how badly his back was burnt.

'Is Alfie all right?' Conrad came round enough to ask, his voice hoarse and rasping like sandpaper.

She loved the very bones of her man. It was so typical of him to ask about the man who'd probably started the fire that had almost killed both of them. She glanced round to look for Alfie. Everyone was out now, standing in small groups, their faces lit by the fire. 'He's sitting with Rob and Maureen,' she said. 'He looks dazed but, as far as I can see, unharmed.'

The paramedic told Conrad he wasn't to talk, turned him onto his side and put an oxygen mask over his mouth and nose. The second man put a thin, wet-looking dressing on his back. They told Nina they were going to take him to hospital now, and she could come in with him.

Janice pushed through the crowd just as Conrad was being lifted into the ambulance. 'Nina,' she shouted. 'I know you're going with him, but you've left your front door open. I'll go in, find you some clothes and bring them to the hospital. You can't sit about in that skimpy nightie.'

It was a silky, knee-length chemise and she was wearing nothing beneath it. 'Oh, shit,' Nina said. 'I didn't think about what I was wearing.'

'It's okay, love,' the paramedic said, with a grin. 'I can give you a hospital gown to make you decent, but we must go now. That burn your husband has is pretty bad.'

Janice gave Nina a brief hug, said she'd be there within the hour, then let her get into the ambulance beside Conrad.

*

As dawn broke Mike Church stood with Brian Alcott and surveyed the smoking ruin that was Alfie's house. Neither man had gone to bed because the firefighters had been working through the night to put out the blaze. The hissing of water, crackling sounds and the shouts of the firefighters were not conducive to sleep.

'I suspect Dee had a hand in it,' Mike said, as the firefighters hauled out what looked like the remains of the staircase. 'One of the men said they could smell petrol as they went in.'

'She was vicious enough to do it, but would she have known how to set a fire? She didn't strike me as that organized. Wasn't Alfie once a gangland figure in London?'

'He did have a shady past,' Mike said, 'but I liked and trusted him, and I can't imagine someone from his past coming up here to try to burn him alive. No, I bet anything you like Dee is behind this.'

'Guess we'll have to wait for the forensic team to find out how it started and why,' Brian said. 'I'd better go in now. May is worrying we might have smoke damage.'

'Young Conrad was a hero,' Mike said. 'What with everything that happened with Chloë we haven't even had a chance to welcome him to the street, or even said hello to him yet. I just hope he isn't too badly burnt. I heard he works with troubled children. It takes a big heart to do that.'

As they spoke Janice drove into the close, parked her car on her drive and came over to the two men. 'Any news? Have they found out how it started yet? I took some clothes into the hospital for Nina and stayed with her for a bit. It seems Conrad will be fine, just very sore for a while.'

'Well, at least that's good news.' Mike gave her a watery smile. 'I was just remarking how brave and quick-witted he was. The firemen smelt petrol, so I think it was arson.'

'Dee's dirty work, no doubt.' Janice sniffed. 'I always thought she was a demon. Looks like I was right.'

'We can rely on Rose and John to keep us informed about the investigation,' Brian said, with a wry smile. 'I'd better get back to May.'

'How are you bearing up, Mike?' Janice asked, once Brian had made his way home. 'This must have added to your distress.'

'Only inasmuch as it's another reminder of how malicious people can be. Ruth and I are just in a kind of waiting room. We need to know who killed Chloë, we need to bury her too, but I don't see it all being wrapped up anytime soon. I kind of hope this fire will stir things up a bit, make the police more dynamic and perhaps the killer more scared because emotions are running pretty high now.'

Janice saw the pain in the man's eyes and wished

there was something she could do to make him and Ruth feel a bit better. But she knew that nothing on earth could help parents who had lost a child. 'Give my love to Ruth and please tell her if she wants to talk, have a drink, whatever, I'm available anytime.'

'I was never a man for praying,' Mike said sadly, hanging his head, 'but since we got the news about Chloë, I've been praying all the time for Ruth. She isn't sleeping or eating, she spends hours in Chloë's room cuddling her bedclothes or her teddy. I'm afraid she'll never come back from this.'

Janice put a comforting hand on his arm. 'I'm sure she will, with such a loving husband beside her.'

20

Monday, 27 July, Day Ten

DI Marshall hurried into the room where his team had gathered for a briefing. He was harassed, worried, desperate for a breakthrough in the case. But as he saw his team, perched on desks, leaning on walls, every one of them looking tired and pasty from too much fast food and coffee, and not enough sun, he felt a surge of gratitude for them.

Sadly, what he had to say wasn't going to cheer them.

'You will be as dismayed as I am that the press has once again claimed we're not doing enough to catch Chloë Church's killer,' he began.

Immediately shock and indignation registered on the faces of the twenty or so people before him. He knew that they wanted the killer caught and locked away, and they cared deeply for Chloë's parents. Most of them had worked each night until late, not even asking whether they would be paid overtime. Some had barely seen their wives, husbands or children all week. But, of course, the public had no real idea how much investigation went on behind the scenes. They only counted arrests.

'There is nothing to be gained by me pointing out all that has already been done to find the killer. Or that we're now even more determined to find him. But today the media spotlight is back on Willow Close because of the fire at Alfie Strong's. I brought you all together to confirm it was arson. I want to know whether this is coincidence or if the fire and Chloë's murder are connected.'

He paused to let his words sink in and looked at each officer with a grim expression. 'The fire could have been started by someone who believes Alfie Strong to be the killer. With us having Alfie in for questioning, the story leaked to the press was enough for a lynch mob to form. But whatever the newspapers and the public choose to believe, I'm not convinced this fire was the work of a vigilante. With a united effort we must endeavour to investigate Dee Strong. She's already tried to frame her husband with false evidence, and he threw her out of their home because of it.' He paused again.

'But as if that isn't enough criminal activity in one small, seemingly serene middle-class close, late on Saturday night the Bromsgrove police discovered that the Alcotts have been running a cigarette racket from their sunbed salon there. The Bromsgrove police came to Cheltenham early yesterday morning to arrest the couple, and some of you were involved in the search of their house. Disappointingly we found nothing unusual, but we have taken their accounts books to check, and as we speak their bank is giving us further information about their financial situation.'

Marshall paused and looked at his team. 'Three crimes, two of them extremely serious, in a street of ten houses. That statistic would be common enough in an inner-city estate in London, Birmingham or Manchester. But here in Cheltenham?' He shook his head as if in disbelief. 'It makes me even more certain that Chloë's killer lives in Willow Close,' he stated firmly.

There was a hum of discussion, which stopped when Marshall clapped his hands together.

'So, our priority is to find the person with a motive for killing Chloë. The child's life was centred on Willow Close. She was born there, saw her neighbours as aunties and uncles, and they were all fond of her too. It should have been the safest place in the world for her. But I think she was killed because she had discovered something serious about one of her neighbours, and they were afraid she'd spill the beans.'

Again, he looked at each one of his officers. 'Who has a secret they don't want to get out?'

'But, sir,' a young fresh-faced constable with curly black hair raised his hand, 'how would anyone know where she would be on the evening of her death?

School had just broken up for the summer – she could've gone anywhere.'

'That might apply to many kids of her age,' Marshall replied. 'But Chloë's parents were conscientious. They didn't allow her to go beyond the local park, and she had to be home at a set time. All the residents in the close would have known that. They'd probably grown used to seeing her father walk down to meet her at seven thirty. There are many unknowns right now. But the evidence tells us that Chloë's murder was unplanned. Had it been planned Chloë would've been lured to a quieter place. The killer would have brought a weapon with him. I'm certain it happened because something was said that made the killer fly into a rage and lash out with the only weapon to hand, a rock. He must have panicked to find himself covered with blood. Who else but a resident would know there was a broken fence panel he could crawl through, just twenty yards away? He must have known it led to the garden of a drunk, who doubtless would fail to notice an intruder. Once there, he could make his way home unseen through the gardens.'

The same young constable put his hand up to speak again. 'Sir, you keep implying the killer was a man, but it could just as easily have been a woman. Dee Strong didn't have a real alibi for that evening – she was actually very vague about when she arrived home.'

Marshall smiled at the young constable. He liked

his enthusiasm. 'I'm sorry, and you're right. Dee Strong is a contender. We know her to be a vindictive and cruel woman. But she's no fool. I think she would have planned a murder better than this killer did. As for yesterday's fire, I'm absolutely convinced she orchestrated it, but no doubt she'll have an iron-clad alibi and would have paid someone else to do it. So, I want a bunch of you to work on digging into her background to find the person who started the fire.'

He paused to take a breath. 'I also think, and I'm sure this will surprise you, that Trudy Singer needs more scrutiny. She comes across as a rather pathetic woman. Her husband has left her, and she doesn't appear to have any friends. She may very well have been simmering with resentment that Chloë was a popular child, a rising star with the kind of parents who are everything she isn't. She also has no alibi. She said she was watching TV in her bedroom when Amy went out and fell asleep after hearing her come home. All very vague. More questioning needed, here at the station, I think. So organize a search warrant. As for the rest of you, I want you to check again on each of the other residents. No softly-softly this time. I want you to search their past, their homes, garages, garden sheds. Find out when they last spoke to Chloë, fish around for any recent disputes in the street. Leave no stone unturned. Shake them up vigorously, because that's when things drop out.'

Several of the officers had questions, and Marshall answered them all. Then he divided them into groups, the first of which was to dig into Dee and Alfie Strong's past.

'I'm going to see Conrad Best in hospital. As you probably all know, the Bests only moved into Willow Close the day after Chloë's murder. Best is known to us already, not for a criminal past but because he is a house-father at Bracknell House, a home for disadvantaged children. I know from Frank Dooley, the manager there, that Conrad is above reproach, a kind, sensitive man. Now the details of last night's fire have come through, we know he's also extremely brave. Without his intervention we'd be looking at another murder.'

Someone clapped, and all the officers joined in.

'Yes, he deserves that,' Marshall said, and smiled broadly. 'I'm told he's very intuitive about people too, so I'm hoping when I visit him, he might share his views on some of his neighbours.'

Conrad was feeling less than his usual perky self when Jim Marshall arrived to see him. The burn on his back hurt like hell, his throat felt like sandpaper and his arms and legs ached, presumably from hauling Alfie away from the fire.

'I commend you for your bravery,' Marshall said, putting down a small basket of fruit on the bedside locker. 'Alfie would have died without your intervention. The chief fire officer informed me that by the time they got there the entire bedroom was on fire.'

Conrad shrugged and felt embarrassed. 'I like Alfie, even if I haven't known him long. I couldn't let him die. But tell me, have you found what started it?'

'It was definitely arson – newspapers doused in petrol at the bottom of the stairs. No fingerprints, but I didn't expect any. This arsonist was professional. He got in via the kitchen window and left the same way. We've looked at CCTV for a sighting of this man, but there's nothing, so I have to assume he planned his route to avoid cameras.'

'So it wasn't Dee out for revenge, then?'

'That doesn't look likely. But I suspect she paid the arsonist to do it.'

'Who has an arsonist up their sleeve?' Conrad laughed lightly.

'People with a chequered past, like Dee,' Marshall said, with a smile. 'I would bet she's got a whole collection of evil blokes in her little black book. But don't quote me on that. The police aren't supposed to share such thoughts.'

Conrad smiled, liking the man for keeping a sense of humour. He seemed honourable too, which he wasn't sure all coppers were. 'Any headway with the murder?' he asked.

Marshall sighed. 'No, not really, though just

between us, my hunch is that the killer is one of your neighbours. We shall be investigating ever more strenuously now, especially after the arson attack. You doubtless heard about the Alcotts receiving and selling on cheap Polish cigarettes in Bromsgrove? Seems Willow Close isn't quite the quiet, crime-free backwater people thought.'

Conrad felt a sudden pang of conscience at Marshall's words. Nina had told him the police came to the Alcotts yesterday morning, but she hadn't known what for. But, in the light of the fire, he felt he ought to divulge what he'd seen the man from number seven engaged in. If someone else got hurt, he'd never forgive himself for keeping quiet.

'Maybe you should check out the man at number seven a little more closely,' Conrad ventured, hardly able to believe he was actually grassing someone up. It went against every rule he'd ever made for himself. 'I don't know his name, but one evening last week he nearly crashed into my car with his, so I followed him, sort of hoping for an apology. He went to a lockup nearby and there I saw him and another man moving wooden boxes into a van. They were both extremely furtive, keeping an eye out, if you know what I mean. I might be totally wrong, but I do know ammunition, explosives and suchlike come in boxes like that.'

'And where was this?' Marshall looked staggered.

Conrad explained where the lockup was. 'If I'm

right, please don't expect me to be a witness for the prosecution. And if I'm wrong, and it was nothing more sinister than a few car parts, please don't let anyone know where the tip-off came from. Not because I'm a coward but because children under my care are vulnerable. They wouldn't trust me with their problems if they thought I bandied information about. I'm only divulging this in the hope it could possibly lead to finding the killer.'

'My lips are sealed,' Marshall said.

'There's one more thing. I did get the number-plate of the other man's van. I put it in my phone at the time. Will that help?'

Marshall's face showed his astonishment that Conrad had had the presence of mind to do this. He was clearly stuck for the appropriate response as Conrad reached for his phone and read out the number.

'I wish there were more public-spirited people like you about,' he said, as he jotted the number down. 'I hope your burns heal quickly so you can go home.'

Nina came in again later to see Conrad. She had been with him most of the previous day, and he'd finally told her she was to go home and get to bed. But he could see by her heavy eyes that she'd had no sleep and she'd been crying.

What a horrible start it was for them in Willow Close. They had built up such a bright, sparkling image of their life there, and now after little more than a week he was burnt, and she must be wondering what would come next. Yet she forced a bright smile and teased him about all the nurses fancying him. 'Is your back any better today?' she asked.

'Not so bad now,' he said, caressing her cheek tenderly. 'Stop worrying about me, Nina. I'm a tough old bastard.'

'I found out the Alcotts were arrested for receiving Polish fags. Rose told me this morning. Where does she get her information from?'

'How terrible,' Conrad said, with a look of mockhorror. 'They should be put in prison for years.'

'Don't tease,' Nina said sharply. 'Rose says they've always acted like they were above everyone else in the street.'

'Easy to be above Rose.' He laughed. 'God, I'd like to find out she watched porn or gave men blow-jobs in the park.'

'Conrad!' Nina said reprovingly. 'Sometimes I wonder about you.'

'DI Marshall came to see me this morning,' he said. 'I like him. I hope he can solve the murder soon.'

'The street was crawling with police when I left,' she said. 'They even asked where I was going. One said how brave you'd been rescuing Alfie. I felt so proud.'

'How is Alfie?'

'I haven't seen him, but Rob and Maureen are

putting him up. There's nothing left of his house but the outside walls and a sagging roof. The roof looks like it could come down in a strong wind. He's worried about the insurance and convinced it was his wife's doing.'

'I think she must have been behind it, but she'll have paid someone else to do the dirty deed,' Conrad said, with a sigh. 'But, my darling, you mustn't gossip with our neighbours now. One of them may have killed Chloë, and therefore they're capable of killing again if they think anyone's getting close to identifying them. I wouldn't blame anyone for killing Rose, but I don't want to lose you.'

'Who do you think did it?' she asked. 'What about that guy we followed to his lockup? Rose told me he's ex-army and he looks capable of killing. His wife is very religious apparently – that could make a man a bit twisted.'

'Don't, Nina! You mustn't try to guess who did it or talk about these people. Keep out of it, and away from Rose, and let the police find the culprit.'

'Meanie,' she said, with a pout. 'I was going to become the street's Miss Marple. But I suppose I'll have to obey you.'

Conrad smiled. 'Yes, you will, my little flower. I'm hoping they'll let me come home later today. Then I can keep an eye on you.'

*

Marshall wasted no time in ordering a further investigation of Terry and Wilma Parkin at number seven. He remembered that they had left early for a weekend away the morning after Chloë was killed, and Terry Parkin by his own admission hadn't got a real alibi for the time of the murder. He'd said he was gardening.

It was his wife being at a Bible study group that had probably stopped the officers who called on them probing any deeper. A quick check with the hotel they'd stayed at in the New Forest revealed Terry had made the booking online at midnight on the Friday night. He had, of course, said it was a surprise for his wife, but now it was beginning to look more like getting out of the way to avoid questioning.

He'd had the opportunity to kill the child. He could easily have come back through the gap in the fence of Gareth Price's garden, leapt over the Singers' fence and into his own. He hadn't been asked for the clothes he was wearing on that Friday night, so he could have washed them before his wife got home, or even stuck them in the garden incinerator. But what motive would he have had to kill Chloë?

Could she have seen him with guns, or whatever it was he kept in the lockup?

Within an hour one of his officers had brought him details about Wilma. She had been brought up by devout Christian parents in a village in the Cotswolds.

She had continued to be deeply religious, working as a bookkeeper and secretary for a publisher of art and inspirational books. There was nothing shady in her past or her present, except perhaps her choice of husband. It did seem a little odd that a shy, mousy woman with strong religious convictions would choose a soldier as a husband. And what would a handsome, bold and charismatic man like Terry have in common with her?

Could his wife be a smokescreen? Maybe he'd married Wilma to allay suspicions of criminal activity.

Men who came through the experience of the army, dangerous postings, the excitement and the camaraderie were statistically more likely to turn to crime in Civvy Street, as they needed the adrenalin rush.

The Transit van's number-plate showed up as being owned by Sidney Ferry of Pyle Hill, Bristol. The detective checking him out soon found he was ex-army too and had joined up in Bristol on the same day as Parkin. So, that was clearly where they had met and become friends.

On the face of it there was no evidence to support the theory that Parkin and Ferry were engaged in anything illegal. Ferry might have been using his old friend's lockup to store some goods, then had to deliver them on somewhere. But the itch Marshall had felt about Parkin when he'd whisked his wife away for the weekend was usually a reliable indicator of something dodgy going on. Besides, why did Parkin get his friend to take the goods away if he had nothing to hide?

Conrad said the wooden boxes could have contained ammunition or explosives. Some would argue that Conrad had seen too many American films. But Conrad had no idea that Ferry was an expert in weaponry and explosives, so his guess might be on the money.

Terry Parkin must be taken in for questioning, his house and the lockup not just searched but forensically checked. Marshall realized he was going to be left looking rather foolish if he found nothing, but he was prepared to take that risk.

Janice opened her front door to find a police sergeant and a female officer ringing her bell at eleven on Monday morning. After the fire on Saturday night, she hadn't gone to bed until after three because she'd stayed with Nina in the hospital. Then last night she'd had a date with one of her regulars and didn't get home again until the early hours. She'd intended to stay in bed all day today to catch up on sleep.

Finding the police at her door was surprising, but to hear they wanted more information about where she was on the night after Chloë was killed was astonishing.

'I already made a statement that I was in a hotel

in the Cotswolds,' she said irritably, wrapping her dressing-gown more firmly around her. 'You checked me out too.'

'Yes, Miss Wyatt, we aren't disputing where you were that night. We're doing checks on everyone in the street and we want to talk with you about general matters. May we come in?'

DS Dowling looked at young PC Stella Coombes. He'd found her to be very insightful when interviewing people, and as such he hoped she could smooth Miss Wyatt down and get her to talk.

'It's nothing to worry about,' PC Coombes said, aware her sergeant wanted her to take over. 'It's just loose ends, really. We won't keep you long. I expect you're still recovering from the fire.'

'Yes, it was pretty scary,' Janice said, and opened the door. 'Do come in. I don't want the whole street to know I haven't got dressed yet.'

She got all three of them a coffee and took a moment to nip upstairs and put on some jeans and a sweater. 'That's better,' she said, sitting down opposite the two police officers. 'Now fire away!'

'We wondered what you do for work, Miss Wyatt?' Coombes asked.

'I'm a professional companion,' she said.

'Sorry,' Coombes said. 'What is that exactly? Do you mean you keep an old lady company?'

Janice laughed. 'Not old ladies. If a man wants

someone to accompany him on holiday, to dinner or the theatre, I'm that woman.'

Dowling's mouth dropped open with shock. Coombes had better control.

Janice smiled. 'I suppose you think that makes me a "hostess" or even a prostitute, but I'm not. They don't buy me for sex. I'm a companion, a date, whatever you want to call it. Sometimes I do sleep with my gentlemen, but only if I want to.'

Coombes took a deep breath to steady herself. 'How long have you been doing this?' she asked.

'Nearly ten years. I used to work in promotions. In fact, some of the gentlemen I see now I knew back then.'

'What sort of men are they?' Dowling had to ask.

'Lonely mostly, divorced and often retired professional men. I have a dentist, a neurosurgeon and two accountants. Almost all are wealthy, but money doesn't protect you from loneliness, does it?'

'Er, no,' Dowling said. 'So is this lucrative enough to live on?'

'Oh, yes,' she said happily, whirling a lock of her red hair in her fingers. 'I run it as a proper business. I pay tax and insurance. I dare say you'll check that out.'

Dowling sensed a touch of acid in her voice. Was she playing with them? Enjoying wrongfooting them? She'd certainly done that: he couldn't even remember what he was supposed to be asking her.

'Fair play to you,' Coombes said, surprising Dowling, who had always thought she was a bit strait-laced. 'I'm sure such work has made you very astute about people, men in particular. Would you share with me any suspicions about the men in your street?'

'People are saying it's Alfie Strong, but I don't agree. Poor man has that dreadful wife to cope with. They talk about Gareth Price too, but then he's into his booze, not violence. I like him actually. He's an interesting, intelligent man . . . well, when he's sober. Terry Parkin would be my first choice, just because he's ex-army. It's been my experience they have a shorter fuse than most. So the short answer is I haven't really got a clue who did it,' Janice said. 'If I had I'd have been on the phone a week ago to tell you.'

'You're remarkably candid,' Dowling said admiringly. 'It's refreshing. Did you ever talk to Chloë?'

'Yes, lots of times. I got to know her and her parents when she fell off her bike outside one day while I was cutting my grass. She'd hurt her leg quite badly, so I picked her up and took her home. After that she always stopped to speak to me. She liked coming in here too because she said it was like Aladdin's cave. I get on very well with her parents. My heart goes out to them – they're such nice people.'

'Did Chloë ever tell you anything, such as a boy she liked or anyone giving her a bad time?' Coombes asked.

Janice shook her head. 'She used to talk mostly about singing and dancing, and how she wanted to go on the stage. She was a confident, happy soul.'

'Do other people in this road know what you do for a living?' Coombes asked.

'No. I tell people I'm a bookkeeper and work at home if they ask. That sounds so boring they never question me about it. I expect they'd tar and feather me if they knew the truth. I hope I can rely on you not to tell anyone.'

'Of course we won't, Miss Wyatt. I'm impressed by your honesty. But we'd better go off now to our next call. Thank you for the coffee.'

'Just don't come back,' she said, and smiled impishly.

21

Rose Freeman had been watching the police go up and down the close all day. She felt she was being left out, so when her doorbell rang, and she found DS Dowling and PC Coombes on her doorstep, her face lit up. But her delight vanished as soon as they told her they wished to question her and her husband about what they were doing on the night of the murder.

'But we told you we were in our garden,' she said, her voice suddenly more shrill, her features sharper.

'We're aware of that, Mrs Freeman, but we have more questions to ask.'

'You'd better come in, then,' she said grudgingly.

Dowling had spoken to Rose Freeman twice before. She'd collared him at the re-enactment, putting on a fine show of being an almost auntie to Chloë in the hope of getting some information from him. The second time was when he'd come to see Gareth Price about his fence and she'd rushed outside as soon as she saw the police car and remained in her front garden, watching to see if he was going to take Gareth away.

The interior of the Freemans' house was exceptionally bland and stuck in the seventies with magnolia walls and a brown brocade three-piece suite. An electric imitation coal fire was set in a very cheap MDF surround. Above the mantelpiece was the *Green Lady* print by Tretchikoff. There were no other pictures or books, and Dowling guessed that watching the neighbours was their main source of entertainment.

Somehow the décor of the room said everything about Rose Freeman. No real heart, imagination or personality. A woman who thrived on the failures, disappointments and tragedies of other people's lives. Whether her husband had become a weak non-person through her constant nagging and interest in anyone but him, or whether he had been born to become her assistant, was anyone's guess.

DS Dowling felt a surge of pleasure in knowing that he was lucky enough to have a wife who was also his best friend, and he hoped that once this killer was caught, they could have a holiday and remind themselves they were lucky to feel the same about each other as they had on the day they married.

'Tell me, Mrs Freeman, do you work?' he asked.

'No. Call me old-fashioned but I always believed being a wife and supporting my husband by cooking and cleaning and making sure he had an ironed shirt was not just a full-time job but the recipe for a happy marriage.'

Dowling took one look at John Freeman's hangdog face and knew there was no point in asking if he agreed with his wife's statement. He wouldn't dare stand up to her.

'This job of looking after your husband seems to take up so little time that you're able to monitor the comings and goings of all your neighbours too?' he asked, wanting to goad her.

'I don't monitor, I take an interest,' she snapped back at him. 'Isn't that right, John?'

'Yes, dear,' John replied, with the minimum of enthusiasm.

'I believe you worked at Cavendish House department store before your marriage?' Dowling said. 'Which department?'

'I was a buyer for handbags and luggage,' she said.

'But that isn't true,' Dowling said, so glad she'd fallen into his hands. 'You were the Ladies powder-room attendant, were you not?'

Her face flushed scarlet, and her husband suddenly looked animated.

'If you lie about this, how do you expect me to believe you were in your garden all evening at the time of the murder?'

'But I was! Tell them, John.' She turned to her husband, with pleading eyes.

'We were in the garden that night,' he said, after a few moments' thought. 'At least I was. My wife spent most of the evening going backwards and forwards to the front window to check on our neighbours.'

'Is that so, Mr Freeman?' Dowling half smiled at the man. 'Did she tell you when Mr Church went down to the park to look for his daughter?'

'I believe it was around half past seven.'

'And at what time did your wife tell you she thought Chloë must be missing?'

'By eight,' he said, hanging his head. 'I told her I ought to join Mike and look for her, but she said I'd just get in the way.'

'So did she go back into the garden to be with you, or did she stay at the window?'

'She stayed at the window. She had pulled a chair over by it. She was there until at least ten thirty when I went to bed.'

Dowling and Coombes exchanged glances. They could almost imagine the roasting John Freeman was going to get when they left. Rose looked furious.

'Well, Mrs Freeman, you were in the best position to see people going in or out of the close. So who did you see?'

Dowling knew she couldn't have seen anyone with bloodstained clothes as she would have reported that immediately. But she might have seen someone she hadn't thought to mention before.

'I saw Wilma Parkin go out about six. I expect she was off to her church. She seems to almost live there.

Then Terry went out a bit later, not in his car, he was walking. He came home about half past eight, and Wilma was brought home by her vicar just after nine. I saw Brian Alcott go out too – that was around seven. He was walking, not in his car, which I thought was odd, as May had left it at home when she went out and took a taxi. I also saw Gareth Price come home so drunk the friend who'd given him a lift had to hold his arm. It was dark then, but I saw him holding on to the lamppost outside his house.

'But it was Mike Church who concerned me most. He kept going out to look in the park for Chloë. When it was dark he took a big torch and he was calling her name too.'

'Did you see Rob and Maureen Willis or Trudy Singer go out?'

Rose shook her head. 'No, but then the Willises rarely go out in the evenings. They're real homebodies. As for Trudy Singer, well, we hardly see her. She once told me that when her husband is away she's in bed before nine. He was away that night. That poor child of theirs must have a miserable life. She's down in the park sometimes till after dark and her mother's in bed!'

'Was she late that night?' Coombes asked.

'No. I saw her on the lawn outside her house about eight thirty. She was in pyjamas. I think she must've been wondering what was going on down at the Churches'.'

'You haven't mentioned Alfie or Dee Strong,' Coombes reminded her.

'I never saw Alfie at all, but Dee went out about half six. She didn't go in the car, she walked down the road. She wasn't dressed up like she usually is at night. She was wearing a black sleeveless dress, and had plimsolls on her feet. First time I ever saw her without high heels.'

'Did you see her come back?'

'No . . . Funny you should ask that but when I went to bed I said to my John, "She never came home to-night." I wondered if she had a fancy man.'

Dowling knew Rose had run out of information about her neighbours when she asked him how long he'd been in the force, then about his wife and kids. It was time to go, and he was very relieved. She might have given him a great deal of information, some of it extremely useful, but he'd never met any woman quite as malicious as she was. She really enjoyed other people's misfortunes.

Brian Alcott was called at Cheltenham Crown Court just before midday. He'd been there since nine thirty, and his solicitor arrived a little later. He'd never had cause to need a criminal lawyer before, so he'd agreed to use the duty solicitor the police had summoned when he was arrested on Sunday morning. Mr Drew didn't look impressive: small, plump and balding, with a permanent look of displeasure on his face.

The police had come for him and May at five o'clock on Sunday morning, Brian had stumbled to the door half asleep thinking it must have something to do with the fire at Alfie's. When they said they were arresting them both for bringing cigarettes illegally into the country and evading tax, he'd nearly fainted with shock and terror.

Regardless of what Mr Drew looked like, the solicitor had managed to convince the police that May had known nothing about the cigarettes so she was off the hook. He'd got bail for Brian too, as he pointed out, 'It's hardly the crime of the century.' But he had lectured Brian on the folly of being involved with the criminal classes.

'The police appreciate you didn't smuggle them yourself, having checked your passport to see if you'd been out of the country,' Drew said, his look of displeasure deepening. 'But I'm warning you, the courts take tax evasion very seriously as it's a crime against the Crown. If you plead guilty tomorrow morning, as you must, it will be dealt with straight away. You can expect a very large fine, and of course the cigarettes will be confiscated.'

May had driven Brian to the court on Monday morning but she refused to come in with him. 'I can't risk people I know seeing me,' she said. 'I told you when you first came up with this idea about cheap cigarettes that it was a bad one. But you wouldn't listen. This is your problem.'

Being furious with his wife as he waited to be called into court at least gave him something other than his fear to dwell on. How could May say such a thing when she had benefited from the sales for over a year? He'd told the police she hadn't known about it to save her skin but now she was turning her back on him.

He was fined five thousand pounds, and he arranged to pay it off at a thousand pounds a month.

When he got out into the street again he felt tainted, as if he'd been in a filthy cell with real criminals, who robbed and wounded people. He went straight into the nearest pub and had several large whiskies, then took a taxi home to tell May what he thought of her.

When he got there he found the front door open. As he stepped into the hall and looked into the sitting room, he saw two police officers pulling open drawers and poking in the sideboard.

'What now?' He held his fists to his head as if losing his mind.

May appeared from the kitchen. 'It's all your fault,' she snarled at him, nudging him into the kitchen so the police couldn't hear them. 'I said you should tell them the truth about where you were the night Chloë was killed. Now they're pulling our home apart looking for evidence that you killed her.'

'But you know I could never do that,' he wailed. 'I've taken the entire blame for the cigarettes to spare you. But no one is going to pin murder on me.'

'You've been drinking,' she said, her lips pursed in disgust. 'You stink of it. I've had more than enough for one day. I'm going to stay with my sister.'

Then he noticed a suitcase packed and ready in the kitchen. She was leaving him to deal with all this. 'What sort of wife walks away when her husband needs her?' he asked, and despite trying very hard not to cry, he failed and tears flowed down his face.

'A wife who is sick of you being stupid,' she snapped.

He lunged forward to strike her.

'Don't, sir!'

The voice came from one of the police officers, stopping Brian in his tracks. The young officer had opened the kitchen door. 'You don't want to find yourself up on an assault charge, do you?' he added.

Brian drove his fist into the wall instead. He made no impression on the wall but instead hurt his knuckles.

'Go now, Mrs Alcott,' the policeman said. 'I'll make your husband a cup of tea.'

Rose Freeman watched from the sitting-room window as a police officer came out of the Alcotts' house with May. He was carrying a suitcase, which he put into the boot of her car.

'May's leaving him,' she yelled to John. 'Does that mean Brian killed Chloë?'

'My God, woman,' John said from the doorway. 'Is there no end to your vindictive delight in other people's problems?'

'You what?' she said, turning to look at her husband.

'You heard what I said,' he hissed at her. 'You've always got to put the boot in, haven't you? What on earth did I ever see in you?'

'Don't be so nasty,' she said indignantly. 'You're just as interested in what's going on as I am.'

'No, I'm not.' He raised his voice in anger. 'Like a fool I've put up with it, but I can't stand it any more. We've got no friends at all in this street. They all hate you and laugh at you behind your back. I like Brian, I like Alfie too, and I can't delight in them having such a bad time.'

'Alfie deserved all he got,' she said stubbornly. 'I still believe he killed Chloë, and as for Brian, May's always led him by the nose. She thinks she's way above everyone else in this street. All she's got is some crummy tanning places in Birmingham but she flounces around with her designer handbags and shoes as if she owned a jeweller's in Bond Street.'

'You are a malicious, hate-filled woman and I can't stand another moment of it,' John shouted at her. 'Who are you to sit in judgement on other people? When I met you, you were a lavatory cleaner, and you come from a rough housing estate in Gloucester. Your mother was a tart and your father was in and out of prison. Would you like me to run up the road and tell our neighbours all that?'

'Why did you marry me, then?' She tossed her hair back indignantly.

'Because, you stupid woman, I actually fell in love with you. You were rough then, but I liked that you wanted to better yourself. When I bought this house and, yes, it was all my money, you put nothing into it, I wanted you to feel safe and happy. I expected us to have a family, and it was disappointing when that didn't happen. But you showed no sorrow – you said you didn't even like children. Remember that?'

John's heart was racing. He didn't like to argue, not with Rose or anyone else, and he'd certainly never attacked her verbally before.

'Why should I like children? My parents never liked any of us. Mum dropped a new one every couple of years and expected me to take care of them.'

'Thousands of people have childhoods as bad as yours or even worse. But they don't all take it out on other people. I've shown you nothing but love and understanding. I even tolerated you becoming more and more obsessed with what our neighbours were up to because I thought it was to do with your childhood. I should have taken you to a psychiatrist.'

'There's nothing wrong with me,' she yelled at him.

'You're the pervert! I know you go to that massage parlour behind the shops. I followed you one night. You filthy bastard.'

'I go there when I can't stand what you've become any more,' he admitted. He had a pain in his chest now and he was finding it hard to breathe. 'You even bring your malice to bed, going on and on about Janice next door and her men friends, or how snooty Mike Church is. I can't make love to a woman who is so filled with hate for other people. It takes all the joy out of me.'

He clutched at his chest as the pain became like a red-hot poker going through him. The room swam and he felt himself falling.

22

Janice couldn't help hearing the row between Rose and John because the windows were open on both houses.

'Good on you, John, tell her what a disgusting person she is,' she said aloud, smiling as she imagined Rose's astonishment at John rounding on her.

Yet Janice was shocked that he'd finally snapped. She would never have expected that from him.

Their voices were growing louder and louder, but when John started on about her job, her family, that she couldn't even read when he married her, Janice wanted to shut the window, she'd heard enough.

But suddenly John's voice became different. His speech had slowed and become a little slurred. It sounded like he was having difficulty breathing.

She heard a crash as if he'd fallen and then Rose screamed.

Janice didn't stop to think. She just ran out of her door to her neighbour. She could see Rose through the reeded glass on her door: she was using the telephone in the hall, and as soon as she saw Janice, she opened it.

'I think he's having a stroke or a heart attack,' Rose blurted out, to the emergency service on the phone and Janice. 'I don't know if he's breathing. Please come quickly.'

Janice found John lying on his back in the sitting room. She listened, but couldn't hear breathing and she couldn't find a pulse either. Loosening his shirt collar, she put the heel of her hand over his heart and, with the other hand above it, began CPR. She'd learnt to do it in a first-aid class, but it was a few years ago and she wasn't sure she was doing it right. When she'd done thirty presses, she decided to do mouth-to-mouth resuscitation.

It was one thing practising on a big doll, quite another doing it to a real person, and the thought that she could be killing him rather than saving him was terrifying.

Yet she thought she'd got him breathing again – there had been a spluttering noise – so she went back to the CPR. Aware that Rose was watching her, she yelled at her, 'Go out in the road and get one of the coppers.'

Rose disappeared and Janice continued, alternating CPR with mouth-to-mouth. All at once a burly policeman came rushing in. 'Okay, miss, I'll take over,' he said.

Rose had never been so silent. Her face was ashen, and she was wringing her hands. 'He isn't going to die, is he?' she asked, in a small voice.

'Not if we can help it,' the policeman said. 'Your friend here has done a good job with him.'

At last they heard the ambulance and Janice had never felt so relieved.

'You go with him,' Janice said, putting an arm around her neighbour because she looked so scared and lost. 'I'll lock up for you. Take some money with you for a taxi home. I've got to go out. If I hadn't, I'd offer to pick you up later.'

She'd always thought Rose was made of steel, yet she was leaning into her now like a child, her whole body limp. 'He's going to be okay,' Janice told her. 'Take a cardigan – it might be chilly later.'

As Janice watched the ambulance driving away, siren loud enough to wake the dead, she thought how odd it was that you could really hate someone but that disappeared when you saw them vulnerable and scared.

Janice got ready for her date with Ralph Kingsbridge reluctantly. John's heart attack and her involvement had left her feeling a little shaky and sad. All she really wanted to do was watch TV and go to bed. But he lived in Bath and she couldn't let him down at the last minute. Also, she had only his work telephone number. She picked out a black close-fitting sleeveless dress, which men always liked. She'd add a red belt and red heels. And put her hair up too.

*

Ralph was already at a table outside the wine bar on the Promenade waiting for her when she got out of the taxi. He was a dentist, a big man of at least six foot two, handsome in a florid way, with floppy fair hair, but a bit overweight.

'You're looking gorgeous, Beau,' he said, jumping up to kiss her cheek. 'I got you a gin and tonic. I hope that's okay?'

She didn't like gin. Vodka was her tipple. But Ralph was one of those pompous men who are inclined to treat women as if they had no mind of their own.

She sat down and was just about to tell him she'd had a rather upsetting experience that afternoon, and any drink was welcome, but he didn't give her a chance.

'I've booked a table at the new Lumière restaurant,' he said gleefully. 'I'm told the food is exquisite, and I kind of pulled rank to get us in. But that's not all. I've booked us a room at the Mayflower Hotel.'

Janice liked Ralph well enough, but she didn't like his leering smile. Neither was she in the mood for his assumption that as it was their third date it was time for her to sleep with him.

She drank the gin in one gulp – she needed it.

'That was rather presumptuous of you,' she said, secretly thinking that if he could book the divine and expensive Lumière, he could have booked a hotel of the same standard. The Mayflower was very down-at-heel, full of people on budget weekends. 'My next-door neighbour had a heart attack this afternoon, and I must be home by ten thirty in case his wife needs me for anything. She's very shaken.'

'That's a poor show,' he said, frowning at her. 'I paid in advance for the room.'

Janice couldn't believe his response. It showed how incredibly shallow he was. 'I'm sorry you can think only of your pocket, not of a man's life being in the balance,' she said tartly, and got up to go. 'You'd best cancel your reservation at the Lumière then – that'll save a few bob – and I'll go home now.'

He was on his feet in a trice, grabbing her upper arm, digging his fingers into her flesh. 'I don't like whores letting me down,' he snarled at her.

Just the word 'whores' was enough for Janice to see red, especially outside a busy wine bar. But coupled with his tone and his grabbing her arm, that was way beyond the pale.

'Get your hand off me,' she hissed back at him. 'Our arrangement was for companionship, as well you know. I'm shocked that a so-called "gentleman" could be so crass. Goodnight.'

She slapped at his hand and he released her. Janice turned and began to walk to the taxi rank.

'Not so fast,' he said, catching up with her and this time grabbing her shoulder. 'I don't like women running out on me.'

'What a shame. Perhaps in future you could try being more sympathetic. Not that you'll have any future with me, of course.'

She didn't see his fist coming at her, he was so fast, and it caught her squarely on her cheek, a red-hot searing pain.

'Leave her alone,' a male voice shouted. 'Pick on someone your own size.'

Janice was stunned by the blow, and it was a couple of seconds before she realized that the man who had intervened on her behalf and another were holding Ralph's arms to stop him getting away. A third was phoning the police. She realized these men in their thirties had also been at the wine bar.

'Thank you for helping me,' she said, holding her cheek and trying not to cry. 'I really can't cope with any more drama today. So if you'd just hold him until I can get into a taxi?'

'You should press charges,' one man said. 'You'll have a real shiner by tomorrow.'

'She won't want the police involved. She's on the game,' Ralph said.

'Well, I'm not surprised she didn't want to go anywhere with you,' another said. 'The lady has class. But we'll hold you till the police arrive to tell them what you did. She can go home.'

Janice ran the rest of the way to a taxi. Her face was

throbbing, and her eye was closing already. If only she'd stayed at home.

As Janice sat in the back of the taxi fighting tears, Dee was less than a quarter of a mile away, being arrested at Langham's Hotel.

She had come down to the bar at six. As it was Monday a lot of the weekend guests had gone home. She surveyed the room and felt a little dismayed. There were several company representatives, all too obvious by their cheap dark business suits, and the loud banter as they met up with men they'd shared evenings with before.

Apart from the reps, the rest of the clientele were older couples. Spencer, her man from Saturday night, wasn't someone she'd forget in a hurry. A gentleman where it counted, but an animal in bed. They had danced in the bar, Dee's way of making absolutely sure no one forgot she was in there. Spencer could dance, something Alfie had never mastered. And it was one in the morning when the night porter told them he had to lock up.

Until she'd met Spencer, Dee had believed she had only to look at a man to know if he'd be good in bed. She'd put Spencer in the camp of the ineffectual. The sort that thought they were good but their too-soft hands, their hurry to get to the main course, and a lack of understanding of what turned women on made the whole thing disappointing.

How wrong she was about Spencer! He had imagination, stamina, a big cock, and he knew exactly what women wanted.

He had to leave the hotel by eight the next morning as he was travelling to Edinburgh to see a client early on Monday. He kissed her goodbye, said it had been a memorable night and left his business card on the bedside cabinet. Dee went back to sleep until ten thirty. She wished he'd been able to stay all day with her.

The fire in Willow Close was on the news at lunchtime. A casualty was reported, but no name or other detail was given.

From then on Dee was on tenterhooks waiting for the police to arrive. While she hadn't told anyone where she was, she knew only too well the police could get the hotel name from the taxi company. So she waited, and waited, and waited. No police came.

Was it possible they didn't suspect her?

Finally, at four in the afternoon she decided she would go to Jason's and give him the money she owed him. It was too far to walk so she took a taxi, got the driver to wait around the corner, then went to Jason's house and handed over the envelope.

He asked how she'd got there and, knowing he'd

be angry with her and claim taxi drivers remembered addresses, she said she'd walked. She was back in the hotel within half an hour and went to her room to doll herself up for the night ahead. She thought she might go to one of the more prestigious hotels for a drink a bit later.

She was on her second vodka and Coke when the police came in. Three men and one woman. She'd known they'd come mob-handed to frighten and humiliate her.

They cautioned her and said they were arresting her for conspiring to commit arson. She pretended she knew nothing of the house burning down, but they waved aside her protests and said they had arrested the arsonist too. She had led them to him.

Her first thought was that Jason would kill her. It had never occurred to her to check if anyone was following her in the afternoon.

Her humiliation was complete when she was handcuffed in the bar, with staff and guests looking on.

The coldness of the officers as they led her out to the police car and bundled her into the back seat told her that her luck had run out. In the past she'd always managed to wriggle out of trouble somehow, but this was likely to end in a prison sentence. If Jason grassed her up about other crimes, which he doubtless would, it was going to be a long one.

*

DI Jim Marshall decided to interview Dee Strong with DS Dowling. She had opted for the duty solicitor, perhaps because she'd never had occasion to need a solicitor before. But as yet he or she hadn't arrived.

'Where were you at midnight on Saturday the twenty-fifth of July?'

'You know where I was. At Langham's Hotel,' she said. 'Dozens of people will confirm that.'

'I'm sure they will, Mrs Strong,' he said. 'Because you purposely set up that alibi, along with paying Jason Pickering to burn down your house in Willow Close. You intended your husband Alfie to die in the fire too, didn't you?'

'I did nothing of the sort,' she exclaimed indignantly. 'I don't know how you could say such a thing.'

Marshall half smiled. He had to hand it to her. She was cool, even if her pants were on fire. 'Interesting you didn't ask how your husband was,' he said. 'If the fire was a genuine accident, it's the first thing any caring spouse would ask. "Is my husband okay?"'

'Why should I care? He threw me out the house.'

'Precisely. We have many witnesses to that.'

'He'll have dropped a fag when he was drunk. He put the chip pan on once when he was drunk. It did hundreds of pounds' worth of damage and I was in bed upstairs. He could have killed me.'

'This fire was set, no accident, and you paid Jason Pickering to do it.'

'Has he told you that?'

'Yes, and one of our men saw you hand him an envelope with money in it.'

'I don't believe he admitted to something he hadn't done and, anyway, that money could've been for anything. You must know he lends money,' she said stubbornly.

Marshall just folded his arms and stared at her for a while. It usually had the effect of making a suspect break the silence with some explanation. But she remained silent and unfazed.

'I think we'll put you back in a cell now,' he said eventually. 'Mr Pickering has given us a great deal of information about you. It will take a few hours to go through it all.'

She merely shrugged. DS Dowling led her away.

Marshall went back to his office deep in thought. He was beginning to wonder if Willow Close was cursed. So many different incidents happening to sidetrack him from Chloë's murder. A report of a woman being punched in central Cheltenham earlier had turned out to be about none other than Janice Wyatt. The young man who reported the incident had jotted down the cab's number-plate, so of course it was followed up, and the address it took her to was number two Willow Close.

Earlier still John Freeman from number one had

been taken away in an ambulance. It seemed he'd had a heart attack.

Marshall had lied when he'd told Dee Strong that Jason Pickering had admitted to setting the fire. He hadn't. He'd denied it with what would have passed for a smile, but with his scars it was a grimace. Whether he was telling the truth, or that he knew they had no proof, was anyone's guess. He said the envelope Dee had handed to him was a repayment on a loan and surely everyone knew he was a loan shark.

Marshall did know that. The reason no one ever came forward with a complaint about this man and his rates of interest was because he terrified them. There had been several other fires too, which the police felt certain he had set, but again no proof.

But Pickering clammed up after that, just replying, 'No comment', to every question.

'He's a bad bastard,' Dowling said, when the two men had a cup of tea together to talk things through. 'He's clever too. Whatever he does he never leaves a trace behind.'

'He must have some weak spot,' Marshall said. 'Everyone does. But we must concentrate on Chloë's murder. That's far more important. But we'll set some men on following Pickering. They'll have to be careful as he's a slippery customer. But if he thinks

Dee Strong has been talking about him, he might be tempted to pay her a visit.'

'Not like you to wish a lady harm.' Dowling smiled.

'She's no lady. I think she has anaconda in her genes,' Marshall replied.

23

Tuesday, 28 July, Day Eleven

It was half past eight in the morning and Nina had just come out of her door, on the way to the bus stop, when she saw Janice putting out her dustbin. Her friend immediately put up a hand to hide her face, but she was too late: Nina had already spotted her black eye.

'What on earth happened to you?' she asked, shocked. Janice's eye was purple and closed, her cheek badly swollen too.

'Traditionally I should say I walked into a door,' Janice said, with an attempt at a grin. 'But as it's you who's caught me, I'll tell the truth. It was a date who turned nasty when I said I had to go home.'

'That's terrible! I can't believe anyone would do that to you,' Nina said, in shocked sympathy. Janice had confided in her about her work a couple of days before. At the time Nina had said she thought it was a risky business, but Janice had insisted they were all nice men she'd got to know well.

As this was no time to say, 'I told you so', Nina

offered to get her any shopping she needed and said she'd pop in after work to see how she was.

'Just some milk, please,' Janice said. 'I don't want anyone else to see me until it goes down.'

'Then hurry back indoors and pull up the draw-bridge before Rose spots you.'

'She's at the hospital still with John. Didn't you hear he had a heart attack yesterday afternoon?'

Nina gasped. 'No, I didn't. There's never a dull moment around here! Is he going to be okay?'

Janice shrugged. 'I really hope so. At least it proves Rose loves him – she won't leave his side. But I'll tell you more this evening.'

Once on the bus Nina considered all the nasty and unsettling things that had happened in the close since she and Conrad had moved in. A child's death, accusations flying around, then the fire at Alfie's, Conrad burnt and in hospital.

They had believed it was their for-ever house, but now it was becoming tainted. When you moved to a new place, you needed to feel you could trust your neighbours, but there were very few people in the close she and Conrad could trust.

It was a very quiet day in the shop. Nina and Babs, the owner, had unloaded the vanload of flowers from the market and there was only one bouquet to make up. Nina did that, and Babs went out to deliver it, leaving Nina to tidy up.

'You must have the afternoon off,' Babs said, on her return. 'It's quiet, and I can manage alone.'

Babs was in her early fifties, an attractive natural blonde with a country-girl look about her, rosy cheeks and wide blue eyes. She'd had the shop for nearly twenty years, and she was a pleasure to work for as she appreciated effort and artistry, often telling Nina she was a better florist than she herself was. 'It's so warm and sunny out there I doubt buying flowers is high on anyone's list of stuff they should do,' she went on. 'Besides, you'll want to visit your husband.'

'He might be coming home today.' Nina was touched that her boss was thinking of Conrad. As the drama had happened over the weekend, and Babs didn't come into the shop on Mondays, Nina had only mentioned the fire and Conrad's part in it briefly on the phone. She hadn't thought Babs would even remember.

'I told the ward sister I wouldn't be able to collect him until I'd finished work. But if you're sure about me going home, I can ring the ward and tell them I'm coming earlier.'

'How bad is the burn?' Babs asked. 'They let people out of hospital so quickly, these days. If a burn was bad enough to be admitted, surely it needs more than a couple of days to heal.'

'Conrad is a law unto himself,' Nina said. 'He's told them he's fine, and of course they really need the bed. But a nurse will come every day to change his dressings. So I suppose he might be right, and he'll heal quicker at home.'

'Well, run along, then,' Babs said, and smiled. 'Wish him a speedy recovery from me.'

As Nina got on to the bus, she spotted young Amy from number six up at the front. Her body language said she was sad, drooping shoulders and her head bowed. On an impulse Nina went and sat beside her.

'It's Amy, isn't it?' she asked. 'I'm Nina. We moved into number three the weekend before last. I haven't had a chance to meet you and your mum yet.'

The girl gave her a watery smile. It wasn't an 'I'd rather not talk to you' smile, more one of surprise that anyone would want to get to know her. She was very overweight, her brown hair was dull and stringy, and the pink floral dress did nothing for her. In fact, the belt at her waist just accentuated her big belly.

It was odd that she was dressed normally: Nina had seen her a couple of times dressed and made up like a Goth. Conrad said it was quite common for shy kids with no confidence to dress that way – they felt it made others think they were arty, strange, but in control. It was possibly easier to make friends with other Goths too, if they were mostly kids who had been marginalized.

Nina had picked up a great deal about neglected children from Conrad, and she felt Amy was a perfect example of one.

'So tell me how you are,' Nina said brightly, wishing she had Conrad's easy way with kids. 'You must feel very lonely and sad without your friend?'

'Yes, I do, and Mum is really getting on my nerves. She keeps crying all the time about Dad leaving. She doesn't think about me at all.'

'Oh, Amy, that's awful for you. What do you do with yourself all day? Have you got another friend to hang out with?'

'Not really. I went into town today to look in the shops, but it's boring on your own.'

Nina could see the girl was close to tears and felt sorry for her. The teenage years were difficult for most kids, all those emotions surging about, thinking you aren't pretty enough or clever enough ever to be a success. From what she'd seen, kids who had a hobby, be that football, dancing, horse-riding or swimming, were mainly happier than those who had nothing but school to occupy their mind.

Nina had been horse-mad from the age of nine, when she'd had riding lessons. Fortunately horses were something her parents approved of. By the time she was Amy's age she was down at the stables every night after school, at weekends and during the holidays, mucking out and grooming. She did it for nothing, just so she could ride the horses and get away from her parents. Maybe Conrad could find out something Amy liked and encourage her to take it up as a hobby.

'I noticed you dress like a Goth sometimes,' Nina said. 'Is that what you're really into? Art, heavy-metal bands? Forgive me if I've got it wrong, I don't know much about Goths.'

'I don't know much about it either,' Amy admitted. 'But I saw some girls in the park like that and I thought if I dressed the same they'd talk to me. They did too – they're nice. That was why I went into town today, to see if I could find some good clothes. But they mostly buy their stuff in specialist shops – there's a couple in Bristol.'

Nina thought how sad it was that a child should want to dress like Morticia Addams to make friends. 'I've got an idea,' she said. 'Why don't you come and have tea with Conrad and me tomorrow evening, about half past five? I've got to collect him from hospital now, but he works with young people and I'm guessing you'll like talking to him. What do you think?'

'That would be nice,' she said, and a ghost of a smile played about her lips.

'What do you like to eat?'

Amy shrugged. 'Anything.'

'Well, anything is cheap enough. Do you want chips with it or mash?' Nina joked.

Amy finally laughed. 'I meant I like everything, except fish with bones,' she said.

They were approaching their stop now and Nina stood up to ring the bell. 'Right! Five thirty to-morrow. No fish with bones!'

Today Conrad looked more like his old self: his face wasn't so drawn, and the sparkle was back in his eyes.

Nina hugged him cautiously, afraid she'd hurt his back, then kissed him. 'How's the burn?' she asked.

'I don't notice it until I lean back on something, or someone slaps it. Not that anyone has slapped it, but I keep imagining how much it will hurt.'

'That might become my secret weapon to make sure you do exactly as I tell you,' she joked. 'So be warned.'

'So what's new?' he said, as Nina drove him home.

'Janice has a black eye, a present from one of her men friends. Rose is still at the hospital with John. There may have been developments today, but I've been at work. However, we've got a young guest coming for tea tomorrow.' She explained that she'd spoken to Amy on the bus and felt she needed an adult to talk to. 'She seems troubled to me. As you're so good with kids, I think she might open up to you.'

'She was happy to come to us?' Conrad seemed surprised.

'Yes, she was. Why?'

'A lot of kids who have low self-worth and feel un-loved can't or won't turn to anyone for help. So it's a good sign that she agreed to come to us. Mind you, she might not turn up!'

'What – and miss the chance of dining with the only relatively normal and happy couple in the close? Not to mention your devilishly good looks!'

Conrad sniggered. 'I like "relatively normal".'

'Well, my fearless champion of the underdog, what would you like for tea? And how can I make you comfy if seat backs hurt the burn?'

'I'll just lie on my side on the sofa and you can spoon-feed me spag bol.'

'I'll do no such thing. I know that sofa's on the way out, but I still don't want it daubed with sauce. But maybe spag bol is a good idea for tomorrow. Kids usually like it. And you can stand up to eat it!'

'Such callousness.' He sighed. 'Have you forgotten I'm the hero of the close and therefore entitled to be spoilt?'

As Nina pulled up on their drive it was half past three. 'Would you mind if I nipped in to see Janice quickly?' she asked. 'I'll explain later, but I got her some milk, so she doesn't have to go out.'

Conrad raised one eyebrow. 'Umm, sounds intri-guing. But don't be long.'

'I'll come in first and make you some tea and a sandwich if you're hungry.'

'I'm not. You go now – I can make myself a cup of tea.'

When Nina helped him out of the car, she noticed he appeared very stiff. 'I won't be long,' she said, kissed him and opened the front door for him.

Nina noticed Janice peep round the curtain as the bell rang. Clearly, she was checking before she opened the door.

'Milk!' Nina said, holding out the carton. 'I can't stay long as the wounded hero needs to be waited on.'

'Come in. Is he okay?'

'Sorer than he's letting on, I think,' Nina said, as she walked in and closed the door behind her. 'But he looks better today, and they've given him some good painkillers. But tell me about you.'

Janice explained what had happened. 'I'm not in the habit of letting men down,' she said, 'but John having that heart attack shook me up. I did CPR on him, but I was scared I hadn't done it right. I really didn't want to go out after that, but I felt obliged to. I certainly wasn't in the mood for some pushy bloke assuming I'd stay the night with him.'

'And he punched you?'

Janice nodded. 'DI Marshall, the head honcho on Chloë's case, called round this morning. Seems the guys who helped me had rung the police and given the taxi reg number, so they traced me. He wanted me to give details about the man.'

'Surely there was no connection with that bloke and the one who killed Chloë.'

'No – well, I doubt it very much. I think Marshall came purely because he thought if I was hurt and low I might spill the beans about my neighbours. I had to disappoint him saying I didn't get involved with anyone here, but he kind of wheedled his way in to getting me to make observations about them.'

'And what observations did you make?'

Janice laughed, putting her hand over her eye as if she thought laughing might make it hurt more. 'I said I thought Dee was capable of anything, even killing a child. I told him about an incident a couple of years ago when Chloë rang the doorbell and ran away. Well, we've all done that as kids, haven't we? We used to call it Knockdown Ginger. I was cleaning the car, so I saw it all. Anyway, Dee came out like a woman possessed, screaming at the kid that she didn't appreciate being wound up.'

'That's terrible. Did her parents call the police?'

'No. Better than that. Mike went up to Dee's and yelled at her with many choice adjectives too. It was great. I wanted to applaud him. Alfie came to the door and stood there smirking. Like he was glad she was getting a taste of her own medicine.'

'Was that it? No repercussions?'

'Well, Mike and Ruth never asked Alfie and Dee to any parties after that. Ruth told me Alfie came to see them and apologized for Dee. But Alfie had always been fond of Chloë, and she of him, and I think he used to go and see her at her house without Dee knowing. If Dee'd ever found out he did that she would've gone ape, I imagine. I don't know if Dee still bore a grudge against Chloë, but I do think she's capable of hurting a child. She really is a nasty woman.'

Nina dwelt on that for a moment. She hadn't seen enough of Dee to be sure she was that bad. 'So, back to you, Janice. Are you going to give up your companion business now?'

Janice grimaced. 'I can't say. Right now I'm too scared to see anyone, but that will wear off, won't it? I mean, what else will I do for a living?'

'I think you need time to think it through carefully,' Nina said. 'This is a little reminder for you that maybe a change of direction is in order.'

'One of my men, the only one I let come here, is a real darling. He's trapped in a terrible marriage, and I know if he could get out of it, he'd be with me in a shot. I used to daydream of being with him for ever. But I don't even want to see him any more.'

'I'm not sure jumping into a permanent relationship is the answer now,' Nina said thoughtfully. 'I think you need space, so you can put things into perspective.'

Janice nodded. 'You're right. Mind you, don't feel too sorry for me as I found myself flirting with DI

Marshall today and felt I wanted to know him better. An interesting man. He knows all about me and seems to like me regardless.'

Nina sniggered. 'You're incorrigible, flirting with the fuzz!'

'One has to seize opportunities when they arise.' Janice laughed. 'I'm so glad you came to live next door. I like you a lot. I trust you, too, and I know without asking you won't talk about this to anyone. Bless you!'

'Your secrets are safe with me.' Nina tapped her nose and pulled a silly face. 'I'd better go back to the old man now, and get the food organized, too. But if you need anything, feel scared or lonely, just ring us.'

24

'Police, open up!' the officer barked, as he could see someone on the stairs through the reeded glass. It was seven in the morning, always a good time of day to catch people unawares. They had a search warrant for the Parkins' house at number seven and another for their lockup. While men were searching here, the Bristol police would be calling at Sid Ferry's home. It was hoped by both police forces that within an hour both men would be in custody.

'What on earth is it?' Wilma Parkin, in a long white nightdress, looked stricken. 'What do you want with us?'

'Your husband, please,' the officer said. 'We have a search warrant for this premises and your husband's lockup. Forensics will be here soon.'

Terry Parkin appeared behind his wife, wearing a plum-coloured towelling dressing-gown, his legs tanned mahogany brown. 'What on earth do you expect to find?' he asked. 'You've searched this house already.'

'We weren't looking for firearms then, sir,' the officer said. 'Now, if you'd like to go and get dressed, we can get on with our work.'

'Firearms? Do you mean guns?' Wilma squawked, and promptly burst into tears. Her husband enfolded her in his arms, held her for a moment, and led her back upstairs.

The search of the Parkins' house revealed nothing, as did the search of the lockup, but the forensics team remained checking for residues of gunpowder, chemicals or anything else that could push the investigation forward.

Bristol police found nothing at Ferry's home or in his van. But they did find an east London postcode in his satnav and they were investigating it now.

When Marshall heard that, he didn't hold out much hope of the postcode being any use to them. Ex-soldiers were thorough. Ferry wouldn't have kept an incriminating postcode on his satnav any more than he'd leave a few bullets or gunpowder in his van. Marshall was glad that this particular investigation had been taken out of his hands. All he wanted was to find Chloë's killer. Nothing was more important than that.

Amy arrived at Conrad and Nina's just before five thirty. Nina opened the door to her and noted the child had pink eyes, as if she'd been crying. But she could also see she'd made an effort with her appearance. She wore a plain turquoise dress and her hair was fastened up at the sides with glittery slides.

'Come on in. Conrad's looking forward to some company as he's been alone all day,' she said.

Conrad grinned welcomingly as Amy came into the sitting room. 'I hope you're hungry – Nina seems to have cooked enough for an army,' he said, noting she looked a little scared. 'Come and sit by me. You look very nice. Turquoise suits you.'

Nina watched from the door through to the kitchen. Conrad's deep and melodious voice made people warm to him, and his kind eyes lured you in to make confidences. She knew this because she'd met Conrad after breaking up with a man who had convinced her she was basically worthless, that her taste in clothes, films, music, décor and everything about her was rubbish but if she was with him he could sort her out.

Her ex had kept her from her friends, meeting her from work so she couldn't go off somewhere. Fortunately for Nina, he met a woman needier than she was, and ran out on her. Yet even though she knew deep down that that was the best outcome, she was left with a huge loss of self-esteem and no confidence.

At the time Nina had worked in the same florist's in Cirencester she'd started with as a trainee at sixteen, and Conrad had come in to buy a bouquet. His appearance and voice were enough to make her take notice, but he was chatty too, which male customers rarely were. He wanted the bouquet for a lady who had let him take four boys in his care for a holiday at a cottage she owned in the Cotswolds.

As he agonized over the colour of the flowers he told her about the lady. His car had broken down one day in the village of Burford in the Cotswolds, it was pouring with rain, he was alone and he couldn't get a signal on his phone to call a breakdown service. So, he'd knocked on the door of the pretty cottage where he was, explained his predicament to the owner and asked if he could use her phone.

As Nina had been taken with Conrad immediately, for his easy manner, beautiful eyes and lovely voice, she could well imagine why the lady had given him tea and cake while he waited for the breakdown people to come. The upshot of this encounter was that Conrad told her he was a house-father, and said he'd love to bring his city boys out to the Cotswolds for a little holiday. Although he'd searched he'd never found anywhere within his budget.

She said she had a small cottage she rented out, which could hold five people, and he could have it for the first week in May for free, as long as he made sure he left it clean.

'So we had a week's holiday, the four boys who could be trusted to behave, and me. It was a huge success. We even had lovely weather,' he said happily, looking hard at Nina. 'So you tell me what colour flowers she'd like. Her home was very classic.'

'Then I suggest we go for pinks and whites,' Nina had said. She felt a bit nervous – she wasn't used to men giving out so much information or being so enthusiastic about flowers.

To her surprise and delight, Conrad telephoned her the next morning and asked if she'd like to go to Westonbirt Arboretum with him on her next day off. He said they could have tea and cake in the café.

Did he know how bruised she was? That if he'd asked her to dinner or even the pictures she'd probably have got scared and said no. But a walk somewhere she'd always wanted to go to, with a man who took care of children, sounded safe and marvellous. So she went. He kissed her in a glade surrounded by rhododendrons that were still in flower. It was the best kiss ever, gentle but with a hint of passion to come, and she felt she was about to climb a stairway to Heaven with him.

As Nina prepared the meal, she was glad she'd made the bolognese sauce last night: she had only the pasta to cook now. She had her ears pricked to listen to what Conrad was talking to Amy about. It was all safe stuff, her favourite subjects at school, her hobbies, what she liked to watch on TV. To Nina's surprise, Amy was quite forthcoming: she said she hated sport and gymnastics because she was useless at them. She liked handicrafts, but her mother complained if she made a mess. She liked cooking too, but was rarely allowed to do any at home, only at school.

'What about films and television?' Conrad asked. 'Do you like the soaps?'

'Not much,' she said. 'I like the true-crime programmes best, when they do a re-enactment of the crime, and show how they put together all the evidence.'

'What job would you like to do?'

'A forensic scientist,' she said, without any hesitation. 'It's really interesting and I'm good at science.'

Nina went back into the living room then and laid the table. She glanced across the room to Conrad and Amy, who looked comfortable together, and Amy already seemed much happier. Nina remembered how happy she'd felt that day in the arboretum with Conrad. He could make the most mundane outing fun, sprinkle stardust on anyone's life, but back then she had felt so good with him she'd had to pinch herself to be sure she wasn't dreaming.

'Would you like me to paint your nails after tea?' Nina asked Amy. Conrad had once told her when his mother remarried he had missed physical touch. She used to ruffle his hair, tuck him into bed, give him hugs. Children and young people deprived of such caring gestures were likely to be unable to show affection to their own children.

Nina thought the simple act of doing the child's nails might help them to create a bond. 'I know when I was your age I used to love it.'

Amy was surprised and clearly pleased. 'But I nibble them a bit,' she said, and blushed.

'Even more reason to paint them, then. They'll look so nice, you won't want to spoil them, and it might stop you biting them.'

'Can I have black varnish?' Amy asked. 'It would make me look more like a real Goth.'

'I flirted with being a Goth for a short while,' Conrad said, surprising Nina, who hadn't known this. 'I liked punk bands and it seemed to me they all became Goths. I looked the part with my black hair, and I had it long then, but I couldn't bring myself to have any piercings, which seemed to be essential.'

'I wouldn't like to do that either,' Amy admitted. 'I'd be scared to have tattoos too. So it's just as well I'm too young.'

'What do Goths believe in?' Nina asked.

'Well, most like to act like they're on the dark side, reading heavy stuff, and listening to dark sort of music. But there doesn't seem to be any kind of rules. I just like the way they hang out together, all kind of spooky.'

Amy had a good appetite. She ate more than Con-

rad, and her eyes lit up when Nina brought in a chocolate gateau and cream for dessert.

Nina put the plates in the dishwasher, then got out
her box of nail stuff. 'You choose the polish you'd
like,' she said. 'I'll just get some warm water for the
manicure.'

Conrad winked at Nina.

Amy found a black varnish. 'I can't imagine you
wearing this,' she said.

'I think I only got it for Halloween,' Nina said. 'I
didn't know Con when he was a Goth, or I might
have been tempted.'

Nina set a side table in front of Amy and put her
equipment on it, then pulled up a stool for herself. Amy's nails were badly bitten, and she'd been
chewing the skin around them. Nina filed the nails
smooth, removed the hangnails and soaked Amy's
hands in a bowl of warm water.

'You must stop biting around your nails, sweetie,'
she said. 'You'll make them sore and you might get
an infection. Does Mum ever do your nails?'

Amy shook her head. 'No. But she doesn't really
notice anything about me, not my clothes, hair or
anything.'

Nina and Conrad exchanged glances. 'Well, you
can come over here sometimes and do girly stuff,'
Nina said quickly. 'I expect Mum's feeling a bit low
since your dad left.'

'He left because she's so boring,' Amy said. 'But she's never done stuff with me anyway.'

'Did you and Chloë do each other's hair or nails?' Conrad asked.

'Sometimes. She had lovely blonde hair, and she didn't bite her nails. Everything about her was perfect.'

'It can be hard having someone close to you who's perfect,' Conrad said. 'There was a boy at my school who was like that, clever, a brilliant gymnast and very good-looking. I admired him, but secretly hated him too. Did you ever feel that way about Chloë?'

'No!' Her retort was sharp, as if his question had been offensive.

Nina took one of Amy's hands from the water and dried it gently. 'Conrad means that clever, beautiful people can be annoying if you feel you can't compete,' she said calmly, picking up an orange stick and gently pushing back the girl's cuticles. 'I had a friend who was captain of the netball team, a great swimmer, very pretty and popular. I liked her a lot, but I always felt I was in the shade next to her.'

'Well, I suppose it was a bit like that with Chloë,' Amy confessed. 'Her dancing, singing and everything. I wished her parents were mine too.'

'There's nothing wrong with that,' Conrad said. 'The boys I take care of often tell me about aunts and uncles they wished were their parents. I had a stepfather I hated, and I used to envy some of the boys I was at boarding school with – their families seemed so loving and happy. I guess it's just the way it is. We all wish for something we haven't got or to change what we have if we're dissatisfied with it.'

'My dad's got another woman in Brighton,' Amy said suddenly. 'Mum says she's a tart and only after his money.'

Nina and Conrad's eyes met. It was as if she approved of her dad having another woman and didn't like what her mother had said about her.

'What do you think about it?' Conrad asked.

'Think about it?' Amy looked puzzled.

'Well, do you think your mother is right, or do you take your dad's side? Or don't you care either way?'

'Mum drove him away.' Her voice grew shriller.

Nina took her second hand from the warm water, patted it dry with the towel, then just held it. 'Why do you think that?' she asked gently.

'She's so useless. She doesn't do anything now, not even cleaning. She just lies on her bed and cries.'

'But she does that because she misses your dad.'

'She's got me!' she burst out angrily. 'Why doesn't she remember that?'

'Oh, Amy . . .' Nina didn't know what to say. It was a cry for help, but how could she and Conrad help her? This girl wanted a fully functioning mum, not a mere neighbour. 'Maybe you need to point that out to her. Have you tried to tell her how you feel?'

'She won't listen. She's too busy thinking about herself. She goes downstairs at night and cooks loads of food, like bacon and eggs. I watched her from the hall one night – it was disgusting. She had about six rashers of bacon, beans and three eggs. She stuffed it in like she hadn't eaten for weeks.'

'Would you like me to try to get some help for you both?' Conrad said.

Nina picked up the nail varnish and began to paint. She was out of her depth now. She knew almost every teenage girl became angry with her mother, usually because the mother tried to restrict her daughter. But this wasn't normal teenage angst. This was full-blown disgust, loathing, and pure anger that her mother didn't care about her.

'I think I told you I'm a house-father at a home for boys who have been in trouble so I'm in touch with good people who could help you and your mum.'

'I don't want to get help for her. I want to get away from her,' she blurted out.

Nina had finished the first coat of nail varnish and she was beginning to wish she hadn't asked Amy here.

'And where would you like to go?' Conrad asked, his voice as gentle as a summer breeze.

'To a place like where you work,' she said.

'I see,' Conrad said.

Nina started on the second coat of varnish. She would leave it to Conrad now. He was the one with experience.

'But I can't go to one of those unless I do something bad,' she said, and began to cry.

Having finished Amy's nails, Nina got up and moved to sit next to her on the sofa. 'Don't smudge them,' she said, put her arms around the child and drew her to her chest. 'Some of these things you're feeling are to do with losing your best friend, and then your dad leaving. But your poor mum, she can't help how she feels either, and her unhappiness is stopping her thinking about anyone else. I think she needs a doctor's help, Amy. Will you try to talk to her and persuade her that's what she needs?'

Amy cried into Nina's chest for a long time, huge heaving sobs that were distressing to both Nina and Conrad. When at last they began to slow, Conrad fetched a flannel, prised her away from Nina and wiped her hot, flushed face.

'I suspect that's the first time you've really cried since Chloë died,' he said. 'Crying can be a great healer, and maybe you'll start to feel better about it all now.'

Amy went home about twenty minutes later, and Nina heaved a sigh of relief. 'Thank goodness that's over,' she said. 'I felt I couldn't breathe because she was so upset. Do you think she'll be all right now?'

Conrad shook his head. 'She's a mass of contradictions, hating her mum and loving her, the same with her father. She's glad he's gone but hates it too. She's lonely, sees no future for herself. She's the sort of kid who could slide into drugs.'

'What can we do to help?'

Conrad reached out and caressed her cheeks. 'You were great with her. Keep being interested, and I'll talk to a couple of people who might have some suggestions. We can't do any more.'

25

Marshall received a message from his contact in the Metropolitan Police that the postcode in Sid Ferry's satnav belonged to Ferry's sister. She worked in a bank, had two children aged five and seven, and her husband was a teacher. An unlikely couple to be gun-running. But Marshall hadn't believed the postcode would lead them to where the guns or ammunition were. In many ways he was relieved at the outcome, glad that the Met were taking over the investigation, and he would get some clear space to concentrate on finding Chloë's killer.

Just a few hours ago he'd asked his team to go over every last bit of evidence once again, every witness report, any notes taken on the house-to-house search. They might find something they had missed.

Terry Parkin had not been charged with anything yet. He admitted that he had stored boxes in his lockup, but denied they were wooden ones as the witness reported. He claimed they were brown plastic, holding men's work boots he'd bought on-line some time ago and thought he'd make a big profit when he sold them on. His friend Sid Ferry had taken them to a market trader in Bethnal Green to sell on his stall.

It sounded plausible. Time would tell if that story was true or false.

Meanwhile Marshall had handed over the investigation into Dee Strong's life to his colleagues. They had found plenty of old associates who had lots of reasons to wish a long prison sentence on her. Extortion, theft, blackmail, shop-lifting, prostitution, she'd done it all. But it was hearsay, and there was no hard evidence yet that she'd paid Jason Pickering to burn her husband's house down. Or that she'd killed Chloë.

Pickering was under surveillance: with patience and some luck he might slip up and reveal something they could arrest him for.

Gareth Price had been sober for a week, and he had found the best way to stop himself yielding to temptation was to keep busy. He'd worked on his garden, cleared the rubbish out of his shed and garage, taken clothes he no longer wore to the Salvation Army, and cleaned his house from top to bottom.

He felt quite proud of himself, but he also knew that one week dry didn't mean he was cured. Tonight he was going over to see the Churches. When he had first bought number five, in the late eighties, he and Gloria had been good friends with Mike and Ruth.

They had comforted the Churches when their first baby was stillborn, and just three years later, when Gareth and Gloria had lost fourteen-year-old Clare in the tragic road accident, Mike and Ruth had been incredibly kind to them. Ironically it was later the same year that Chloë was born, and although Gareth and Gloria were broken by grief, they were glad to see their friends so happy with their new baby.

After Gloria had left him, and before his drinking had become serious, Gareth had gone to dinner with Mike and Ruth quite often. He'd liked to play with Chloë and enjoyed watching her progress from baby to schoolgirl. When she'd started singing and dancing, he'd always gone to watch. When he learnt she'd been killed it had brought back all the pain of losing his Clare.

He knew only too well that in the last few years he had lost his way and his old friends.

However, in the last couple of days, his new sobriety had made him remember people he had once been close to, and he felt guilty that he'd neglected them. This evening he was going to make a start on putting that right. He'd bought some flowers and made up a little basket of treats for Mike and Ruth. It included pâté, good cheese, special biscuits and a fruit cake. He didn't expect them to invite him in. When Mike opened the door Gareth held out the flowers and basket. 'I should've come before. You were both so kind to Gloria and me when Clare was killed. I wanted to support you through this terrible time you're going through, but I couldn't because of the drink. I'm not drinking now, and this is my long overdue apology.'

Mike took the basket and flowers and smiled. 'Drinking or not, it's good to see you, Gareth. Do come in.'

'Just for a few minutes,' Gareth said. 'I remember only too clearly all the well-intentioned people who call and never seem to know when it's time to leave.'

Mike smiled. 'There have been a few. But there's not many people who really know how we feel. You're one who does.'

He ushered Gareth in. Ruth was on the sofa, and she got to her feet to kiss him.

'I'm ashamed I haven't been over before,' he said. 'No excuse, except the bottle, but Chloë's death helped me to see I must give it up. A whole week so far.'

'Mike and I can see why bereaved parents turn to drink. We have too, though we're trying not to. But do sit down, Gareth.'

'I can't even ask how you are,' he said, taking an armchair by the window. 'I know that already. But are you managing to sleep, eat, go for a walk?'

'We don't do much of all three,' Mike said, sitting down beside his wife. 'We watch TV but don't take anything in. Neither of us has any appetite. We live for the day when her killer is caught. Then I think we might be able to deal with it. Her funeral will be a week on Monday, and many people have said that's always a turning point.'

'It wasn't with Gloria and me,' Gareth said. 'People behave as if it's like a full stop, and you don't grieve after that. But of course you do. My only piece of wisdom is that it's like waves breaking on a beach. Some days you get just the smaller ones, but then, when you least expect it, a big one comes crashing in and knocks you off your feet.'

'Tell me, Gareth, have you been going to A A, or just doing it alone?'

Gareth understood that Ruth's question was to stop any further talk of grief. 'Yes, I joined a local group. I've only been twice so far, but it helps to know you aren't the only one suffering. I've been finding jobs to do to keep my mind off the drink.'

'We heard John had a heart attack. Do you know how he is?' Mike asked.

'Maureen said he's improving. She and Rob have gone back to work now, but she called on Rose. She said Rose seemed like a different person, kinder, not probing for gossip. But that'll be shock. She'll be back twice as nasty, you'll see,' Gareth said.

Mike and Ruth laughed. 'We're concerned about the Alcotts too,' Ruth said. 'Since their court appearance they've been lying low. I know they're in there – I can hear them through the open windows – but I suppose they're afraid everyone's talking about them.'

'Selling smuggled cigarettes isn't my idea of a major crime,' Mike said. 'Not compared with murder or arson. I don't think anyone's horrified by cheap fags.'

'Who knew there were so many secret things going on in the close?' Gareth grinned. 'Once it was just me everyone talked about. Now I'm old hat as they're spoilt for choice.'

'Gareth,' said Ruth, 'how are Trudy and Amy? Amy used to spend so much time here, she must feel so alone now without Chloë. And Roger left Trudy, we heard, so she must be in a bad way.'

'I don't like to stick my nose in,' Gareth said. 'Especially after that night when Trudy thought I'd accused Amy of being in my garden. But things are not good for them. I've heard Trudy crying, and shouting at Amy. Of course the poor kid wants to go out to get away from her mother's misery, and of course that's making Trudy even unhappier.'

'Did I see her dressed like a Goth?' Mike asked. 'With that white make-up and black eyes I couldn't be sure it was her.'

'Yes, that was her. Who knows where the poor kid's head is? I suppose she's met a different crowd and just wants to fit in. Weird or not, I think it's better than being on her own all the time.'

'It couldn't have happened at a worse age,' Ruth said, her voice soft with concern. 'At thirteen you're standing with one foot in childhood, the other in adulthood. Amy doesn't have any other resources to fall back on either. She doesn't dance, sing, do sport, paint or ride horses. I don't think there are any close relatives either, or real friends. I used to mother her a bit when she was here, and that's been snatched away from her too.'

'I always thought she and Chloë were ill-matched friends,' Gareth said. 'That's just an idle observation. Shoot me down if you don't agree.'

'Sadly, you're right,' Mike said, and sighed. 'Just a few weeks ago Chloë said she'd be glad when we moved as Amy was getting her down. She hung on her coat tails, wanting to be with her every day, evenings and every weekend. But she stuck with her because she felt sorry for her.'

'I just wish I could shake Trudy and make her see she's got to get over her husband leaving her and be a proper mother,' Ruth said. 'It's never too late. She could take Amy on a little holiday, talk to her, find some common ground.'

Gareth thought it was time he changed the subject. 'Will you move, like you planned?'

Mike and Ruth exchanged glances.

'Eventually yes,' Mike said. 'It's all become a bit poisonous here. But maybe a cottage in a Cotswold village rather than a Cheltenham townhouse. I'll have to go back to work soon too, but I don't want to leave Ruth.'

'I should return to work too.' Ruth gave a glum, half-hearted smile. 'But maybe a return to general nursing, or even district nursing. I don't think I could face a school again.'

Gareth got up. He felt he'd been there long enough. 'Whatever you do, cling to one another. If only Gloria and I had done that, we might have been together still. Now I must go.'

'We'll take that on board,' Mike said. 'Thank you for your gifts and for coming to see us. We know how hard it must have been for you. But stay on the wagon, Gareth. You're worth so much. Remember the laughs we used to have? Maybe one day we can bring that back.'

Mike hugged him, and for a moment Gareth thought he was going to collapse in tears. It was so good to feel an old friend's affection, especially from a man who was hurting so badly.

'Anything I can do, just ask,' Gareth croaked, his voice breaking with emotion. 'I can cut your grass, clean your car, whatever.'

'Bless you,' Ruth said softly. 'You just stay on the wagon and we'll feel that at least Chloë's death achieved something.'

*

'I think you must find somewhere else to live, Alfie,' Maureen said gently. 'We invited you to stay as it was an emergency but, as I'm sure you know, we didn't want a permanent lodger.'

She looked down at Alfie sitting on the sofa with his feet up on a stool. He'd made himself a sandwich and coffee earlier, while she was at work, and the plate and cup were still there. His breakfast things were still on the side in the kitchen. He hadn't even put them in the dishwasher. Worse still, she could smell cigarette smoke. He knew very well she didn't like smoking in her house.

She and Rob were in the habit of snuggling up on the sofa to watch TV in the evenings, but Alfie had commandeered the big sofa and the television remote. He flicked from channel to channel constantly, and never asked what they wanted to watch.

He snored, and the house almost shook with it. He didn't clean the bath after using it, and he asked what was for dinner as soon as Maureen got in. Yesterday she'd said they were having salmon, new potatoes and salad, and he said he didn't like salmon or salad. It was on the tip of her tongue to tell him to go to the supermarket and buy his own food.

'I'm a nuisance, am I?' he said, looking up at her with a fake-mournful expression.

'I wouldn't call you a nuisance, Alfie, but Rob and I like our own space and company. We helped out as we know what a shock it must have been to have your house burn down. But your insurance will cover accommodation until your house is rebuilt. I take it you've contacted them?'

'No, not yet,' he said. 'I've had a lot on my mind.'

'I'm sure you have,' she said, ice creeping into her voice. 'But your insurance is a priority. You should've phoned them the day after it happened. Most insurance companies have the phones manned until eight or nine in the evening. Why don't you phone them now?'

'All my papers were burnt,' he said.

At that Maureen felt like slapping him. 'I'm quite certain you can remember the name of your insurance company, and they can find your policy with your address. You had your own replacement windows business for years, so you must have had lots of dealings with insurance companies.'

'I'm watching the news now,' he said, flicking the remote to BBC1. 'I'll do it later.'

Maureen saw red. 'No, Alfie. Now,' she said, snatching the remote from his hands. She had never imagined she'd ever feel any sympathy for Dee, but she was beginning to now, if this was how Alfie had been with her. 'I'll google the company to find their number, and then you'll ring them.'

'That was a bit harsh,' Rob whispered to Maureen a little while later. She'd found the insurance company's phone number for Alfie, moved him into their small home office and stuck the phone into his hand.

'Possibly, but someone had to do it,' she said, and grinned. Rob could never get heavy. 'It might be a year or more before his house is rebuilt, better he moves to a place of his own now.'

At number seven Wilma was laying down the law too.

'I'll never be able to hold up my head in this street again,' she said plaintively. 'Or in my church. You can insist all you like, Terry, that you weren't storing guns or explosives in that lockup, but I'm not stupid. You definitely had something illegal or dangerous in there, and I cannot believe an ex-soldier who fought for his country would do such a thing. You're a disgrace.'

Terry was shaken by Wilma's reaction. He'd always thought she would believe him, regardless of what others told her. He'd banked on that too, the one person who would always be on his side. Now she was saying she couldn't stay with him and that she was going to her parents'.

But on top of this blow to his pride and the loss of the security he'd always felt being with Wilma, it was only a matter of time before the police in London discovered there were no work boots. Sid had slipped a market trader friend four hundred pounds to pretend that was the amount he'd sold the boots for, and they'd all gone. Terry would trust Sid with his life, but this other man was an unknown quantity, and once police officers began sniffing round him and his stall, he was quite likely to cave in and admit there never were any boots. Meanwhile the guns, which were now in crates somewhere Sid insisted was safe until they were sent to Libya, might be discovered. Then Terry, Sid and the agent arranging the shipping would all be for the high jump.

Terry wished he'd never got into this business. The first time Sid and he had done it, with a much smaller consignment, everything had gone like clockwork and they'd made a couple of thousand each. Even that cash was stashed away for fear the police could check their bank accounts. This time they were expecting to make five times as much, but was it worth it?

Terry didn't think so now. He was every bit as scared as he had been at times in Afghanistan. It was debilitating: he couldn't sleep, he'd lost his appetite and now Wilma was leaving him.

26

Thursday, 30 July, Day Thirteen

'Tex?' Marshall held the telephone receiver away from his ear, peering at it in disbelief. Tex was an unlikely person to call him. He hadn't imagined the man ever would.

'Yes, it's me. You said I could phone you if I had any information.'

'Would you like to come in, or shall I come to you?' Marshall asked.

'Can't do either. I might be seen. Meet me at the train station. I'll wait outside for you and we can find a quiet place to talk.'

'When, Tex?'

'Half an hour, that okay with you?'

Marshall checked his watch. It had only just gone eight in the morning. 'Okay. I'll see you at half past.'

It was raining and, with the schools being on holiday, the traffic was light. Marshall parked his car and walked across the forecourt. Tex was already there, but without his signature Stetson. Instead he was wearing a dark blue baseball cap and a tweed jacket that looked two sizes too big for him. This was clearly intended to be a disguise and Marshall felt a flicker of excitement. The man must have something worthwhile to tell him.

'The train to Birmingham just left so the benches are empty,' Tex said, leading the way past the ticket office and on to the platform. He went to the last bench that was under cover and sat down.

'Do you know Jason Pickering?' Tex asked, as they sat down. 'He's got bad scars on his face.'

Marshall nodded. 'What about him?'

'Well, I heard he started a fire in Willow Close, the road where Chloë lived. I overheard a couple of the guys at my place laughing about it, like it was good to burn people's houses down. Then one man, I can't tell you his name, said he knew Jason was going to start a fire tonight at an antiques shop in Montpelier. He called it Bygones – I remember that cos he said, "Bygones will be gone."'

'Are you sure of this?'

'Well, it's what I heard. Of course, those men at my place brag about stuff all the time, so it might not be true. From what I've heard about Jason Pickering, he don't tell no one nothing. But one of the men, bragging or not, worked at Bygones on Tuesday. He was moving some pieces of furniture to a storage place, and he said he heard it. It can't have been Jason who talked. He wouldn't, would he? But there must be some truth in it, or why say it? Anyway, it's weird that a bloke with an antiques shop would hide stuff away in a storage place, ain't it?'

'It is,' Marshall agreed. It was all too common for businessmen, like Max Harding, owner of Bygones, in financial straits to hide the valuable things and, after the fire, claim on insurance. 'Well, Tex, I'll put some men on it. Thank you. If it's true it could be an invaluable piece of information.' He got up, preparing to get back to the police station. 'Can I give you a lift somewhere?'

'No, thank you. Better I'm not seen with you. I don't like to tell tales, but I was afraid someone might get hurt if I didn't tell you about the fire.'

Marshall watched Tex walk away with his curious loping walk. It occurred to him that people had put this man down as having low intelligence, yet in many areas he was probably brighter than the very people who labelled him.

He would put Bygones under surveillance tonight. If they could catch Jason Pickering in the act that would be really good news. Also they needed to know where Dee Strong had vanished to: she hadn't been seen since she left Langham's Hotel. The hotel might have asked her to leave, but Jason might be induced to tell them where she was now.

*

At midday it had stopped raining and Conrad was cutting the grass at the front of the house. He was bored at home while Nina was at work, so he'd been looking for jobs he could do. The burn on his back was much better, and he thought by Monday it would be fine to go back to work.

When he saw Amy coming down the road, he waved. She looked very unhappy, head down, shuffling her feet. That unhappiness had to have come from the way her mother was now, and he was tempted to go over to see Trudy and suggest she take her daughter out somewhere. A walk in the Cotswolds, maybe a cream tea in one of the villages, might cheer them both. But it wasn't his place to interfere.

'Hi! Where are you off to?' he asked, when she got closer.

Her eyes looked very pink as if she'd been crying and she'd reverted to wearing her normal clothes, abandoning the Goth look. But she had outgrown her yellow dress, which was too short and tight. She looked neglected.

'Just to the shop to get some milk,' she said, her voice sounding bone weary, but she crossed the road towards him. 'Is Nina home?'

'No, she's at work. There's lots of weddings this weekend so she'll be flat out making buttonholes and corsages.'

'It must be nice to be a florist,' she said, 'looking at flowers all day.'

'Yes, but Nina has to work very hard sometimes,' he said, smiling. His wife was always remarking that people imagined being a florist was the easiest and most pleasant job in the world. 'Do you still want to be a forensic scientist? That's hard work too.'

'I've been looking it up on the internet and you need three A levels to go to university and be really good at maths,' she said, her mouth turning down at the corners. 'I'm useless at maths, so that's another fail. I'm not very good at anything, really.'

'A lot of the boys I care for say that,' he said. 'But it's just because they don't look at the bigger picture. I tell them there's work with computers, in science, on farms, in power stations, as mechanics, engineers and in the forces. There are thousands of different fields and you can find one where you'll fit right in. When I get back to work, I'll bring some career leaflets home and we can talk about it if you like.'

She smiled and for a second the world-weary look left her eyes. 'That would be nice. When we go back to school in September my year is being streamed so you do subjects that interest you or would help you get a job. But, so far, because I didn't know what I wanted to do I'm left just doing the same old stuff.'

'It's hard to imagine yourself in a job when you're only thirteen,' he said, with a smile. 'I wanted to be a zookeeper. I thought you could just roll up and feed elephants or giraffes. I didn't know you had to get a degree, and learn about animals, insects and reptiles. It takes years.'

'I'd better go and get the milk now or Mum will be moaning,' she said reluctantly.

Conrad felt a little pang in his heart for the unhappy, lonely girl. He had no doubt she believed her mother didn't care about her. Thirteen was a horrible age to be, especially if you felt you didn't fit in anywhere.

Terry Parkin threw the phone on to the sofa in anger. He'd rung Wilma to try to persuade her to come home. But she'd refused point blank.

'But I haven't been charged with anything,' he said. 'The police have checked every last thing and there's nothing to charge me with.'

He guessed she was crying, and he thought that was a good sign: a religious woman would feel bad about leaving her husband for nothing. She believed marriage was for life.

'I know you better than you know yourself, Terry,' she said, after a moment's pause, possibly to wipe her eyes and nose. 'You can't deceive me. I know you've been dealing in firearms, and that you and your army chum have just been smart enough to deceive the police. You're trading in death.'

'No,' he yelled down the phone. 'You're badly mistaken, Wilma. I don't know how you can think that of me.'

'I don't just think it, I know it's true, Terry, and you're making it even worse by lying to me. I am not coming back. Our marriage is over.' She rang off and he knew it was her final word.

He had never been a man to cry but he found himself crying now, because Wilma was his anchor. He loved her dearly, and without her, he knew he would drift, chasing excitement, money and possibly treacherous women. He was likely to end up on the rocks, with nothing, his integrity and pride in tatters.

27

After his meeting with Tex, Marshall returned to the police station, deep in thought about Jason Pickering and the intended fire at Bygones.

Dowling, his sergeant, wouldn't be in until later in the day so he couldn't discuss and plan a stake-out now. But he could go for a discreet reconnoitre of Bygones this morning with DC Susie Forbes. They could pretend to be a married couple looking for an antique table.

Susie was a very attractive willowy brunette, and her taste in clothes made sure no one ever guessed she was in the police. When Marshall glanced into the operations room, where she was looking at some files, he saw she was wearing a red linen jacket and jeans. Her shoulder-length hair was loose, held back by a wide, stylish red band.

He called her over and explained what he had in mind. 'If Max Harding is in the shop, and I hope he isn't, we must be very careful we don't make him suspicious of us. How much do you know about antiques?'

'Not a lot. My wages are more Ikea than Cheltenham antiques, but I can fake it.'

'Come on, then, let's go.'

Marshall was already familiar with the shop and knew when they walked in that Tex had been right. All the quality antique furniture the shop was known for had been removed. The valuable pieces had been replaced with reproduction items, and very ordinary Victoriana.

He didn't know the woman looking after the shop. Late sixties, middle-class, well dressed and probably working because she was lonely. Max Harding must have taken her on just recently.

This was confirmed when she engaged Marshall and Susie in animated conversation, saying how grateful she was to get the little part-time job just a few days earlier: most shopkeepers wouldn't look at anyone over fifty. 'If you need any details about the background of the furniture on sale you might need to contact Mr Harding, the owner. I'm afraid my knowledge of antiques is very limited. I'm good at dusting, though.' She laughed.

Susie played her part well, calling Marshall 'darling' and being effusive at how lovely a scrubbed pine table would look in their kitchen.

Marshall wandered about while Susie kept the assistant busy and managed to get a look into the back room. He noticed a huge amount of scrunched-up packing material in wooden tea chests. A quick flick of a lighted match was all it would take to get a fire going. With piles of old books and packing straw it would be an inferno in minutes.

At the back of the building a door and a barred window gave on to the area he'd just parked in. It was such a narrow space he'd had to let Susie out before parking, and it was enclosed by a high brick wall at the far end. The flat above the shop seemed unoccupied, but he intended to look into this once he was back at the station.

They left a little later after Susie had taken the pine table's measurements, saying they would check how it would fit into their kitchen and come back to her.

'I think Dowling can handle this job,' Marshall said, once they were back in the car. He had observed two wheelie-bins right at the top of the parking area, about six feet from the back door, which would make an excellent hiding place for the right man to nab Pickering as he came out of the building. 'I'll suggest you go with him and play at being his girlfriend while you wait for Pickering to appear tonight.'

'What if he doesn't come?' she said, as they drove away.

'We'll cross that bridge when we come to it,' he replied.

Later that afternoon, after he'd liaised with Dowling about the job that evening, Marshall went to call on Conrad Best in Willow Close.

'Well, there's a surprise,' he said, when Nina opened the door. 'I thought you'd be at work.'

'I came home early because the shop was very quiet and I'd gone in an hour early today to do a couple of wreaths,' she said. 'Come on in. Janice from next door is here too. We can have a party.'

As soon as that last bit came out of her mouth, Nina felt silly. You just didn't say things like that to a senior policeman. But there was something very human about DI Marshall that invited jokey remarks.

'Great idea.' Marshall laughed. 'But don't tell anyone I said so. I've just come to see how you are, Conrad,' he said, as he came into the lounge. Conrad was sitting on the sofa, Janice beside him. They both had a glass of wine in their hands.

'A glass of wine, Detective Inspector Marshall?' Nina said. 'Or tea or coffee?'

'I'll have a small wine, please,' he said. 'I don't want to be a party pooper. How's the back, Conrad?'

'Less painful every day,' Conrad said. 'Good to see you.'

'And you also, Miss Wyatt,' Marshall said. 'Your eye is looking better.'

'Amazing what make-up can do,' she said, with a wide smile. 'And it's Janice.' She was pleased to see him again. In fact, he was even more attractive than she'd first thought.

Nina brought him a glass of wine and urged him

to sit down. 'Are you here to arrest one of us?' Janice asked teasingly.

'Certainly not. You three are not on my list.' Marshall grinned. 'I was just checking Conrad was okay, and if I'm honest, I hoped you might tell me if there's been any more news in the close. It's two weeks tomorrow since Chloë's death, and I'm beginning to wonder if I'm missing something that's right under my nose.'

'Alfie Strong is starting to outstay his welcome with Maureen and Rob Willis,' Janice said. 'We're all dying to know where Dee is too. Rose Freeman spends every day at the hospital with John, and when we do see her, she appears to have had a brain transplant. She doesn't ask about anyone any more! Or offer any opinions.'

Nina noticed how Janice sparkled when she spoke to Marshall, and he couldn't take his eyes off her.

'What about Terry Parkin? Is he behaving?'

'Are you trying to turn us into informers?' Conrad said light-heartedly.

'No. Just want some observations,' Marshall said.

'We haven't seen him since his wife left him,' Janice said.

'She left him? I thought they had a very solid marriage.' Marshall was really surprised.

'I was surprised too,' Janice went on, 'Wilma being so religious and all. But maybe she caught him seeing another woman. Anyway, he's at home, or his car is, and the lights come on in the evening, but I don't think he's been to work.'

'I have a more upbeat observation,' Nina chipped in. 'Gareth Price is staying sober and he and Conrad have become mates.'

'You have?' Marshall looked at Conrad in surprise.

'"Mates" is a bit strong.' Conrad grinned. 'But we talk. He's a really interesting, clever bloke. I admire him for getting on the wagon too. From what I understand it's really tough to stick at it. But he's determined, keeping busy and even talking about doing a few hours back at his old firm of architects.'

'That's excellent news,' Marshall said. 'Police officers normally get all the sad, bad and horrible news, so it's great to hear something good has come out of the tragedy in this road.'

'I'm thinking of turning over a new leaf too,' Janice said, and there was no doubt she was aiming this at Marshall. 'An old friend who is an estate agent suggested I'd be good at selling houses. I'm excited by it. Imagine a job where you could poke around in other people's homes!'

Everyone laughed. Marshall finished his wine and stood up. 'I must go. It was good to see you three, very cheering.' He looked at Janice. 'I think you'd make a great estate agent. Just don't make it too obvious you're poking about!'

*

Nina showed him out but when she came back, she pointed a finger at Janice. 'You really do fancy him, don't you?'

Janice smiled. 'What if I do? He's single, solvent, has his own house, and is highly intelligent. He also knows about me and doesn't seem put off by it. The problem is, how does one ensnare a police officer? I can't try while he's investigating people on our road. When that's over, he'll probably disappear.'

'I'll invite him to a dinner party,' Nina said. 'Conrad likes him, so do I, and four is a nice round number.'

Janice giggled. 'Now there's a thought to keep me warm in bed tonight.'

28

DS Ian Dowling, DC Susie Forbes and the rest of the plain-clothes team took their places near to Bygones in Montpelier at eleven that night. Knowing that Jason Pickering was a slippery customer, and likely to disappear like smoke if he got the slightest hint of police close by, Dowling had chosen officers who would never be suspected of being police. Cars were unmarked and parked on side-streets, with one constable remaining close to each in case a chase was necessary. The other men and a couple of women were on foot, mingling with the people chatting outside pubs and restaurants before they went home.

DC Alan Brown was Dowling's ace card. His police nickname was Ninja as he had a black belt in karate, and had a reputation as a fast-moving, fearless warrior, a man not to be messed with. He had concealed himself behind a wheelie-bin at the top of the parking space, right by where Pickering would enter and leave.

It was imperative to catch and arrest him red-handed as he left from setting the fire. That way Forensics could still find traces on him of the accelerant he used. If they arrested him beforehand, with his track record he was likely to find some way of wriggling out of any charges.

A fire engine was on call, ready to come and put out the fire before it did much damage. But Dowling privately thought it would serve Max Harding right if his shop was gutted, on top of being prosecuted for insurance fraud.

Dowling had given the team a pep talk before they left the station: there must be no mistakes tonight – it was imperative that Pickering be caught and put away. After his arrest, they all hoped Pickering would tell them where Dee Strong was.

It had been a long, frustrating fortnight since Chloë Church was killed, and Dowling, like Marshall, had begun to think they would never solve the case.

He had also believed Jason Pickering would never be locked up for his crimes. The man had always managed to evade prosecution for jobs they knew were his. Each time they managed to get him to court either the witnesses vanished into thin air or refused to go to court, or his solicitor managed to find some technicality that let him go free.

But tonight Dowling and his team were feeling optimistic about his capture. There were only two ways out of the building, the back way or through the shop. And both exits would be covered. It was also Thursday: people tended to go home after coming out of the pubs or restaurants as they had to work the next day. This left the streets clearer. Crowds hanging around often hampered a stake-out like this one.

Yet Dowling knew he could not take anything for granted tonight. Pickering was cunning, organized and violent. He could also run like the wind and knew every alley and side road in Cheltenham.

Dowling's car was across the road from the shop: he was ready to move and block Pickering's escape once he was inside. He had Susie with him, so if Pickering noticed them, he would assume they were just a courting couple having a chat before going home.

At eleven thirty Dowling used his radio to check everyone was in place and paying attention. Then the wait began.

Midnight came and went, the streets became gradually deserted, and the only sight was the circle of golden light beneath the lampposts. A fox walked casually across the road intent on checking out rubbish bins.

The officers waiting in twos moved along, continuing to pretend they were deep in conversation, but in fact they were so hyped up they said nothing of any consequence. The men waiting in cars yawned and opened the windows to stay awake. Quarter past, then half past: Dowling and Susie counted no more than six people passing Bygones in that time.

Then, just as Dowling was considering telling the

officers to stand down, the radio crackled, and DC Pete Fairway reported Pickering in sight. 'Coming your way,' he whispered.

Dowling put his arm around Susie, their heads together as they saw Pickering in their mirror; he was about twenty yards behind them on the other side of the road. 'Don't react, or even glance at him,' Dowling whispered to her. 'Look at me like you're in love because he's smart and will be looking for coppers.'

Dowling watched Pickering as he held Susie in his arms. The man had a long bouncy stride, the walk of a man who felt invincible.

Pickering paused at the space beside the shop, looking all around him, and Dowling held Susie as if oblivious to the world outside his car.

'That's enough, Sarge,' Susie whispered at his neck. 'I know it's in the line of duty but don't get carried away.'

Pickering turned into the space and was swallowed into the darkness. Dowling had to hold his nerve, give the man time to get inside, and for Alan the Ninja to be braced for him when he came out. Then he could start the car, block the parking area and make it far more difficult for the man to run.

When Dowling was certain Pickering was in, he gave one word on the radio. 'Ready.'

This was it now. He didn't think he'd be able to see fire from his viewpoint, but another officer had slunk to the front of Bygones and he gave Dowling a thumbs-up that he was watching through the shop window. They all knew Alan the Ninja was unlikely to fail in felling Pickering as he came out of the shop, but just in case, everyone had to be ready to play their part in catching and holding him.

Dowling's stomach growled as he started his car with the lights turned off and drove it across the road so the bonnet blocked the space. His stomach always growled on jobs like this. His mind slid to the idea of being a postman, or a window-cleaner, anything where he didn't feel his life and career might be over in the next twenty seconds.

He opened the car window. He could see nothing by the shop, just deep velvety darkness, but he imagined Alan poised to leap into action. But then, suddenly, he saw a faint orange glow in a small window, which told him the arsonist was doing his job.

'Fire,' he said into the radio, the signal for everyone to move closer, including the fire engine.

He watched two officers appear, stealthily pass his car and move into the darkness of the shop's wall.

A click of the back door opening made Dowling and Susie Forbes prick up their ears and lean forward to try to see into the darkness. Then Alan the Ninja made a whooping sound. Everything happened so fast that later Dowling was unable to tell Marshall the exact order of anything. He was aware of the other two officers moving closer to the action to be ready to help Alan.

Alan had certainly met his match in Pickering, for even though the man had no martial arts in his arsenal he was a strong and agile street-fighter, as light on his feet as he was fast. One of the officers said he saw a flash of a knife in Pickering's hand, but Alan kicked it away and it fell to the ground while he leapt on to Pickering's back, like a monkey.

The other two officers said later it was so dark in the lane, and with Alan and Pickering in dark clothes and locked together, they couldn't make out which was which man. But they ploughed into the fray as the fire in the shop suddenly whooshed up and gave better visibility. One officer punched Pickering in his belly, and as he doubled up momentarily, Alan kicked his legs from under him. Once he was on the ground, they were able to handcuff him. But even as they hauled him to his feet, he still managed to head-butt DC Graham White and send him reeling.

As the men frogmarched Pickering out to the waiting police van, he turned towards Dowling, standing by his car, and scowled. A chilling moment intended to terrify.

'Well done, all of you,' Dowling said to the team, once they were back in the police station and Pickering had been charged with arson, then locked into a cell until his solicitor arrived. He had fought the officers every step of the way and screamed abuse at them. It had not been an easy arrest. 'I've just heard they were able to put the fire out easily and it doesn't appear to have caused any serious damage.'

Marshall came into the room as the team were dispersing. 'Well done, all of you,' he said, his smile stretching from one ear to the other. 'We've got him at last. It's late now, I'll leave questioning for the morning, give him time to calm down and his brief to get here. Good night and thank you.'

Back in Willow Close, Conrad was wondering what on earth was taking Nina so long in the bathroom. 'When are you coming to bed?' he called. 'You haven't gone down the plughole, have you?'

The bathroom door opened, and Nina came out in her nightie, a towel wrapped round her head. 'I've been dyeing my hair,' she said. 'Are you ready for a shock?'

'I want to snuggle up in bed and go to sleep,' he said plaintively. 'I don't want any shocks.'

'Well, you're going to get one,' she said, whipping off the towel to reveal deep burgundy-coloured hair.

'Yikes,' he said, and stared at her. 'That's astounding.'

'Astoundingly horrible or good?'

'I'll give my final verdict when you've dried it.'

As Conrad watched her hair drying, he had to admit it looked gorgeous. The auburn dye she'd used before had made her hair dull. Now it was shining like a new conker. 'Janice recommended this one,' she said. 'I think she was right. It's the colour for me.'

'I have to agree,' Conrad said, and yawned. 'I might just wake up in the night and think I've got a new woman in my bed.'

'Do you think DI Marshall does fancy Janice?'

'Yes, I do. But he may worry that her previous career will be bad for his own. The police are funny about that sort of thing. If he goes public with her, there are quite a few junior officers who know what she's done. They'll all tell other people.'

'Maybe they won't go public then, just have a torrid affair next door.'

'Come to bed, Burgundy Bonce, and stop worrying about Janice and Jim Marshall. They can sort it out themselves.'

Further up the close at number six, Trudy Singer was lying in her bed sobbing loudly. Earlier in the evening she'd had a phone call from Roger, and he'd told her he was going away for a couple of weeks.

'Where?' she asked, thinking he just meant with his work.

'Thailand,' he said. 'I need a holiday. I'm leaving from Gatwick at nine a.m. tomorrow.'

Trudy's heart seemed to lurch in her chest. 'You can't go away,' she croaked. 'What about us?'

'What about you?' he responded. 'If you want a holiday, you'd better get yourself a job.'

She heard the steel in his voice and knew nothing she could say would change his mind. Or make him feel bad. 'I can't work with Amy to take care of,' was all she could think of to say.

'She's not a baby,' he said sharply. 'At thirteen she can look after herself for a few hours. God! My mum went out to work when I was six – she had to – and I let myself in after school with a key.'

'That's against the law,' she argued.

'Possibly, but Amy isn't six. She's in her teens and she has a key anyway. Look, I'm going now, Trudy. I've got a lot to do before the flight.' He put the phone down before she could say anything more.

Trudy burst into tears. She couldn't cope. Without Roger coming home at weekends she had no focus in her life. She stayed in bed until at least eleven. Then there was lunch to get ready, but Amy mostly went out and didn't want hers, so Trudy ate it all. Once she would have been dead-heading the flowers in the garden, hoovering, washing or ironing, cutting the grass, even cleaning the windows, but since she last saw Roger, she hadn't done any of those things. She wasn't even shopping because she was using food from the freezer. If she needed bread or milk, she sent Amy. In the afternoons and evenings she watched TV, but she couldn't tell anyone what programmes she saw as she couldn't concentrate to take them in.

Amy never asked what was wrong, but even if she had, Trudy wouldn't have known what to say. Was she ill? Or was she depressed? She supposed that must be it. Though what the difference was, she didn't know. All she did was cry.

Amy lifted her head from the pillow in the room across the landing and sighed with exasperation because her mother was crying again. She didn't understand how anyone could cry so much. She looked at her clock on the bedside table. It was after midnight. She'd have to shut her up or Terry and Gareth would be complaining. She got out of bed and padded in bare feet across the landing to her mother's room. Without bothering to knock she went in.

Her mother was sprawled across the bed wearing her quilted dressing-gown over her nightie, and her face was blotchy from crying.

'Mum, you've got to stop that racket,' Amy said firmly. 'The neighbours will complain, and I can't go to sleep either.'

'He's going on holiday to Thailand tomorrow,' she sobbed. 'He never took me anywhere.'

'No one would ever want to take you on holiday looking the way you do,' Amy said, and moved over to the bed to peel the thick dressing-gown off her mother. She could smell wine on her breath – she'd obviously had a whole bottle to herself – and she smelt of sweat. 'Now get into bed and shut up. I'll fetch you some water.'

Amy got a glass of water from the bathroom, and also wrung out a face flannel. Going back into the bedroom she saw her mother hadn't moved: she just lay there.

Putting down the water, Amy manhandled her mother so that her head was on the pillow, then pulled the duvet over her, carefully wiped her face with the wet flannel and looked down at her. 'That's enough crying now. I can't stand it any more, Mum.'

'Why are you so hard? You're getting like your dad,' Trudy whimpered.

'You've made us like it,' Amy snapped back. 'No one else I know has such a pathetic mother. What good does crying do? Dad is not coming back. Why would he? He's got a nice life away from you. Now listen to me. Tomorrow you're going to get up, wash your hair and put something nice on.'

'I haven't got the energy to do anything,' she whined. 'And you're never here. I'm so alone.'

'Is it any wonder I go out? I can't stand being with you when you're like this.' Amy's voice grew louder, and she was flushed with anger. 'I'd like to be taken into care. Anything is better than being here. You disgust me. Do you know that? Disgust, like you make me feel sick and my skin crawl. Now shut up and go to sleep or I'll phone the police and tell them I'm scared of you, so they take you away.'

'What happened to my sweet little girl?' Trudy asked, her voice breaking. She gazed at her daughter in despair.

'You made her this way,' Amy said. 'Are you proud of that?'

'I'd never have married your father if he hadn't got me pregnant. Don't be so full of yourself. I never wanted a child,' Trudy snapped back.

29

Friday, 31 July, Day Fourteen

Conrad was bored, so bored he'd taken to staring aimlessly out of the window.

He'd got up early that morning with Nina, made her a cup of tea and some toast. Her hair looked great in the daylight, and he said they should go out for a meal tonight so he could show her off.

She'd patted his cheek and reminded him that Fridays were always frantically busy in the shop as she'd be making wedding bouquets and buttonholes all day. And she had to be up early on Saturday to mind the shop while Babs did the wedding deliveries.

'You cook something nice,' she suggested. 'What about that linguine with prawns you used to do? We haven't had that for ages. We can go out on Saturday night.'

After Nina had gone, he went back to bed for a while. He hadn't been sleeping well because of his back. Every time he turned, he woke himself up. He must have dropped off as, suddenly, it was half past nine, and he thought he ought to cut the grass.

By half past eleven that was all done, and the thought of being alone for the rest of the day was depressing. He went upstairs to make the bed. He couldn't see why people bothered to make beds. You just got back into it at night and messed it all up again. But Nina liked it made, so he did it as carefully as she would, plumping up the pillows, smoothing the duvet cover, and arranging the cushions.

That was the point when he began staring out of the window.

He watched Alfie come out of Rob and Maureen's and wondered if he'd made any attempt to find a new home yet. He looked happy enough, bouncing down the road like an eighteen-year-old. Perhaps getting shot of Dee had done that.

His old house looked awful. They hadn't cleared the site yet, and burnt timbers and piles of charred bricks weren't a pretty sight.

Terry Parkin was getting into his car. He obviously wasn't going to work as he was wearing a smart light grey suit, not his BT overalls. Conrad wondered where he was going.

After the police had taken Terry in for questioning, rumours had flown about that he was a drug dealer. Conrad felt bad that he'd grassed him up to the police about those boxes he was taking out of his lockup. They clearly couldn't have contained drugs. If they had, it would've been the biggest drugs haul ever. But maybe it wasn't guns or explosives either. It was possible it was something perfectly legal, which was why he hadn't been charged with anything.

So why hadn't he told his friends and neighbours what was in the lockup? That was what innocent people would do. And why had he and the other guy been so furtive that evening when he was watching them?

What was it about this street? He felt angry that ever since they'd arrived it had been one thing after another. First the murder of a child. Now Brian and May Alcott had become virtual hermits since they'd got caught with those fags. Alfie's house had burnt down and Dee had gone. As for Rose and John, it was said John was recovering, and she was now a changed woman, though Conrad doubted she'd stay that way once her husband was well enough to come home.

But thinking back to Terry Parkin, Gareth had said Wilma had left him. Why would a religious woman give up on her husband? It must have been something bad. Had he killed Amy? Had she found him out?

'The madness of this street is getting to you,' Conrad said aloud. 'You've got to block it out.'

He laughed then: talking to yourself was supposed to be a sign of madness so perhaps it was too late for him.

Of course he knew he wasn't really going mad: next week when he went back to work he'd be fine. He'd just had too much time alone lately.

He made himself a cheese and pickle sandwich and a cup of tea, then decided he'd go to see Gareth.

Gareth had called on him after he came back from hospital, to see if there was anything he could do to help. Over coffee they'd struck up a friendship. Gareth was an intelligent and perceptive man with a lively sense of humour, and Conrad really admired him for going on the wagon. He could well understand that losing a child, then your wife leaving you, was enough to make anyone drink to dull the pain. But today Conrad wanted to talk to him about extending the back of their house, making a bigger kitchen and living room. He wasn't angling to get an architect's drawings for nothing, just a bit of advice and costings.

'Come in.' Gareth looked delighted to find Conrad on his doorstep. 'I saw you mowing the lawn earlier and tried to find an excuse to come and talk to you.'

'You don't need an excuse.' Conrad smiled. 'I'd be pleased to have a chat anytime. I can't do much until my back's healed properly and it's so boring doing nothing.'

Over tea and some fruit cake on Gareth's patio, Conrad told Gareth about his plans, and that he wanted some advice.

Gareth's garden was very lush, with many large

bushes and attractive trees. The earlier rain had freshened everything, especially the willows the close was named after, which had been looking a little dull.

'I wouldn't have a conservatory,' Gareth said thoughtfully. 'Too hot in summer and too cold in winter. If I was you, I'd make it a brick extension with a tiled roof, but put some glass in the roof so you get plenty of light, and big glass doors you can open wide in summer.'

They batted ideas back and forth for some time, both drawing sketches and discussing their merits.

Conrad felt comfortable with Gareth, as if he'd known him all his life, and he admitted to him how he'd been feeling earlier, about there being so much bad stuff happening. 'It isn't fair,' he said. 'It's our first real home, Gareth, and we were both so excited to be living here, but now I can't help feeling we ought to cut and run.'

'It is bad luck that so much awful stuff has happened since you moved in, but hold on, Conrad, it can't last for ever. Chloë's death started something. A lot of the other problems were, in one way or another, brought about by that. A kind of chain reaction. Once the killer is caught it will all simmer down, and things will return to normal.'

'You're probably right, and any potential buyer would be put off, knowing there had been a murder here. So I suppose we just need to sit it out.'

All at once the sound of Trudy shouting at Amy came from over the fence, something about Amy not eating her lunch.

'I told you I didn't want anything,' Amy yelled back. 'Why don't you listen to me?'

Trudy responded with something about growing girls needing three meals a day.

'I don't want to grow any more,' Amy shouted, her voice sharp with anger. 'You've made me fat by pushing food into me. You've ruined my life with it.'

Trudy's reply was muted, something about puppy fat and she'd grow out of it.

The argument went on and on, loud one minute, then quieter as if they were moving from room to room.

But whatever Trudy was saying it was just making Amy more het up, and her voice was growing louder and louder. 'You pushed food on Dad too. He hated that about you. Once he said to me, "She thinks the answer to everything from a headache to a broken leg is to stuff some food in your mouth."'

'You can be as cruel as him,' Trudy retorted.

'He wasn't cruel, he was honest. I don't blame him for leaving. You're so fat you wobble when you walk, like you're made of jelly. And you want me to be just like you.'

Trudy made some reply, but it was clear she was crying, and her words were indistinct.

The two men raised their eyebrows and half smiled, both feeling awkward at overhearing all of this. Conrad guessed Trudy and Amy were back in their kitchen, but with the windows wide open they might as well have been in the garden, shouting.

'You've ruined all my chances,' Amy went on, her voice sounding hoarse because she was so angry. 'They laugh at me at school. They call me Awful Amy and Amy the Tank. They made Chloë hate me too. She said she'd be glad not to see me any more when she went to that new school in London.'

Conrad's ears had pricked up now. He had seen boys in his care spiral out of control when they felt the whole world was against them, and he thought Amy was already on that spiral.

'You didn't need that stuck-up little cow with all her airs and graces,' Trudy screamed back at her. 'Or her bloody perfect parents who look down on me.'

'They don't look down on anyone,' Amy shrieked. 'I wanted them for my parents. I hate you, Mum, hate your fat face, your endless snivelling, the way you lie around eating and blaming other people. No wonder Dad left.'

Conrad got up. He sensed something bad was going to happen.

Gareth caught hold of his arm. 'Sit down, Con. They go on like that all the time. It never lasts long.

They'll both be crying in a minute and eating chocolate bars together.'

Conrad was aware Gareth knew them better than he did, but he'd heard the escalation of anger in Amy's voice, and he worried someone was going to get hurt. He shook off Gareth's hand, ran across to the hedge between the two gardens and vaulted over it.

As he landed in the Singers' garden, he could hear a strange kind of high-pitched sound, almost like the whine of a dog.

He couldn't see either Trudy or Amy through the kitchen window and he hesitated for a moment or two, thinking perhaps the row was over, as Gareth had said it would be, and they'd moved to the lounge. If he went crashing in there, he'd look foolish and Trudy would be angry.

But that whining sound worried him, and he moved to the open door.

The sight that met him was far worse than anything he could have imagined. It was the worst nightmare. Trudy was on the floor, slumped back against the kitchen units, drenched in blood. Amy was holding her in place by her hair with her left hand, and in the right, she had a big French cook's knife. She had slashed her mother's throat with it.

Amy was covered with blood, and there was an ever-increasing pool on the floor, gushing from Trudy. Her wound was a fearsome four-inch gash.

Amy's expression was terrifying. Her face was mottled, eyes bulging, and she was grimacing in a maniacal way.

'No, Amy,' he yelled, and threw himself at her, knocking her away from her mother, and forcing the knife out of her hand until it fell to the floor.

'Gareth, call the police and an ambulance,' he bellowed, hoping he could hear across the garden.

Amy fought to get away from him. Her eyes were those of a wild animal, and she screamed like a stuck pig. He caught hold of one of her forearms, pulled her up and grabbed her other arm. 'Calm down,' he roared. 'I need to stop your mum's bleeding, or she'll die.'

She continued to scream and fight him, so he had no alternative but to drag her to the door in the hall that led to the garage, and push her in. He locked the door, knowing she couldn't get out on to the street as he could see the keys for the outer door on the hall table.

Rushing back to Trudy he got a tea-towel from a drawer and held it to her throat to staunch the blood, at the same time pulling her flat on the floor. Her eyes were rolling back in her head, and there was a strange gurgling, wheezing sound as if she was trying to speak.

'Hold on there, Trudy. The ambulance will be here in a minute. Don't try to speak. I've got you.'

It didn't look good for her. He had only had a brief glance at the gash in her throat, but it had looked deep. He prayed silently that Gareth had rung the emergency services and that they really would be here any minute.

'Oh, my God!'

Conrad looked up to see Gareth in the doorway, his face ashen. 'Did you call the police?'

'Yes,' he said. 'On their way. What can I do? How bad is that?'

'As bad as it can get, I suspect.' He glanced down at Trudy and saw her eyes were rolling back in her head. 'Go and open the front door for them to come in. I've locked Amy in the garage.'

They could both hear her pounding on the door, shouting, swearing and crying all at once. Gareth moved to pick up the knife.

'Don't touch it,' Conrad said. 'Leave that to the police. Just open the front door.'

'There's the ambulance,' Gareth said, as they heard the siren coming closer. 'I'll go and show them in.'

The paramedics took over, and as soon as Trudy was in the ambulance and it was pulling away down the road, the police unlocked the door to the garage.

'Don't you come near me or I'll hit you with this,' she yelled at the two officers. 'I'll only let Conrad come in.'

The officers looked back at him. Gareth caught

hold of his arm as he had earlier. 'Leave it to them,' he said. 'She's got some kind of weapon.'

'What is it?' Conrad asked the officers, as he couldn't see past them.

'A lump hammer,' one said.

Conrad got between the two men. He saw Amy was in a terrible state, soaked in blood, her face purple with rage, and she brandished the hammer as if she meant to use it.

'I'll come in with you if you put that down,' he said. 'Everything's okay, Amy, we understand. Put the hammer on the floor and I'll come in with you.'

'You won't! Grown-ups always lie,' she shouted.

'I don't,' he said calmly. 'I promise you that if you put the hammer down, I'll come and put my arms around you and make you feel safe again.'

She kept her tear-filled eyes on him, her nose running and lips trembling, but slowly she lowered the hammer, then dropped it.

Conrad stepped into the garage and slowly walked towards her, his arms open. As he reached her he closed them around her and held her tight.

He stayed that way, holding her, till he felt her anger subsiding. 'You have to go with the police now, but they'll look after you,' he said softly. 'I'll take you out to the car.'

He kept one arm firmly around her, and with his other hand, he held hers, and slowly walked her to the door, past several officers who had all fallen silent and out to the waiting car.

'Nina and I will be thinking about you, and in a day or two we'll see if we can come and visit you,' Conrad said, once they were outside.

'Where are they taking me?' She looked up at him, her dark eyes troubled and frightened.

'Just to the police station for now. They'll get a doctor to check you over, give you clean clothes.'

He kissed her forehead, then handed her to the officer who was waiting to see her into the car.

It was sometime later as Gareth accompanied him home that Conrad realized how much his back hurt, and that he was drenched in Trudy's blood. He was shaky and close to breaking down. The police had informed him that Trudy had died shortly after being put into the ambulance.

He would never forget the pleading look on Amy's face as she stared at him from the police car window. He couldn't help but wonder if there was anything he could have done to avert her attack on her mother.

The sad fact was that Amy would be locked away now for years, possibly most of her life. She would be branded a monster, and her story would be told without any understanding of what had made her kill.

It looked to him as if she had killed Chloë, too. If

she had it would have been in response to the cruelty and bullying from other young people, and lack of love or interest from her parents, that had made this terrible thing happen. Conrad felt certain she wasn't born bad.

30

DS Dowling took out his phone and called Marshall. 'Can you come immediately to Willow Close, boss? Trudy Singer is dead.'

There was only silence. 'Did you hear me, boss?'

'I heard you all right. I'm just rigid with shock. I'll be there in ten.' As Marshall sped into Willow Close, he saw faces at the windows, but there was no one on the street, except a uniformed officer guarding the Singer house, which had been cordoned off with the usual tape. There were a great many cars parked on the street too, presumably Scene of Crime and Forensics.

Marshall parked in the only spot available at the bottom of the close, then walked up. Dowling emerged from the house, handed him some plastic shoe coverings and began to talk him through what the first officers on the scene had reported.

When Marshall got to the kitchen door he gasped involuntarily. The room was awash with blood, not just the floor but up the cupboard doors and splashes on the walls. It was like a scene from a horror film.

'Tell me what happened.' He had thought it was going to be suicide, not this.

'It seems Conrad Best heard a row between mother and daughter while he was in the garden next door with Gareth Price,' Dowling said gravely. 'As it grew louder and more aggressive, Best jumped over the fence to intervene. He got to the kitchen door just as Amy had slashed her mother's throat.' Dowling pointed to the knife in an evidence bag on the worktop.

'Amy did this?' In all his years in the police Marshall had never been so shocked as he was by this.

'Yes. I know, it's truly appalling. Conrad Best said he knocked the knife out of her hand, and when she fought him, he put her in the garage while he tried to save the mother. Mrs Singer died in the ambulance.'

Marshall looked down at the blood-spattered units, the pool on the floor, and the long smear where Conrad had pulled Trudy right down on to the floor. There were some of Conrad's and presumably Amy's footprints too. He could imagine the whole scene as if he'd been there. It fitted exactly with what he'd been told.

'Did Amy say anything? Any explanation?'

'I don't think she said much at all, just a lot of screaming and shouting. But one of the first-response officers is over with Conrad Best now, getting his statement. When I arrived Amy had just been driven away and Mr Best said he had no doubt she'd killed Chloë too.'

'He did?'

'Yes, he thinks it was in a fit of rage. Then, after two whole weeks of punishing guilt, her father leaving and her mother falling apart, it was all too much for her and it tipped her over the edge.'

Marshall pulled at his chin reflectively. 'I trust that man's judgement. We could do with him in the force. I want a couple of men to go through this house and the garden checking absolutely everywhere for a school dress. With hindsight I think Amy must have given the officers a different one from the one she was wearing that night. She's hidden the bloodstained dress somewhere. Possibly plimsolls or sandals too.'

'What about the Churches?' Dowling asked. 'They must be watching all the activity and wondering.'

'Umm,' Marshall murmured. He was silent for a moment, looking thoughtful. 'It's a difficult one. I shouldn't really say anything until we've got a confession and charged Amy – after all, we could be wrong. But it would be inhumane to leave them wondering what's been going on here. I think I must go down there and talk to them.'

'I don't envy you that, boss,' Dowling said.

As Marshall walked down the road to the Churches' house, not for the first time he wished he'd picked any career other than the police. Mostly he loved his job, the solving of complex crimes, catching villains and putting them away. Murders were always fascinating: he never ceased to be staggered by how often seemingly gentle, rather staid people could plan and execute the killing of a family member. But child murders were hideous, and when it was done by another child that made it a hundred times worse.

What on earth was he going to say to Mike and Ruth?

Mike opened the front door before Marshall even knocked. The expression on his face said that he'd already worked out at least some of what Marshall was going to tell them.

'Come in, DI Marshall,' Mike said formally. 'So it was Trudy, after all, and she killed herself rather than go to prison?'

Marshall hadn't expected Mike to come to the wrong conclusion and he was thrown. Mike continued, 'We might have known. Trudy was always sniping in a jealous way about Chloë's talent. But we never thought for one moment she could get angry enough to hurt Chloë. Well, who would?'

Marshall swallowed hard. 'I'm sorry, Mike, but that isn't what happened. I came to tell you just what we know for sure. It may take a day or two to get the whole picture.'

Ruth appeared behind her husband. 'Come into the lounge, both of you, and shut the front door,' she said. 'We would appreciate a full and frank explanation.'

Marshall admired the way the couple were holding it together, dignified, strong and willing to listen without becoming hysterical. Ruth appeared to be serene, as if she'd already faced the worst and nothing else could be as bad.

'Trudy is dead, but not by suicide. Amy killed her,' Marshall said gently, once they were all seated. Ruth and Mike gasped. Ruth clamped her hand over her mouth. Her blue eyes grew darker at the horror of what she'd just heard.

'Now, I expect you'll think, as I do, that Amy may have killed Chloë too. But until we can get her confession and charge her, this must go no further than these four walls.'

The couple had fallen silent. They were holding hands, their faces set like stone, and for all his experience Marshall didn't have the right words to try to comfort them. 'I'm so sorry, this must be unbearable for you,' he said. 'But I felt I must tell you rather than leave you wondering what was going on up the road. My men are searching now for vital pieces of evidence that could prove Amy killed Chloë. But tell me, did you two ever suspect her?'

'I did,' Ruth admitted. 'Though I felt ashamed of myself for thinking it. It wasn't that I ever saw any violence. It was just a look, an odd sarcastic remark, nothing more, really, when Chloë spoke about her dancing, the shows she was in, and the possibility of going to a stage school in London. She seemed sullen, a kind of darkness, but I told myself I was wrong and it couldn't be true.' She paused for a minute. 'Then there were remarks from Chloë. She said a few times she was tired of Amy hanging on to her. She said she thought she was jealous. I told her off. I said it was unkind to be like that.'

'When Ruth told me what she thought I didn't agree,' Mike said, moving closer to his wife, putting his arm around her. 'How could I think such a thing of a child who'd been in and out of here since she could walk? Who saw us two as her auntie and uncle? Besides, most kids get a bit jealous sometimes. It doesn't usually mean anything. But now I'm thinking I should have trusted Ruth's intuition and even told you, Detective Inspector. But I found it impossible to think such things, let alone say them to you.'

'I squashed my suspicions because I didn't want to believe it,' Ruth said, her eyes filling with tears. 'But I have to say Amy hasn't spoken to me once since Chloë died. I saw her the other day in that Goth outfit she's taken to wearing and I waved. She turned away and pretended she hadn't seen me. I thought at the time it was because she didn't know what to say to me. I just wish I'd mentioned it to you now.'

'You two have nothing to reproach yourselves with,' Marshall said. 'You were dealt the cruellest blow in losing Chloë, but you've kept your dignity and compassion for others too. That says so much about you both.'

Ruth tried to smile, but it was just a slight movement of her lips and her eyes were dead. 'I must go now,' Marshall said, getting up from the armchair. 'I'll be in touch as soon as I have something positive to tell you.' Ruth was now slumped against her husband on the sofa. He knew the news had rubbed salt into the wound, making it worse, and his heart went out to them.

Next, he went across the road to Conrad Best's: he felt the man deserved acknowledgement for what he'd done today.

Nina had just arrived home. She was clearly concerned for her husband, and rightly so as he was very pale. From what he said, it sounded as if the burn on his back had broken open.

'What more can happen?' Nina said, her eyes sparking with anger. 'Ever since we got here there's been one thing after another. For two pins I'd go and rent a place while we sell this house.'

'You *were* very unlucky to arrive when you did,' Marshall said. 'But if you think of what might have happened to Alfie if Conrad hadn't been on the spot to rescue him that must make you feel better. And today Conrad acted instinctively and bravely to intervene in a family row, and although it had already turned to tragedy, he prevented anything worse happening. All this drama will be wound up very soon, then you two can enjoy the rest of the summer.'

'I told him just now that if any further nasties crop up, he's got to ignore them,' Nina said, with an attempt at a smile. 'He is a bit of a star, though, isn't he?'

'Yes, he certainly is,' Marshall agreed. 'I'd like you on my team, Conrad.'

Conrad tried to smile, but as he moved, he winced. 'So what's next? Has Amy been charged?'

'I haven't seen her yet as I was out on another case. She's in custody, of course, and they'll be finding an appropriate adult to be with her as we question her. I've got my men searching the house and garden.'

'I can't help but feel sorry for her.' Conrad sighed, his dark eyes sorrowful. 'She isn't entirely to blame. Surely her parents and teachers should have picked up on her getting more and more disturbed. It would have been a long time coming.'

'Speaking of things a long time coming,' Nina said, 'I'm taking you to the hospital to get your back looked at. Let us know how things go, Inspector?'

'Of course. You'll be the first to hear about any developments. Once again, thank you, Conrad. Without you intervening it might have been even worse. I do hope you haven't done further damage to your back.'

Marshall was about to cross the road to his car when Janice Wyatt drove into the road and pulled on to her drive. She was wearing sunglasses to hide her black eye and gave him a little wave as she parked.

He knew that, with the seriousness of the day's events, he should just make an excuse and get into his car, but he couldn't. 'Hello, Miss Wyatt,' he said, as she got out of her car.

'I thought we'd agreed it's Janice.' She grinned cheekily. Clearly she knew nothing of the earlier events. 'Now you know all about me I can't hide behind Miss Wyatt!'

She glanced up the road, saw the scene-of-crime tape, the officer outside the house, and frowned. 'Gosh! What's been going on? That looks bad,' she said, then turned back to him. 'But you've just come out of Conrad and Nina's. Is it something to do with them?'

'No, not them, but it's really serious, Janice. Trudy Singer is dead. I'm afraid I can't stay and talk now, it wouldn't be right. Nina will explain, I'm sure, though she's just about to take Conrad back to the hospital.'

Janice's eyes widened and he realized he had made the situation worse. 'I must go, but perhaps I could phone you later, or tomorrow.'

Back at the station Marshall went to the viewing room next door to where Amy was being interviewed by Sergeant Carol Unwin, a police officer known for her success at questioning children. She was supported by Detective Constable Brian Mayhew, and the appropriate adult for Amy was Pearl Hardy, a social worker.

He had been told by the desk sergeant that Amy

had been hysterical earlier, screaming at anyone who tried to talk to her, fighting off anyone who tried to touch her. She was quiet now, but Marshall thought she looked too pale, almost haunted, and the grey cotton trousers and shirt they'd given her to wear, while her own clothes were being tested by Forensics, made her look smaller and younger. She still wasn't answering questions, though. She had folded her arms on the table and rested her head on them, as if intending to sleep.

'Amy, if you answer my questions, you can go to sleep properly,' Unwin said gently.

Surprisingly Amy lifted her head, the first time she had shown any intention of cooperating. 'Have I got to sleep here, or will they take me to a home?'

'Well, that rather depends on you answering my questions,' Unwin said.

Amy thought about that. 'What do you want to know?'

Marshall could sense Unwin's relief that she was finally getting somewhere. 'Did you intend to kill your mother?' she asked.

'No, of course not.' Amy looked horrified.

'You may not have intended to do it, but you did kill her, didn't you?'

'Yes, because she made me so angry.'

'Tell me what she said that made you so angry?'

'Well, for days she's kept going on and on about

Dad leaving for another woman. I tried to be sympathetic, but that just seemed to make her worse. She isn't interested in me at all. She never asks where I've been during the day, or who I've been with. I could feel myself growing madder and madder at her each day. Then today I snapped.'

Marshall thought it was interesting that she was speaking of her mother in the present. As if she hadn't yet processed that death was final.

'What led up to it?' Unwin asked. 'Was there something in particular she said or did?'

'She'd just made a toasted sandwich for herself. I had watched her eating it. She was stuffing it in her mouth like she was starving and it made me feel sick. She saw me looking at her and she said, "Eating is the only thing that makes me feel a bit better about being abandoned."'

'Did she always eat like that, or was this something new?'

'She was always greedy and eating too much, but not like that. I was disgusted by it. I said, "Why would any man want to stay with you when you're such a slob?" I know that wasn't a nice thing to say but she had butter smeared on her chin and another blob of it on her dress. Her hair was greasy and stuck to her head. She looked awful.'

'And then?' Unwin prompted, because Amy had paused.

'She screamed at me, "I hope you never find out how terrible it is to be rejected by a man you love." That got me. I felt she was blaming me for Dad going. So I told her she brought it on herself.'

'And then?'

'It sort of calmed down. I went into the lounge to watch TV, and the next thing I know she's telling me lunch is ready. I couldn't believe it. I had a bacon sandwich only about two hours earlier. I told her I wasn't hungry yet. She went back into the kitchen muttering, and a couple of minutes later I went in to see what she was doing. She'd made sausages, mash and baked beans, for both of us. Loads of it. She was sitting at the table eating it. She had four big sausages! Mine was there too. I couldn't believe she was eating again, and I said something about was she trying to make me as fat as her.'

'And what did she say to that?'

'I can't remember the exact words, something like I was as cruel as my dad, that I didn't appreciate anything she did for me. She started crying again, but she was still shoving food into her mouth as she cried. My stomach heaved.'

Amy paused again and covered her face with her hands for a moment as if the memory was too terrible to contemplate. 'There was a lot more. She shouted at me and I shouted back. It was all stuff Dad used to say that she was always pushing food on him too and no wonder he left. But I remember saying just how fat she was getting, that she wobbled like jelly as she walked.' She stopped and once again covered her face with her hands.

'Go on, Amy,' Unwin encouraged her. 'What happened then?'

Amy sat up straighter, and she looked at each of the three people in the room. Her expression, which had been woeful, was now defiant. 'I remembered all the times I'd tried to talk to her about my weight,' she said, her voice louder and clearer. 'Of being bullied about it at school and other things, and she wouldn't listen. In that moment I knew that all she cared about was food. And she was never going to change. I saw that big knife on the work surface. I picked it up and grabbed her hair.'

'So you intended to kill her?'

'No. I wanted to frighten her. But I was too angry to stop. I pulled her off the chair by her hair and she sank down to the floor, her back against the cupboards. She kept saying sorry, sorry, then all at once I slashed that knife across her throat.'

No one spoke for what seemed minutes.

Then DC Mayhew took over. 'When Conrad Best came in and caught hold of you, what did you think then?'

Amy looked right at Mayhew, her eyes despairing now. 'I don't know. I was still furious and caught up in the moment. He shook the knife out of my hand and pushed me into the garage. I was scared, angry, and it was all mixed up.'

'Is that what happened when you killed Chloë?'

Marshall found he was holding his breath, afraid she would deny it. He could see Mayhew and Unwin were tense, willing her to tell the truth, but he guessed, like him, they weren't sure that, in her mental state, she was capable of talking about something that had taken place two weeks ago.

'Not quite the same,' she said at length, looking down at the table in front of her and chewing her nails. 'I went up the slope at the park with Chloë because I wanted to know why she'd been avoiding me. She laughed at me and said, "Don't you get it, Amy? I've moved on. I'm going to stage school. We're going to move to a house in Montpelier. I don't want you hanging round me any more." Wouldn't you be angry and hurt if your best friend said that?'

'Yes, I would,' Unwin said. 'So you hit her with a big stone?'

'No, not then. She carried on walking really fast and I had a job to keep up with her. She said, without even turning round to look at me, "Are you still here? For God's sake, Amy, what do I have to say to get rid of you? That you are an embarrassment? That people ask why I'm hanging around with a fat freak show?

335

That I'm sick of you coming round my house? Is that enough for you?"'

Amy was crying so hard now she couldn't speak. The social worker put a comforting hand on her shoulder and gave her a tissue.

Marshall sensed this was all true: Chloë really had said that and the cruelty of it shocked him.

'She'd been going on about the stage school in London for weeks, about how they were going to make her a big star,' Amy sobbed. 'I didn't mind that because I was proud, she was my friend. I believed in her. But after she turned her back on me and said I was an embarrassment and she was sick of me coming round her house, I just felt like I was going to explode with rage. A big, jagged stone was on the ground right in front of me. I picked it up and hit her on the side of the head. I only meant to hurt her. But she fell down sideways on to the long grass, and I just hit her some more. Over and over again. I couldn't seem to stop.'

'And then what did you do?'

'I dragged her a bit further into the bushes, but I got really scared then and I ran towards the fence at the back of my house. I've got in there before, through some broken slats, into Mr Price's garden. Once I was in his garden, I got even more scared as I was covered in blood. I thought I'd run to my mum and tell her what I'd done. But once I got over the fence and went in, I found she was fast asleep in her bedroom, the television still on. So I took my dress and sandals off and bundled them into a plastic bag.'

'What did you do with it?'

'I went and washed myself first and put on my pyjamas. I was thinking about the best place to hide them. In the end I poked the bag right under the shed at the back and pushed some old flowerpots in front of it. I planned to take it away somewhere else, but there's been so much going on in the road since then, I couldn't.'

'And then?'

'I could hear Mr Church talking to people about Chloë not coming home so I went out in the street in my pyjamas to watch what was going on. Then I went in and went to bed.'

Marshall felt chilled by the matter-of-fact way she'd explained what she'd done with her dress and sandals. And how she went out to see what was going on. She must have seen Mike Church getting disturbed because his daughter hadn't come home. She'd known she'd killed her, yet she still watched his anxiety coldly from her front lawn.

He had thought malice was behind Chloë's death, but that wasn't the right word. There was rage and jealousy, but also deep hurt, which had driven Amy to kill Chloë and her mother. Trudy and Chloë had been so caught up in themselves, they had seen Amy

337

as a nuisance, not someone who loved and depended on them. There was some mitigation on both sides. Trudy had neglected Amy, but then she, too, had felt neglected and unloved. Chloë was cruel, spoilt and pampered: she had turned away from her childhood friend because Amy didn't fit the image of what her future life would be.

But Amy had known what she was doing. Now they must charge her.

31

Monday, 10 August

DI Marshall had a heavy heart as he looked at the small white coffin festooned with beautiful garlands of simple garden flowers. He knew that Nina and Janice had made them, and for some reason, the knowledge that two women who weren't mothers had spent hours over this task moved him deeply.

The crematorium chapel was packed with family, friends, neighbours, and children and teachers from Chloë's school. From his position, right at the back with Dowling and other officers who had been involved in the case, he looked over bowed heads to see Mike and Ruth Church. Ruth's back was bent, as if she was sobbing, and Mike had his arm around her, drawing her towards his chest. An older lady with a black hat, possibly Chloë's grandmother, was also bent over and almost certainly crying too. He hoped that now they knew who had killed Chloë, and that she was finally being put to rest, they could begin to deal with their loss.

At least Chloë had people mourning her, missing

her and remembering her with love. Trudy's parents and husband had already said they wouldn't be going to her funeral. He had spoken to all three. The parents had said they didn't want the press to find out who they were and hound them for information.

Roger Singer was even more callous. 'She was always a pathetic, needy woman and a useless mother. It's her fault Amy became twisted. I don't want any part of it.'

They wouldn't see Amy either. In fact, it was clear they wanted to forget she had ever existed. Amy had been charged with two counts of murder, though the charges might be dropped to manslaughter if her legal team could show the crimes were not premeditated. She had been taken to Brocklehurst, a young offenders' unit in Somerset.

Extraordinarily, she was reported to be happy there. But, then, she was getting almost one-to-one attention from the staff, and the other girls were not judging her, neither for her crimes nor her size or appearance. Dowling had been to see her yesterday and said she seemed as normal and well-adjusted as his own children.

They had found her school dress under the shed, exactly where she'd said it was, along with her sandals. It was soaked in Chloë's blood so there was no chance of a smart lawyer getting her off.

Marshall glanced around him during the first

hymn, 'All Things Bright and Beautiful'. It took him back to his infant and junior schools, a time when everything had seemed bright and beautiful to him.

He wished he lived in a world that really was like that. Yet his glance took in Nina in a navy dress with a white lace collar and her hair, which was now a glorious burgundy colour, tied back with a navy ribbon. Conrad, by her side, was unusually smart in a suit, his dark curls tamed. They were a bright and beautiful couple, both inside and out. If they stayed in Willow Close, he felt they'd create a healing process for the remainder of the residents, just through their caring and honourable characters.

Rose Freeman was indebted to Janice for helping John when he had his heart attack. She was there today, John beside her – he had been discharged from hospital a couple of days ago. Rose was dramatic in total black, but she was holding her husband's hand, and Marshall had a feeling that his near death had taught her a life lesson.

Rob and Maureen, safe, sensible, and so very proper always. Nothing would change them, though he had a feeling they would be selling up soon and moving to somewhere they could be in isolation.

Janice! Muted glamour today: a small hat, a severe black suit and very high heels. She was deep in sorrow trying to support Chloë's parents. He hoped he could ask her out to dinner soon.

Gareth was sitting at the front of the chapel with the Church family as an old and trusted friend. He was to be applauded for remaining sober, for helping Mike and Ruth when they most needed it. Today would be equally hard for him as he remembered the loss of his own daughter.

Terry Parkin stood as straight as a guardsman. Wilma had not come back to him, even though Marshall was unable to prove he was involved in gun-running. Her continuing absence was further indication that he was guilty, and eventually he'd find a way to catch him out.

Alfie Strong looked handsome in his dark suit. Marshall had heard that just the day before he had found a small flat of his own and was moving in tomorrow. Maureen and Rob would be very relieved, and he expected they'd promised each other they would never again offer accommodation to anyone, not even in an emergency.

Brian and May Alcott's happy life together had been blown apart by the smuggled-cigarettes business. May was smartly dressed in a black and white belted dress, her hair, make-up and nails done to perfection. But she wasn't standing close to her husband, and the gap spoke volumes. Brian was smart, too, in a dark suit, but he had a hangdog expression. There was no doubt in Marshall's mind that they had lost their way, and before long May would leave him.

Only Dee Strong was missing. No one here cared whether she was alive or dead. Yet he could imagine all those pairs of ears pricking up if they were to hear where she had been, and where she was heading.

Musing about Dee made Marshall think back to when Pickering was arrested and taken into custody after the fire at Bygones. Although they had told Dee they had followed her to Pickering's place and seen her hand over an envelope, that wasn't true. Pickering refused to give them his address, and Marshall had had to go to Tex and ask him. Tex only knew the road, and had been reluctant to divulge that much, but it was enough. The first neighbour to whom Marshall mentioned a man with a scarred face had pointed out his house.

Pickering's 1940s home looked no different from the rest of the rather shabby houses in the street. Except that his was detached. It had been an end-of-terrace, but ironically, eight years ago, a fire had burnt down the house next door. Pickering had bought the plot, perhaps to ensure he would not be overlooked or overheard. But apart from occasionally clearing the weeds, he'd done nothing else with it.

They'd got a search warrant immediately, and Marshall was there: he wanted to find evidence of past arson attacks and details of the man's loan-shark racket.

Once inside the house, any similarity to the others in the street vanished. It was like a fortress, electrical steel shutters on the windows, the doors lined with steel. His décor was 1970s bachelor pad, black-ash wall units, smoked-glass coffee-table, huge stereo with even bigger speakers, faux-leather sofas, shag-pile carpet and framed advertisement pictures of Porsches and other top-of-the-range cars. Upstairs it was cream shag pile, flock wallpaper and more black ash. But a sound like a cry for help from a locked room made them force the lock, and crash in.

What they found made the men stop in their tracks with shock. It was Dee, but not the glamour girl they knew and had interviewed just a week before. She was lying on the floor, too broken and hurt to get on to the bed. Her face was swollen and bruised, her leggings and T-shirt torn and bloodstained from various injuries.

They had hoped to find evidence of where she was living, but they hadn't for one moment expected to find her in Pickering's house.

'I thought I was going to die here,' she croaked.

She was too weak and hurt to explain anything, so an ambulance was called and an officer went with her to make sure she was put into a private room where they could keep her under surveillance as she recovered.

They went to town on searching the house, tipping out drawers, raking through cupboards and, with some cocaine and other drugs, they found the books he kept for his money-lending. They had dates, amounts paid out, money recovered, and his clients' names and addresses.

They'd almost given up hope of finding anything else when, pushed right down the back of the sofa, they found a notebook. In it, Pickering had written dates with amounts of money next to them, then another sum, perhaps the final amount when the job was done. The last date was the one on which they'd arrested him: six hundred pounds was entered next to it – presumably he was due to get the balance after the job was done.

The previous date was that on which Alfie Strong's place was burnt down. They would check all the others, some going back four years or more, with suspected arsons on file.

The following day a female police officer and a detective constable went to the hospital to question Dee. They reported back to Marshall that the ward sister wouldn't let them into her room. She said that Mrs Strong had been beaten and held captive for several days. She had been severely dehydrated: another day without water and she could have died. She told them to come back the next day.

They could see that this, added to the evidence of arson they already had, would put Pickering away for a long time.

Marshall dragged his mind back to the present and Chloë's funeral. He was glad the murder investigation was wound up at last. While the file on Terry Parkin remained open, his work was done. Putting the Pickering case together and making sure it was watertight would be a joy.

When he got to question Dee, two days after they rescued her, she tearfully tried to convince him she was the innocent victim of a brute. She wouldn't admit she'd paid Pickering to set fire to Alfie's house. She even pretended she hadn't known him before he abducted her in broad daylight and took her to his home. She said he'd raped and beaten her, then locked her in the room where they'd found her without any food or drink.

Marshall suspected the truth was that she'd gone to him hoping that by twisting his arm with a little blackmail he'd give her some money. He in turn had realized she was the one person who could have him convicted of arson, so he had beaten her and locked her in that room while he considered what to do with her.

Marshall was looking forward to playing them off against each other to get at the whole truth. He suspected Pickering would have killed Dee if not for being arrested. Marshall just hoped he could get Dee sent down for a long stretch too.

The funeral service was beautiful and heartbreaking in equal measures. Chloë's singing teacher played a recording of Chloë singing 'Fly Like A Bird', by Nelly Furtado. She said she believed Chloë could have become a star in London's West End as she had shown great promise. Marshall wasn't up to date with current songs, but he thought the words said so much about a young girl on her way to a bright future. She sang it beautifully, and he sensed he would have it spinning in his head for weeks.

After the funeral, everyone was invited back for drinks and refreshments at the Garden Hotel in Montpelier. Marshall and his officers were not going, but they stopped for a short while, looking at the huge amount of flowers and wreaths for Chloë, before leaving.

'How are you feeling now it's over?' Janice said at Marshall's elbow.

'Just very sad today, but it's a relief to know we got the killer,' he said.

'Yes, incredibly sad. There's nothing as awful as a child's death. I wonder how Mike and Ruth will cope now. People say once you know who did it and the funeral is over, you can get on with your life. But I suspect that isn't true.'

'Me too.' He nodded. 'Are you going over to the Garden Hotel?'

'Just to show my face. I'd rather go home and watch something mindless on the TV, but it would look like I didn't care. And you?'

'Back to the station,' he said. 'May I ring you?'

She looked surprised. 'Well, yes, of course.'

He leant a little closer to her. 'I wanted to ask if you were free for lunch on Sunday, but it seems wrong to ask here.'

She smiled and looked round. 'No one is watching us. And lunch would be lovely.'

He smiled broadly. 'I'll phone you when I've made a reservation. I thought somewhere in the Cotswolds.'

Her face lit up. 'That would be perfect.'

As Marshall walked back to his car, he had the desire to do one of those leaps, kicking his heels together sideways as they did in films. But he knew if he attempted it he was likely to fall over.

32

'So here we are again,' Jim Marshall said, taking Janice's hands across the table. They were at the Wild Rabbit, in the Cotswolds. 'Our third Sunday lunch, and I'm wondering when we can progress to dinner.'

Janice laughed. He was wonderfully old-fashioned sometimes. Most men she'd met would think three meals meant bed was next on the agenda. In fact, most thought that after one meal. 'Great,' she said. 'In fact, I'll cook it.'

It was right at the end of August now. The children would be going back to school soon and the days were shortening. It was raining today, and when Janice glanced out of the window next to her, she couldn't see more than two hundred yards. It reminded her of what Conrad had said when she'd popped in to see him and Nina before Jim had come to pick her up.

'Thank heavens it's raining hard,' Conrad said. 'It calms things down.'

Nina raised her eyebrows. Maybe she'd heard him say such odd things before.

'Who needs calming down?' Janice asked.

'Everyone,' he said. 'There's been tension in the

road ever since we moved in. Understandable, in the circumstances. But I've noticed everyone is still behaving as if they expect another drama. And there will be one, if they don't put aside what's happened and get on with their lives.'

There was a thread of logic in this. Janice had noticed people were tense, as if poised for something unpleasant. But she wasn't sure rain could change that.

'You're certainly right about the tension, Con,' she admitted. 'I've noticed the Alcotts have got stiff faces, like they've forgotten how to smile. Even Rob and Maureen, who always were the most laid-back couple in the close, seem agitated. As for Rose and John, they hardly put their noses out of the door any more.'

'I don't think it's that people are tense. I think being serious is a way of showing respect to Mike and Ruth,' Nina argued. 'I mean, who would clown around or throw a party and invite loads of people? I know I wouldn't think it was right. And we didn't even know them before all this happened.'

'Well, Mike and Ruth told me yesterday they're moving into a little cottage out in the country for a while,' Janice said. 'I think most of the problem with everyone is the amount of press sniffing around. You can't put the dustbin out without someone waving a notebook at you. Mike said they'd disconnected the front doorbell as so many journalists were calling. They try the neighbours too. I don't think any of us would tell them anything, but it creates a kind of fear. Mike and Ruth need to grieve in peace, and the rest of us want to put the whole ghastly business behind us. But why do you think rain will help, Con?'

'I've observed at work that rain does have a calming effect,' he said, in a manner which didn't invite argument. 'And I think Mike and Ruth going away to the country for a while is another positive. So, Janice, you go and gaze into your man's eyes. Nina and I might go back to bed – that's a good thing to do on a rainy Sunday. Let's hope the rest of the residents of Willow Close find something nice to do today.'

As she left, Janice thought that Conrad was possibly the best-balanced man she'd ever met.

'You'll cook me a meal?' Jim said. 'I didn't put you down as a cook.'

'I'm a gardener too, and I knit,' she said. 'I doubt you imagined either of those talents. So what hidden talents do you have? Or secret vices?'

'I make models, boats and planes. That's almost as bad as trainspotting, isn't it?'

'No, it just proves you like constructing things and have nimble fingers. What else?'

'Reading, though I don't have much time for it. I think I'd like gardening too, with some encouragement.'

'I'll give you some,' she said, with a grin. 'So when's this dinner going to be? Mostly when we arrange something you get called off on a job.'

'Yes.' He sighed. 'That's the worst thing about being in the police. Your time is never your own. But you haven't said anything about your new job yet. Is that because it's not good?'

'Not at all. I really like it. Though some of our clients are so up themselves I want to slap them. The bigger the house, the worse they are. But I'm not talking about it because of a greetings card I saw recently.'

'And?' Jim raised one eyebrow questioningly.

'It said, "What's the difference between an estate agent and a morris dancer?"'

'Go on. What is the difference?'

'None. They're both wankers.'

Jim spluttered with laughter.

'In general I'd say it's true,' she agreed. 'But it's stopped me admitting what I do.'

'You could say you're an escort. You escort people round houses.'

'Speaking of which, have any of your colleagues said anything about you seeing me?'

'Nothing that makes me think they know about your past. A couple of the women have said it's good to see me happy.'

'You weren't before?'

'I was just treading water, doing my job, probably putting in extra hours because there wasn't anything much else in my life. I wasn't unhappy but meeting you has put a spring in my step, a grin on my face and some hope in my heart.'

'Well,' Janice said, pulling a silly face, 'maybe you'd like to tell me what you hope for.'

'I'm sure you think I hope to go to bed with you,' he said, in a whisper. 'I do, but it's not just that. I'm hoping we can share a life.'

The waitress arrived to ask if they wanted dessert, which saved Janice answering as she was thrown by what he'd said.

She really liked Jim Marshall, but she'd convinced herself that a woman with a past like hers couldn't possibly expect to have a future with a man like him.

'I've embarrassed you,' he said, as the waitress left with their order. 'I'm sorry.'

'You didn't embarrass me. I liked what you said,' she admitted. 'It was just unexpected.'

The rain had stopped, and the sun was out again as they left the Wild Rabbit.

'Shall we walk for a bit?' Jim suggested.

'That would be lovely,' Janice replied. 'I like the smell of the earth after rain. When will Amy be in court?'

'I don't know. It's out of my hands now. The CPS, the lawyers and Social Services decide that. But my guess is it will be close to Christmas.'

'Any idea how long she'll get?'

'Again, it depends on what doctors and psychiatrists say. They check how she is. What her behaviour has been like since she was arrested. Is she showing remorse? Is she mentally ill? Dozens of things. But I'd be very surprised if she gets less than ten years.'

'That's a very long time when you're only thirteen.' Janice sighed. 'The growing-up years, the fun time, first love and first job.'

'Yes, but justice has to be seen to be done, and they have to make sure she isn't a danger to anyone. It would have helped her case if her father was standing by her, but he's washed his hands of her. Her grandparents on both sides are the same.'

Janice took Jim's hand and they walked in silence for a short while. The sun on the puddles in the road was making rainbows, and a steamy heat was coming from the wet hedgerows.

'What about Dee? What's happened to her?' Janice asked. He had told her how she'd ended up in hospital after Pickering had locked her up, but nothing since.

'She's on remand. She couldn't get bail as the judge deemed her a flight risk. She's tucked away in a women's prison near Bristol, waiting for her court case too. We've connected her to several historical crimes, along with charging her for paying Pickering to set Alfie's house alight. We're gathering proof and finding witnesses. Most surprising is that Pickering has given us a couple of good leads. It's out of character for him, but he probably thinks she grassed him up. She's safer in prison. He's got plenty of contacts on the outside he could use to intimidate her.'

Jim stopped walking, put his arms around her and bent to kiss her. His kisses up till now had been mere pecks, but this one was the real deal. Sensual, tender, and Janice literally felt herself going weak at the knees. While she'd had a good life in the main, she'd certainly had too many lovers and not enough love. It was great to be wild and free when she was younger, but being free sometimes created an invisible cage, stopping her committing to a person, a job, or even where she lived. But now she felt as if a door was opening on to a path that would lead her somewhere wonderful.

'That was a lovely kiss,' Jim said, holding her tightly and dropping little kisses on her forehead and cheeks. 'I really want you, Janice, not just for a night or two but . . .' He paused. 'But saying "for ever" sounds so juvenile. No one can commit to for ever anyway,' he went on.

Janice's heart fluttered a little. She was relieved he wasn't trying to say it couldn't work. 'I think I'd like to hope for "for ever",' she said. 'But we'll have that dinner first and take it from there.'

*

Conrad and Nina lay snuggled up in bed. Nina was almost asleep.

'I've made an appointment to go and see Amy tomorrow,' he said, shaking her out of her sleepiness. 'I'd like you to come with me.'

'What brought this on?' Nina asked.

'Whatever she's done, she needs to feel that someone cares about her. She doesn't know us well, but we did connect with her, and that, in my experience with troubled kids, is half the battle in helping them to help themselves.'

'I had planned to go into the shop to do a stock-take,' she said, 'but that can wait till next Monday when we're closed,' and she felt a warm glow because, once again, Conrad was choosing to do a good thing.

The next morning Amy woke early. Light was coming around the edges of the curtains and the birds were singing. She had no watch or clock, but she sensed it was very early as there were none of the normal morning sounds of staff walking along the corridor outside the room she shared with three other girls, or feet on the stairs. Her roommates were fast asleep – one of them, Nicky, was snoring.

She didn't mind it in Brocklehurst. No one bullied her, called her names or asked a lot of questions. The food was pretty good, the staff kind, and she had company when she wanted it. In many ways she was happier now than she had been for a long time.

But she had a ball of guilt and sorrow inside her, and nothing made it go away. By day she could deal with it. Playing rounders with the other girls, watching television in the common room or just mooching about the grounds with another girl, it wasn't too bad, but the moment she was in bed, it all came back.

She could hear the sound the stone had made on Chloë's head, see her blood pumping out. She relived her frantic dash home through Mr Price's garden, then hiding her clothes under the shed.

Before she was arrested she had never thought of how Mr and Mrs Church must feel. But as soon as she'd got here their grief played on her mind. They had been so kind to her, treating her like she was another daughter, and she had repaid them by killing the person they loved most of all.

As if that wasn't enough, her mind would then show her holding her mother by the hair and taking that knife to her throat. She could see the blood on the kitchen cupboards, the pool on the floor and the splashes on the walls.

These scenes played on an almost continuous loop until sleep finally shut it down. She had tried to explain how it was to the doctor, who listened politely enough but then said, 'It's excellent you're feeling remorse.'

Of course she was sorry for what she'd done, but the nightly reliving of it was torture. She knew, too, that once she'd been tried she would come back here or somewhere similar until she was eighteen. After that it would be an adult prison. Just the thought of all those years locked away with no visitors, the guilt pressing into her constantly, was too terrible to contemplate.

Sliding out of bed silently, she pulled her jumper and jeans over her pyjamas. Then, picking up her trainers, she tiptoed out of the room and shut the door quietly behind her.

She had no plan, just a wish to go somewhere to be alone where she wouldn't be found for a few hours. But as she got to the stairs she heard someone walking around down there, and didn't want to be questioned.

Looking around her, she noticed on her left a narrow door, which she knew led to the attics. It was normally locked but when she first arrived another girl had taken her up there to smoke a cigarette. The under-sixteens were not allowed to smoke, but some of them bartered sweets with the older girls to get some.

Amy didn't like the taste, but she wanted to be accepted so she'd gone along with it. The attic rooms were in a bad state of repair, but it felt like a bit of an adventure.

Just recently men had been doing repairs up there,

so Amy tried the door in the faint hope they'd left it unlocked. To her surprise they had and she slipped through, closing it behind her. The views from the small windows between the eaves were beautiful. She could look down on to the green canopy of trees, getting glimpses of grass or flowerbeds down below. Beyond the trees, which encircled Brocklehurst, there were open undulating fields dotted with grazing cows. Did the people who lived in the few houses she could see wonder about the girls locked up here?

The men she'd seen coming up here had clearly been replacing old windows. As she wandered from room to room she noticed several old frames stacked against walls, broken glass in boxes and new frames waiting to be put in.

It was the window with no frame at all that caught her attention. Not only was it closer to the ground than all of the others, but it had a two-foot-wide ledge between the eaves outside it.

She climbed out on to it and sat there cross-legged. The eaves kept the breeze off her, so it felt warm. After a minute or two of listening to birdsong and watching a buzzard hovering on a thermal as it searched for prey, she felt at peace. The sun was coming up, still cool as yet, but with the promise of a warm day ahead.

All at once she knew what she should do. It was the only way, and it didn't frighten her in the way a trial would.

Getting to her feet she looked straight ahead of her, past the trees to a church spire in the distance. Then she stepped forward into the space before her.

Conrad and Nina set off to Brocklehurst just after nine, taking the motorway past Bristol, then winding country lanes for what seemed miles.

They didn't speak much. Nina was aware that Conrad was considering what he should say to Amy. They had stopped at a local shop and bought some chocolate and fruit. Nina had dug out a gift box of luxurious shower gel, body cream and shampoo she'd been given last Christmas and never opened. There hadn't been time to buy something special for her.

Nina glanced at her husband a few times, wanting to ask what he was thinking about, but not doing so. He took people's problems to himself, especially children's. 'At least the centre's in a pretty area,' she said thoughtfully, as they finally approached the large iron gates to the juvenile detention centre.

Conrad opened his window, pressed a bell and a voice asked him for his name. The gates opened slowly, and they drove in past enclosed areas with high fences, topped with barbed wire.

Yet once they were close to the house, it wasn't as forbidding as Nina had expected. Just a tall Victorian building that might have been a school, hospital or workhouse during its history. There were various newer extensions and a couple of Portakabin rooms too.

They parked up and made their way through more security points to reach the front entrance. They waited some time after ringing the bell and eventually a harassed-looking middle-aged woman in a dark suit opened the door. 'Mr and Mrs Best,' she said, looking at a notebook in her hand. 'I've been instructed to ask you to wait in the sitting room. Miss Jackson will be with you soon.'

'Miss Jackson is the governor,' Conrad whispered to Nina, once they were in the sitting room.

There was no reason to whisper, but it felt that way. It was a sparsely furnished room with the kind of rather tall, upright armchairs you would expect to see in a nursing home. The walls were painted a glacial blue with one solitary seascape. A low table held a variety of well-thumbed magazines.

'Why would the governor want to see us?' Nina whispered back.

Conrad shrugged. 'Maybe she just wants to check we're bona fide neighbours who care. I mean, they don't allow just anyone to visit here.'

They waited for about fifteen minutes. Then the harassed woman in the black suit came back. 'Miss Jackson will see you now,' she said. 'Follow me.'

'They always say follow me, so they don't have to

talk to you,' Conrad whispered, as they went down dismal corridors painted cream, but very scuffed.

Nina grinned and put one finger to her lips to shush him.

When they went up a staircase and looked through the window, they saw they were at the back of the building. Beyond the high fence and razor wire there were green fields and woods.

The woman rapped on a door, and on the command of 'Come', she waved Nina and Conrad in and left them.

Miss Jackson was younger than they had expected. About forty, slender, a blonde bob with a few low lights, and she wore a pale blue belted linen dress. 'Good morning,' she said, coming from behind her desk to shake hands with them. Hers was icy cold, and her smile seemed forced. 'I was looking forward to meeting you, Mr Best. I've heard great things about your work with difficult boys. So I wasn't surprised that you had befriended Amy Singer.'

'How is she?' Conrad asked eagerly.

'Well, that is why I asked for you to be brought up here,' she said, and her expression told them she didn't have good news. 'I'm at a loss as to how to tell you this, but I guess the best way is just to come out with it. Amy is dead.'

'Dead?' Conrad repeated. 'How did she die? What happened?'

Nina heard the break in his voice, saw his stricken face, and knew he was trying to hold back tears. She was as shocked as he was, but he had been much more involved with Amy than she had.

'It was suicide, Mr Best,' Miss Jackson went on, her lips trembling. 'It's truly shocking for all of us, and none of us saw it coming. It was before breakfast. I tried to ring you, just after nine, but you must have already left and I didn't have a mobile number for you.'

All colour had drained from Conrad's face, and he reached out for the chair to support himself, then sat down.

Nina sat beside him and reached for his hand.

'I can see what a shock this is to you both,' Miss Jackson said. 'I have some coffee coming up. I'll do my best to explain it all to you.'

'How did she do it?' Nina asked. She couldn't imagine how any child in an institution like this could find the means to kill themselves.

'She flung herself out of a window on the top floor,' Miss Jackson said, her voice thick with emotion. 'The girls are not allowed up there, because it all needs repairing. The windows are gradually being replaced – some are practically falling out. We can only assume that Amy had been up there at some stage, and kept it in mind. Yesterday we saw nothing to alarm us into thinking she was suicidal. One of the gardeners found her, and our first thoughts were that it might have been an escape plan and she'd fallen. But we ruled that out. There are other windows much lower down she could have climbed out of, but all the girls know they'd still be inside the wire, and in range of the security systems. So it was suicide.'

'But if the girls are not allowed up to the attic, why isn't it made secure?' Nina asked.

'It's normally locked. But workmen have been going up and down with wood, paint and other materials, and it looks as if one of them failed to lock it last night.'

'And she took her chance and slipped through,' Conrad said, a lone tear trickling down his cheek. Nina squeezed his hand.

'Didn't the other girls or any of the staff spot her going up there?' Nina asked.

'Everyone would have been asleep. The doctor we called said she'd been dead at least an hour when the gardener found her. So it appears she went up there at first light. Half past five, six o'clock. We have had girls getting up there before to smoke. Maybe Amy had gone up with one of the older girls and liked the peace, and the view.'

'Poor Amy,' Conrad said softly. 'I expect she couldn't face what was to come.'

Miss Jackson nodded in agreement. 'We weren't worried about Amy as she had settled in so well. Just the other day she wanted me to recommend she come back here after she was sentenced. That isn't the sort of thing someone asks if they're struggling. During my last talk with her, I really felt she was coming to terms with what she'd done and what her punishment would be.'

'I wish we'd come before,' Conrad said. 'She must have felt so alone.'

'I found a couple of letters in her locker. One is for her father, the other for you two.'

She opened her desk drawer and pulled out an envelope.

Conrad took it and stared at it for a minute or two. He handed it to Nina. 'You read it,' he said.

Nina opened the envelope. Inside was a single piece of paper. 'Dear Conrad and Nina,' she read aloud. 'I'm not good at letter-writing, but I wanted to thank you for being the only two people in my life who seemed to care about me. I'm scared about what's going to happen to me. I feel so bad about it all, but I can't put anything right. I hope you stay happy together and have children, and if you have a daughter one day, listen to her. No one ever listened to me. Amy xxx.'

Conrad had his hand across his eyes. Nina took his hand away and kissed it. 'My darling, you have nothing to regret or blame yourself for. You are what you always were, one of the most caring, understanding people on this planet. Amy saw that and so do I.'

Miss Jackson cleared her throat to remind them they weren't alone.

'That doesn't read like a suicide note,' Conrad said, tears running down his cheeks. 'I think she went up to that room maybe to look at the view, and once there she thought death was the best way out.'

'You could be right,' Miss Jackson said. 'Keep the letter, and don't forget Amy, but don't blame yourselves for what she did. I sense that if you have a daughter one day, she'll inherit all your fine qualities.'

They had some coffee with Miss Jackson, but left immediately afterwards. Once in the car they collapsed into one another's arms and cried. After a little while they looked back at the building from the car park and, although they had no idea which of the attic windows she'd gone out of, it was chilling to imagine such a young girl feeling that was the only thing to do.

'I'm so glad you came with me,' Conrad said, as he started the car. 'I don't think I could've held it together without you.'

'That's what being married is all about,' Nina said. 'Supporting, backing up, loving each other, no matter what.'

'Let's go to the coast instead of home,' he said, with a weak smile. 'We could paddle and eat fish and chips and talk about trying for a baby.'

'Oh, Con, you are wonderful.' Nina sighed. 'You always seem to think of something nice, even at the darkest times.'

'Let's make for Exmouth, then.'

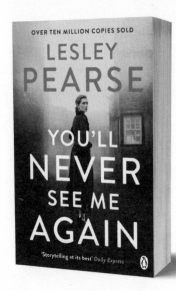

You'll Never See Me Again

When Betty escapes her marriage, she goes on the run, armed with a new identity. But she never imagined starting again would end in murder . . .

The House Across the Street

Katy must set out to uncover the truth about the mysterious house across the street. Even if that means risking her own life . . .

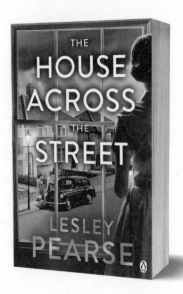

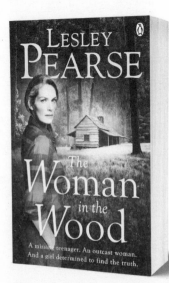

The Woman in the Wood

Fifteen-year-old twins Maisy and Duncan Mitcham have always had each other. Until one fateful day in the wood . . .

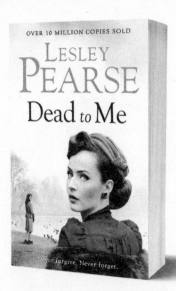

Dead to Me

Ruby and Verity become firm friends, despite coming from different worlds. However, fortunes are not set in stone and soon the girls find their situations reversed.

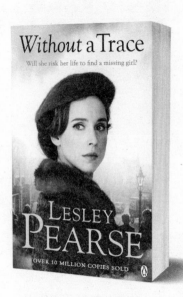

Without a Trace

On Coronation Day, 1953, Molly discovers that her friend is dead and her six-year-old daughter Petal has vanished. Molly is prepared to give up everything in finding Petal. But is she also risking her life?

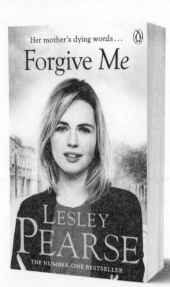

Forgive Me

Eva's mother never told her the truth about her childhood. Now it is too late and she must retrace her mother's footsteps to look for answers. Will she ever discover the story of her birth?

Belle

Belle book 1

London, 1910, and the beautiful and innocent Belle Reilly is cruelly snatched from her home and sold to a brothel in New Orleans where she begins her life as a courtesan. Can Belle ever find her way home?

The Promise

Belle book 2

When Belle's husband heads for the trenches of northern France, she volunteers as a Red Cross ambulance driver. There she is brought face to face with a man from her past who she'd never quite forgotten.

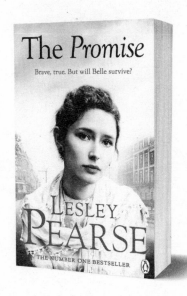

Survivor

Belle book 3

Eighteen-year-old Mari is defiant, selfish and has given up everything in favour of glamorous parties in the West End. But, without warning, the Blitz blows her new life apart. Can Mari learn from her mistakes before it's too late?

Stolen

A beautiful young woman is discovered half-drowned on a Sussex beach. Where has she come from? Why can't she remember who she is — or what happened?

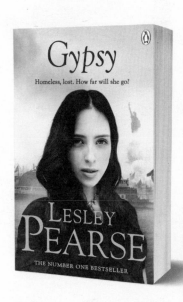

Gypsy

Liverpool, 1893, and after tragedy strikes the Bolton family, Beth and her brother Sam embark on a dangerous journey to find their fortune in America.

Faith

Scotland, 1995, and Laura Brannigan is in prison for a murder she claims she didn't commit.

Hope

Somerset, 1836, and baby Hope
is cast out from a world of privilege as proof of
her mother's adultery.

A Lesser Evil

Bristol, the 1960s, and young Fifi Brown
defies her parents to marry a man they
think is beneath her.

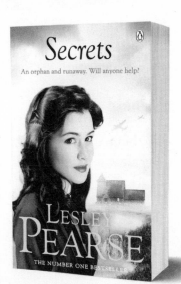

Secrets

Adele Talbot escapes a children's home to find
her grandmother — but soon her unhappy
mother is on her trail . . .

Remember Me

Mary Broad is transported to Australia as a convict and encounters both cruelty and passion. Can she make a life for herself so far from home?

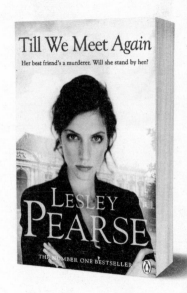

Till We Meet Again

Susan and Beth were childhood friends. Now Susan is accused of murder, and Beth finds she must defend her.

Father Unknown

Daisy Buchan is left a scrapbook with details about her real mother. But should she go and find her?

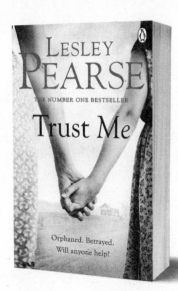

Trust Me

Dulcie Taylor and her sister are sent to an orphanage and then to Australia. Is their love strong enough to keep them together?

Never Look Back

An act of charity sends flower girl Matilda on a trip to the New World and a new life . . .

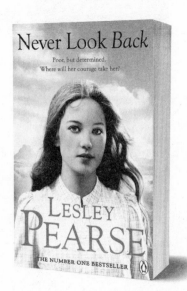

Charlie

Charlie helplessly watches her mother being senselessly attacked. What secrets have her parents kept from her?

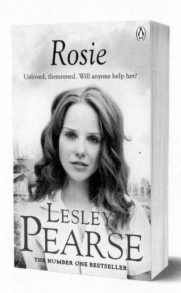

Rosie

Rosie is a girl without a mother, with a past full of trouble. But could the man who ruined her family also save Rosie?

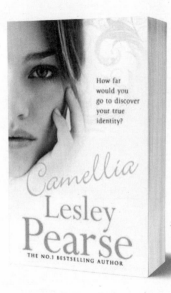

Camellia

Orphaned Camellia discovers that the past she has always been so sure of has been built on lies. Can she bear to uncover the truth about herself?

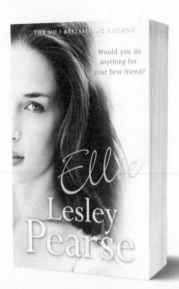

Ellie

Eastender Ellie and spoilt Bonny set off to make a living on the stage. Can their friendship survive sacrifice and ambition?

Charity

Charity Stratton's bleak life is changed for ever when her parents die in a fire. Alone and pregnant, she runs away to London . . .

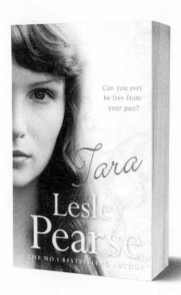

Tara

Anne changes her name to Tara to forget her shocking past – but can she really become someone else?

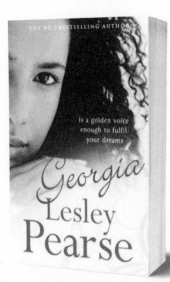

Georgia

Raped by her foster-father, fifteen-year-old Georgia runs away from home to the seedy back streets of Soho . . .